ADVAN

"Dazzling, daring, and darkly hilarious, *Little F* is a novel that breathes new life into the gay coming-of-age story from a writer whose work has helped define the tradition of queer writing. Gritty with a hopeful twist, this gorgeous book is sure to join the canon of classic young adult coming-out fiction."

—KAI CHENG THOM, author of
Fierce Femmes and Notorious Liars: A Dangerous Trans Girl's Confabulous Memoir

"*Little F* is the book I've been needing all my life. It's like Michelle Tea has a magnifying glass pointed straight into every angsty teenage queer's soul. I can't wait for everyone to meet Spencer, her heart-breakingly tender and deliciously messy hero, whose cross-country odyssey is equal parts *To Wong Foo* and *My So-Called Life*. I saw the best parts of myself in this book. The anger. The hunger. The private, indestructible yearning. I laughed so hard I cried."

—EDGAR GOMEZ, author of
High-Risk Homosexual: A Memoir

PRAISE FOR MICHELLE TEA

"Michelle Tea's is a singular voice—brilliant but also irreverent, optimistic but also abrasive, as curious as it is critical.... Reading Tea can feel like conversing with your smartest friend, and it's one of those hangouts you never want to end."

—BUZZFEED

"Tea's conversational tone and her way of writing deeply personal experience... presents a very necessary counternarrative to mainstream histories of American punk, feminism, and sexual identity."

—*THE BROOKLYN RAIL*

"Tea's writing continues to make the world worth living in."

—*LAMBDA LITERARY REVIEW*

LITTLE
FAGGOT

LITTLE FAGGOT

— A NOVEL —

MICHELLE TEA

THE FEMINIST PRESS
AT THE CITY UNIVERSITY OF NEW YORK
NEW YORK CITY

Published in 2025 by the Feminist Press
at the City University of New York
The Graduate Center
365 Fifth Avenue, Suite 6200
New York, NY 10016

feministpress.org

First Feminist Press edition 2025

Copyright © 2025 by Michelle Tea

All rights reserved.

 This book is made possible by the New York State Council on the Arts with the support of the Office of the Governor and the New York State Legislature.

No part of this book may be reproduced, used, or stored in any information retrieval system or transmitted in any form or by any means, electronic, mechanical, photocopying, recording, or otherwise, without prior written permission from the Feminist Press at the City University of New York, except in the case of brief quotations embodied in critical articles and reviews.

First printing October 2025

Cover design by Tree Abraham
Text design by Drew Stevens

Library of Congress Cataloging-in-Publication Data is available for this title.
ISBN 978-1-55861-356-0

PRINTED IN THE UNITED STATES OF AMERICA

To TJ, the one I love to run away with

1

SEPTEMBER 2010

What do you think about when you're getting your ass kicked? I mean after you've realized it's futile to fight back, that you do in fact fight like a girl, a combat style that has proven ineffective against your opponent. After you've ceased to throw your flailing sissy punches, after a crowd has formed to cut off your hope and escape, like ancient people watching some doomed fool get ripped apart by a lion or a hippopotamus.

Did you know that in the Roman Colosseum they sent men to fight hippopotami? Can you imagine facing down a beast like that? It's almost funny at first, but that's because when you think of a hippopotamus maybe you are thinking of a cartoon, a hippo who's sort of lumbering and goofy with square teeth and a big jaw that almost looks like a smile. But a cartoon hippo is not history. History is different.

Sometimes, when I'm feeling very sorry for myself, for the fact that I, a *gay teen*, was born in a suburban hellhole with no appreciation for elegance, kindness, wit, or flair—feeling sorry that I wasn't born to, say, an elegant gay dad in some mythically accepting place like Provincetown, Massachusetts (you can google it, I did)—I like to turn to history for perspective. History reassures you that it could *always* be worse. I could have been one of the undeniably effeminate men who were used to stoke the fires that burned the witches in Europe. *That's* real. Every day I offer thanks to whatever may be listening—a blur of the

Catholic God my family gave me and the cosmic Goddess that Joy, my best and only friend, is into; a blur who in my mind winds up looking like a gigantic hippie woman with a long beard and a toga (which Joy insists is actually perfect)—every day I thank this murky deity for not having me born in the medieval era. At the very least, medieval people would certainly force me to walk around town in a scold's bridle, a terrible metal mask they liked to lock onto the face of whoever they wanted to shut up.

I found out about the scold's bridle on the internet, which is also where I learned about how the ancient Romans took such a sweet and interesting animal as a hippo and turned it into a killing machine. The real hippo of the ancient Roman Colosseum was a mad giant, a sumo wrestler with all that bulk, that fat and muscle, and a giant snapping jaw coming at you with teeth like bricks. Imagine getting murdered by a hippopotamus. That's what I think of as Douglas Prine—don't call him *Dougie*—sends a clenched fist into my face again. First I think, Well, my nose seems suitably broken or something, I can taste the dark and rusty blood coming down my face, so why does he keep on punching me? What, exactly, is his goal?

And then I think of the hippo. I think to count my blessings, thoughts like, Well, at least you're not getting killed by a hippo. Imagine the stink of its breath out of that enormous mouth! You would die in that cloud of breath. Your last thought would be *Oh God, ewwwww* as it took your head into its jaw and snapped your neck. At least *that's* not happening, I think as my head snaps back like a punching bag.

Block yourself. I put my hands over my face but it's too late, sort of a pathetic gesture at this juncture; I only look like I am cowering—which I am, of course—but it's just not *helpful*. What does my therapist say when I fuck up?—*Not a skillful thing to do*. She is teaching me skills, the therapist. Her name is Peyton. Mostly she just nods her head and says yes in the most compassionate voice possible, trying to work her face into a sympathetic

LITTLE F—

frown so I can see that she cares, but because she has had so many syringes of Botox loaded into Frown Town, she just looks sort of calm and smooth, and her breathy yeses make her seem stupid. I wish Peyton had taught me how to throw a punch, or how to block a punch, or even how to dash away. I should take, what is it called, capoeira. Joy has an older sister who took it; you sort of slide around and maybe kick or flip, kind of like a sneaky dance.

Douglas Prine's sneakered foot rises up and into the near nothingness of my abdomen. The blow sends my torso upright, and my arms clasp the pain, my head falls back, and the sun blinds me for a second until a light frosting of clouds drifts across it like a parasol. Above the ring of kids watching me get stomped, I can see more kids, crowded into the windows on the second floor of my high school looking down, clasping their hands to their mouths. Are they scared for me, or are they laughing at me? Is that a teacher—a grown-up!—at the window; is that their eyes and mouth going round in shock, before Douglas's sneakers—Nike, of course, Air Force 1s, duh—connects with my shoulder and sends me back to the ground.

I am not a hippopotamus. I do not have cushions of fat and muscle. I hope that Douglas Prine feels totally great about himself because truthfully anyone could kick my ass. I am not a very large person at all, in fact you could say I am the opposite of large, which would be little, as in *you little faggot*. Being little is one thing, being a little faggot quite another.

But I am little, and not only a faggot but the kind of faggot who never even told anyone I was a faggot, never even kissed a male person or anything, therefore hardly even a faggot, really, not yet, not unless faggot isn't something you do, like a dance—Do The Faggot!—but something you deeply, irrevocably *are*, something others can see on your skin before you have even fully come to grips with it yourself. You know it's something, you're not sure what—or maybe you're *trying* not to know, maybe

I was trying not to know—and then Douglas Prine, someone with a large and low voice, a slightly golden voice, a voice like a lightly toasted marshmallow if lightly toasted marshmallows could be pure, rotten evil, he yells, *Hey little faggot*, and all eyes are on me. I flood with heat and stutter in the glare of all the kids in the schoolyard, all of them always half looking at Douglas anyway because he's *popular*, and now they can just stare openly, and stare at me, their eyes hotter on my skin than all the sun in Arizona, and I'm like—*Who, me?* So now guess what? I look like I don't even know how much of a faggot I am, like maybe I was under the impression I was *normal*, or trying to hoodwink my classmates into thinking I'm *just like them*, and now they're all showing me that I'm not getting away with anything. Or maybe everyone thinks that I hate that I'm a faggot just as much as they hate it. And maybe I do, maybe I don't. Like I said, I haven't really figured anything out yet, that's why I'm in therapy.

Whether I hate being a little faggot or not may not matter to Douglas. Whereas someone like Douglas might feel ashamed for kicking the ass of, say, Ramon Descardo, who is also very small—it is so clearly an unfair match—Douglas feels vindicated for kicking my ass. It is not hard to sort this out. Ramon is small, but Ramon is normal, which means he has some girlfriend with a ponytail and he laughs at Douglas's dumb jokes, either because he is a simpleton and thinks they are funny or because he is quietly wise and, due to his stature, especially aware of the pecking order and knows to laugh at the unfunny jokes of the largest and most violent in the pack. Because Ramon is normal, all he has to do is not stick out too much and be a good sport when Douglas and his henchmen make predictable jokes about how short he is, then life goes on.

Anyway, as I lay curled up on the dirt like a pill bug, my thoughts move from hippopotami to gratitude. Peyton believes thinking grateful thoughts can help me feel less depressed about the extent of my bad fortune. My bad fortune to not have been born to a pair of well-adjusted gay men in Provincetown, or maybe even to lesbians in San Francisco, who would be so into me being a little faggot. *Oh!* they would cry. *Oh, come meet our little faggot! What a cute little faggot you are, do that swishy little faggot dance again!* That is if my parents were lesbians. If my parents were gay men, maybe they would be a little more uptight and say things like, *Son, it's okay if you want to self identify as a "fag," but just respect yourself. You are a proud gay man.* And then one, the faggier one, would go *Heeeeeeeey!* and give me a high five, then we'd go out for brunch at the Castro and the waiter would pinch my faggoty cheeks when I ordered my pancakes. This is a bit of a mishmash from the sorts of things I've seen on the internet, but the two dads in my head are almost always Cam and Mitchell from *Modern Family*.

Regardless, no soulful yet cheery gay parents for me. I was born to solid, stable, functional, miserable straight people. You will meet them soon enough, so let's just stay here, let's stay where the action is.

The dirt is muddy with my blood and spit and drool and tears. What am I grateful for? At least I won't die here today, right now, any minute. And if I do die, surely someone will be upset about it and there will be some justice, right? Douglas will probably go to jail, someone will care, my friend Joy, who by virtue of being my only friend is also my best friend, she will care, and maybe my therapist Peyton will care, maybe she will work very hard to squish down her brow and convey an emotion of grief at my funeral. Or maybe not, as the payments will have necessarily stopped.

Grateful to be alive, grateful not to be battling a hippo. Grateful not to be smelling the breath of a hippo, as my sense of smell is very sensitive, so sensitive I have often wished I didn't have a sense of smell. There are more vile and repulsive smells in the world than there are pleasant smells. Trust me. You have to go out of your way to smell something nice, but people are farting all the time, farting and cooking gross food and not brushing their teeth well or not emptying trash, etc. A fact that may prove the general unfairness of life on Earth may be how bad smells are powerful and inescapable—like the oily, charred stink of the black gunk they use to make roofs, a smell that is always everywhere due to the amount of homes always being built around Phoenix, a smell so loud you can smell it a mile away. Whereas a more pure and interesting scent, like that of the creosote bushes that grow out in the desert, is so faint you have to stick your whole face into the scratchy green leaves to really experience it. Why? Why is the more terrible thing always bigger, badder, and smellier than the good thing?

All this said, I must admit that I am grateful not to be getting killed by a stinking hippo but by this boy, Douglas, who actually smells quite nice, like the sweat he is working up by wounding me is activating some sort of cologne, something that smells like cedar, like a crisp woodland landscape. Merging with the salty stink of his sweat, it's like a piece of the sea ringed by pristine forest, like a lovely seaside forest where a deer has just been shot.

But guess what? As Douglas's Nike hits my chin and I get a whiff of rubber—these are new sneakers, Douglas is breaking them in on me—guess what, these thoughts about how much worse I could have it do not make me feel gratitude, as Peyton had hoped. All these thoughts I console myself with have actually happened to real people. Thinking of the cruelty of humanity takes my breath away, or maybe it was just the kick in the ribs. People are horrible, unfathomable jerks to each other. It makes me feel incredibly worse, a ladder of tragedy in my brain that I crawl down rung by rung. At least I'm not cooped up in a cage being tortured for information I don't have. At least an invading people hasn't bulldozed my house and killed everyone I love. At least I'm not forced to flee my homeland on a raft, watching my raftmates die as we get lost in the vast ocean, bloodthirsty sharks circling the slowly sinking craft. At least I'm not in a concentration camp. At least I'm only a thirteen-year-old boy, I'm healthy, I don't have leukemia, and at least I have a home to live inside, a big home with an enormous bedroom, and there is a pool—at least when this is over I can soak my battered body in a nice, refreshing pool.

The actual structure of my home and the things it provides—food, a pool, a place to sleep—these are good and solid. What Joy refers to as the "energy" of the house, that is a different story. The *energy* seems to be coming not from the blameless, chlorinated pool or the soft carpet of the living room but from my mother and father. Joy says their vibes are so bad that she has to walk through a cloud of magical-burning-herb smoke—once before she visits me and once again when she leaves. But though my father may have lousy energy, at least he has some kind of great job so I have health insurance and can get whatever bones fixed that will need to get fixed. At least I am still thinking thoughts, so I know I am not brain dead, at least my mother cooks me food all the time and doesn't have Munchausen by proxy, at least she isn't quietly sneaking me Drano, at least I'm not locked in an attic with a sibling I wind up having gross sex with while our grandmother tries to poison us with arsenic-laced cookies. I have a lot to be grateful for. This moment will end . . . this moment will end . . . this moment will end—and like a spell I cast upon myself, the moment *does* end, and the last thing I smell is a whiff of peppermint breath as Douglas Prine crouches down and knocks me out with a punch to the head.

2

I COME TO in the hospital. Just like in the movies, with a doctor shining a light in my eyes, prying my lids open, and lasering me with a beam of brightness. I try to squint them shut, but he won't let me.

"Hello," I say. It hurts to talk. My face feels like a piece of fruit that got kicked around the produce aisle and left to rot.

"Hello," says the doctor, releasing my eyelids. I'm blinded by the ghost of the light. "You are a very lucky kid."

"I know," I say. "I could have been thrown to a hippopotamus in the Roman Colosseum."

"You mean the lions." The doctor, being a doctor and thinking he knows everything, attempts to correct me. My vision comes back. He looks like a movie doctor. As in, he's handsome and has a scruff of whiskers on his chin that suggests he is dedicated to something bigger than grooming.

"I mean the hippopotamus," I say. "The lions are the most famous, but they also threw people to the hippos."

The doctor chuckles, probing the bruises on my face. "A hippo," he says. "That's sort of funny."

"At first," I said. "At first it's funny. But think about it."

The doctor thinks about it. I can see the point where he understands how terrible it would be to get killed by a hippo. His face deepens.

"Humans do horrible things to each other," I tell the doctor, in case they didn't teach him this in medical school. "Humans are doing terrible things to each other right now, right at this moment."

"Spencer, you are lucky," he informs me, changing the subject. "This could have been a lot worse. Your nose isn't even broken."

"It's not?" I ask. "Are you sure? It felt so broken."

"It felt how it felt." The doctor shrugs. "It's not broken. You got out of this a lot better than you might've. Stay out of trouble, okay? A little kid like you is only going to get hurt fighting bigger guys." He looks at me for a moment, gives me a businesslike nod, and stands tall. "All right, then. I will send in your mom."

ALONE IN MY tiny hospital room, nestled in my crunchy sheets, I patted myself gently, testing what hurt and what didn't. Most things hurt, but the doctor was right; I could move, I could see, I could think. I wasn't connected to some terrible beeping machine. I guess I hadn't come very close to death, and in this funny way I wished I had. Maybe I'd like to be laid up in traction for a year or two. It's not that I wanted flowers or attention—I actually don't like attention, though I do like flowers. Basically the only thing I like about Phoenix is how the cacti bloom in the desert each winter, the blossoms popping out to form a little crown. While I welcome all flowers, even cliché blooms like roses, the cacti seem more special because you don't really see those flowers coming. Then suddenly, they're there, just for a moment, until the brutal sun shrivels them up and beats them down.

But flowers or no flowers, the idea of languishing in a hospital for a bit is alluring because it would be nice to have an excuse not to "participate" for a while. In life. Stuck in a comfy bed, pleasant nurses bringing me pills, and I could just doze for days.

I imagine that it would be like when you wake up just before your alarm goes off. You're filled with dread at a new day, but then you realize you get to sleep for another half hour or so, and that half hour of sleep is the best, most luxurious sleep ever. Your bed is suddenly a cloud, and you're just drifting. It would be nice to have a bunch of days like that, all in a row, forever. Maybe that's what happens when we die, we just drift and drift, and no one has to think any more about how they were beaten up, or how they were waterboarded, whatever that is. You don't even have to think about how other people are being waterboarded. You have forgotten all about the stink of the hippopotamus's horrible, fat tongue as it sucked your face off. You're something else now, a drifting thing, and you have forever forgotten the feeling of Douglas Prine's shoe in your stomach. That was some other life—and thank God *that's* over.

3

MY MOTHER HAS hair that is sort of thin and arranged in wisps around her head like a helmet. It's a very shiny helmet. It's blond and it glows like gold. She looks old and it bugs her. Like my therapist, she has begun getting shots of Botox, but it looks different on her, not so severe. She just started doing it. She looks relaxed from the eyes up, but from the eyes down it's a tragedy. She just looks sad, her lips in a forever grimace. Once, when I asked her if she was going to get Botox-y stuff on the rest of her face, her eyes got big, but nothing around them moved.

"You think I should?" she asked.

"Maybe," I said. Stopping at just her mouth was like redoing one wall of a room but leaving the rest in shambles. I really understood how a person could wind up with a fully plasticized face. I mean, I don't think there is anything wrong with looking old, but I do think if you are going to commit to a look, you should commit all the way.

Now here she was, pushing the door open and speeding toward me. "Baby," she said, and then she stopped abruptly in the middle of the room as if she'd struck an invisible force field. "Baby. Look at you." Tears rolled out of her eyes, and her mouth dragged clownishly. I kept my eyes on the smooth expanse of her forehead, a little dome.

"Hi, Mom," I said. I don't actually call my mother "Mother" except in my head, where all this is happening, so I'll keep referring to her as such because it conveys detachment. Peyton says detachment is good. It's like when bad things are happening all around you, and you can be like, Oh, look at all that misery and awfulness over there, but *I* am over *here*! You don't need to curl over sobbing about it. It sounds like a good thing. I try to have a certain detachment with Mother and Father. Like, let them do their thing, and I will do my thing—whatever that thing even is—and in five years I can move out and be my own person. Five years! Five years ago I was eight years old, and I can hardly remember what was happening, except I don't think anyone was beating me up at school. Five years.

"Baby, that looks like it hurts," Mother said, hovering just beyond the electric-force field.

"What part?" I asked, truly curious.

"Oh, all of it, baby," she said, slurping at the tears that rolled out her eyes.

"I look bad, right?" I asked. I must have sounded detached. What is this strange body of mine, all clobbered up?

"Baby, you can't go starting fights with people! Look at what you've done to yourself!"

Her voice was like a million little rubber bands snapping at my bruises and wounds. At the same time, it felt nice to have her crying eyes on me. Would she hug me? I wasn't sure how I felt about that, honestly—hugs from Mother can feel a little dramatic, like she's playing a mom in one of the movies she likes to watch on Lifetime. But for a moment it felt like she was really seeing me, and maybe that would summon a hug that felt real. Then again, if she thought that I had started a fight with someone—a fight! Me. Me!—she obviously didn't see me at all.

"Mom, I didn't start anything. Douglas started it with me."

Mother knows exactly who Douglas Prine is. The school I go to, Milford Junior High, is attached to Milford Elementary School, and it's not that big, and all the kids I am in class with are kids I've been in class with my entire life. I say *Douglas*, and Mother's brain pulls up a file of "Douglas through the ages," beginning when he had no front teeth and was as much a goon as anyone else, moving onward toward his growth spurt, his awkward phase, when it was predicted he would fill out, grow into his body the way a puppy grows into its paws. And this prophecy came true, and he looks just excellent, like a boy on a sitcom with floppy, shiny hair and clothes that look perfect on his new muscles and a smile that everyone likes to say is such a *nice smile*, as if Douglas has a nice smile because he is a nice person, rather than because his face was just made that way by God, or by whatever cruelty arranges everything.

"Baby, Douglas told the police that you came at him like a crazy person!" This was hard for Mother to say. A fresh spring of tears sprung from her eyes. "He told them he tried to fight you off, but you just kept coming back!" She paused and daubed at her face with the white sleeve of her blousy blouse, soiling it with tan foundation and pink lipstick. "And his friends all said it was true."

I think this was when I realized that my parents—probably everyone's parents but for sure my parents, my mom—are nothing but awful high school kids who grew up and got jobs and houses. My mother is a girl at school who thinks Douglas is a hunky Ken doll come to life, someone I would *never* be friends with, but I have to live with her, and she rules my life.

"Mom," I said. "Why would I do that?"

"I don't know why!" Mother yelled. She took a breath. "Maybe you could tell me?"

"Douglas totally jumped me after school, right out front. Look at me!" I opened my arms, inviting her gaze like an embrace. She looked me over and bit her lower lip.

"Why would Dougie just attack you like this?" She shook her head. "He wouldn't just hurt you for no good reason. He's not an animal."

It appeared that the choices were either I was crazy or Douglas was crazy, and that my mother had already decided that the crazy person was more likely to be me. If an animal didn't do this to me, then what did?

Her teary eyes stared, huge on her thin face. She wasn't *not* friends with Mrs. Prine. All the moms weren't *not* friends with each other. It was hard to see them as friends because it didn't look like the way that Joy and I are friends with each other. They were friends in that depressing way adults were friends with each other. It probably would suck for her to not get invited to the Prines's house for book club and whatnot.

"I don't know why he did it," I said sulkily.

"Really? You really don't know why?"

Because I'm a little faggot. I guess if everyone in my class knew—even though I have never said anything and also have never even kissed a boy or done anything gay, ever—if my classmates knew it on sight, then probably my parents knew it, too. I'd read blogs by gay people who had nice parents who really saw them, and when they came out their parents said, *We always knew, parents always know.* Or the gay guys who couldn't hide it because they really were just like all the stereotypes of gay hairdressers on TV. I had a feeling I was one of those gay people. I've heard my parents laugh at those stereotypes that were on TV, so how could they not notice the one living inside the house with them? Watching me swish around the kitchen in my swishy little faggot body, pausing at the TV to watch little faggot things on Bravo. Watching me eat dinner in a way I can only imagine is totally faggoty, my limp wrists lifting delicate forkfuls of food to my faggoty mouth. Did Mother want me to come out to her like this, hate crimed on a hospital bed? Life was so stupid. I wasn't going to tell her anything.

It was interesting that Mother called my attacker by his little-boy, not-yet-an-asshole name, *Dougie*, because it was exactly that name that made him lose it. He'd been calling me a little faggot. He'd been asking his friends, Didn't I walk like a little faggot? Like I'd had some faggot's dick up my faggot ass? It's hard to remember that he was ever any Douglas but this terrible one, hard to place him with the sort of loud, class clown-y but not monstrous boy he'd been just last year in middle school. But high school seemed to take all the little, quirky pieces of our kiddish personalities and pump them up on steroids. The boy-crazy girls were really *going for it*, obsessed with flaunting their love lives. The quiet, nerdy kids had bloomed into full-blown poindexters and gave up trying to be part of the group, sitting alone or in tiny clusters of two or three. Douglas's edgy attention seeking had exploded into a bully stereotype that was as classic as the sissy cliché I had apparently become.

I will spare you how truly ugly Douglas's insults became, because I would like to not be made ugly myself by exposure to such ugliness, you know? Believe it or not—and probably a lot of people will find this as a surprise—but I don't walk around thinking of dicks going into my butt. It really doesn't do anything for me.

After about five minutes of harassment that felt like five hours, with all these terrible feelings tumbling around inside me, I snapped. I said, "Sorry, *Dougie*, did it hurt your feelings that I wouldn't let you put *your* dick in my ass?"

"I really don't know why, Mom," I sighed. "I'm really sorry."

"Oh, baby." My mother struggled against the invisible force field, but her faint maternal instincts were no match for its power. She stayed where she was, sort of swaying. "It'll be okay, baby. We'll get you some help, okay?"

I didn't bother pointing out that she already got me some help: Peyton. Peyton started helping me after Mother learned I'd cut myself with a razor I'd found in the garage. What was cool was that everybody knows about cutting now. Mother had even read something about it in one of her mothering magazines and is now an expert. She knew I wasn't trying to kill myself, so that spared us all a lot of drama. What was *not* cool was that it was the first time I had ever cut myself. I was just trying it out because it seemed like something a lot of unhappy people do, and I am an unhappy person, so I thought maybe I'd be into it, but I wasn't; it just stung and made a mess, and I got all frantic trying not to get blood on everything, and it was in this state that Mother intercepted me, swishing into the bathroom, cradling my limp little wrist.

Of course, no one believed it was my first time, even though I have no scars on my body and they could just, like, strip-search me or something. Instead they sent me to Peyton, who also didn't believe it was the first time I cut myself. I stopped trying to convince her. It is generally easier to go along with what other people think of you rather than trying to explain your truth. Peyton *claims* to be interested in my truth, but I assure you, she is not.

None of this matters now, anyway.

4

IF I COULD have my home be anywhere on the World Wide Web, I would have it be in Provincetown, Massachusetts. Over the summer, while I was hanging out on my computer in the air-conditioning all day, googling various gay things and gayness in general, I searched *gay cities* and Provincetown came up a whole bunch, even though it is not really a city. It's more of a village. It is very, very gay. Gay people live there all year round, but then in the summer even more gay people come from everywhere because it is so gay. There are lots of not-gay people there, too, but with so many gays all over the place, they must be okay with it. Here in Phoenix, there are not a lot of gay people that I have ever known or seen.

If you look at a map of Massachusetts you will see that Provincetown is on the very tip of the part that spins out into the sea. The very tip! I imagine walking to the edge of that tip, what it must feel like to be on the very edge of the continent. It must be breathtaking. Imagine if you were lucky enough to have your home right there, on the tip of the world, looking out at the ocean spanning into infinity. I think it would make you feel wonderful. I bet there is a breeze that comes off the ocean that blows all your anxiety away. According to Peyton, I have a lot of anxiety. In Provincetown I could take my troubles to the ocean and sit on the shore and be filled with soothing, philosophical thoughts.

Also, I like the way the houses look on the internet. They are wooden and old-fashioned, like they've been there forever, the salty air chipping their paint away. The gardens in the summer are blowsy; the flowers look drunk, fat bushes of roses and greenery woven into archways, like something in a storybook. You could wear nice outfits like loafers and striped shirts and little belts and you would fit right in because it's New England and preppies are from there, and also there are so many gay men that no one will beat you up for dressing like that. You could decorate your house with seashells you found right on the beach! An anchor would not seem ridiculous in such a house. Or those nice glass balls in little nets.

A natty gay man who had a gay, teenaged nephew he adored would also not seem ridiculous in such a house. I would not seem ridiculous. I would, perhaps for the first time ever, make perfect sense. I imagined this fantasy uncle of mine. Perhaps he would work in an antique shop, putting aside charming treasures to bring home to me. To be given a gift by a person who really saw me, who could actually guess what would bring me delight. I imagined my grateful gasps as I accepted a vintage figurine, my uncle turning it over in his palm to show me the signature on the base, the impressive name of the artist, how it was valuable, a collectible. The rarified education I'd receive! Days surrounded by beauty in my uncle's boutiques, evenings grilling on the patio; the salty breeze blowing our cares away.

Alas, there are no ocean breezes in Phoenix to blow anxiety away—Phoenix only bakes it into you with the merciless sun, as mean as Douglas Prine, kicking you in the face with cancer rays. As I've said, I do like the desert okay, especially when the cacti have their flower bonnets on. But usually the desert feels very far away from all the ugly houses, the wide freeways that always seem to shiver in the distance. The chain stores that ensure everyone dresses the same—the chain restaurants that guarantee everyone will be eating the same pasta dish on a special occasion and the same bottomless nachos on a Friday night. The same too-big department stores stuffed with things that nobody needs, maybe nobody even wants, but everyone is so bored, why not see if this doohickey stimulates some happy brain chemicals? Zombie moms looping their carts through store aisles like they're trying to free themselves from a maze and sunburned white dads with their wraparound sunglasses flipped to the back of their heads—the indoor way to wear them.

My real house seems like it was dropped from a terrible planet right into the desert, which it basically was. It looks like all the other houses and is not interesting. The exterior is a lighter beige than the roof, which is a darker beige than the rest of it. There is a rectangle of grass in the front next to the driveway that curves up to the garage. Bumped up against the house are a few round bushes, not even cacti. I don't know that there is any point to living in Phoenix, but at least a tiny perk would be having a couple of round cacti blooming heads of flowers in your yard each year. That at least would be *something*. The way it is now, if I had amnesia—which I probably only just barely dodged with those blows to my head—if I had amnesia and wandered outside to deduce where in America I was, I would have no idea at all.

Inside the house, Mother has decorated it in this Southwestern way, with patterns created by Native Americans. This seems phony in a way that an anchor in Provincetown does not. I guess in Provincetown you really are experiencing the ocean, whereas Mother does not "experience" Native Americans.

To enter my neighborhood, you aim the car up a little hill and then turn into a labyrinth, turning from this curving street onto that curving street until you arrive at the house that looks like all the others but happens to be yours. When I was a child, I would ride in the car with my eyes closed, tracing every twist and turn with my body. This was in case I was ever kidnapped by a kidnapper, so I would be able to sense where they were bringing me through my blindfold. Mother was so worried about kidnappers, it took me a while to realize they weren't necessarily there, waiting for me. Like, it wasn't a certainty. Eventually I also realized that being kidnapped would be a wonderful opportunity for me to get out of Phoenix, and I stopped being frightened of the possibility.

"I am going to talk to Peyton about this," Mother said in the car as we twined through our neighborhood, more to herself than myself. The houses we passed asserted their individuality with a variety of colorful wind socks blowing from their front doors, the way dull men accessorize with wacky ties. Father has a tie sprinkled with ducks playing golf. The wind socks are kind of like that.

"And your father," she continued. "What is he going to do with all this? You know, your father was against therapy from the beginning. He doesn't believe in it. He thinks your problem is you sit around thinking of yourself too much, and Peyton only encourages that. I really had to go to bat for you to make him agree to it, and now?" Big sigh from Mother. "There is no way he is going to pay for therapy if he learns about this. We'll all be lucky if he doesn't try to sue poor Peyton." She shook her head. "I don't believe it's Peyton's fault this happened. We just didn't realize how troubled you are, baby." Her hand reached through the invisible force field that slinked into the car with us and she gave my thigh a squeeze, right atop what felt like a thigh-sized bruise.

"Dad has insurance," I pointed out. "Insurance pays Peyton."

"There's a co-pay," Mother said, pulling into the drive. Our wind sock was a red, white, and blue teddy bear motif. Mother bought it for the Fourth, but apparently such a sentiment is always timely. With a click, the mouth of the garage opened and Mother slid her car besides Father's. The car shuddered as she turned it off. Instead of getting out, she sat, chewing the pink of her lip.

"I told your father we were running some errands together," she said. "That's where we've been."

I stared at Mother. Another word I learned from Peyton is

denial. It's not just saying no, denying something. It's more like a state of mind, when you deny things all the time, things that are happening right in front of you. Mother believing that she could pretend to Father we were running errands when in fact I look like I was mauled by a bear is evidence of extreme denial. "Really, Mom?"

"Wait, let me collect myself," she chirped, sounding very uncollected. "You know your father. He can make things worse when he flies off the handle." Her hand reached bravely toward me and once again clutched at some painful part of my leg. "I want to make a plan with you, baby. How we'll spin this. What we'll tell Dad."

"We're not going to just tell him the truth?" I asked, although it is true that I was uncertain what the truth was at that point, or which version I was suggesting we share.

"You want to tell him the truth?" Poor Mother, if only she could raise her eyebrows, these statements would feel more pointed, there would be a certain flair to them. Mother is not without drama. But with her paralyzed face, the punch of her comments was weak, like the punch of a limp-wristed sissy. "You want to tell him you went crazy and tried to beat Douglas Prine up and got whipped so bad you wound up in the hospital? You want to tell him the police are involved? You want him to take you out of therapy and sue poor Peyton? Well, fine. We can tell him whatever you want. You just let me know. Better yet, why don't you go tell him." She reached across me and flicked my door open. The automatic seat belt lifted away from me and smacked her in the head.

I wouldn't be telling Father the truth-truth, and the terrible lie that Douglas had manufactured and my Mother believed, *that* lie wasn't good enough for Father. So now here is Mother, passive-aggressively insisting that we create *another* version of events—my third! My head buzzed with heat and hits and lies and Mother. What if my head were to simply explode from it all?

I imagined my exploding head as a popped ball, leaking air with a disappointing fizz, my skull softly caving in on itself.

"Well, won't Dad find out anyway?" I asked. "From people talking?"

"How?" She reached back over and pulled my door closed again, perhaps a tad apologetically. The seat belt settled back against me painfully. "Spencer, you know as well as I do that your father does not pay very close attention to your life. Fathering is just not his cup of tea, never has been. He doesn't know anything unless I tell him or you run down the hall bleeding and crying and carrying on."

"I wasn't crying," I said, referring to the cutting incident. She didn't have to make it worse than it already was.

"I'm just saying, I can handle this, Spencer. I'll handle the school, the police, what have you. I'll have a conversation with Peyton so she knows what really happened, not whatever version you give her."

This was what Mother's maternal instincts looked like in the wild. It wasn't like those hug-y, tender mom's instincts that she awkwardly emulated from her Lifetime shows. Those only served to make her look like she had no true motherly instincts at all. But she did: She had the instincts of a CEO sort of mother, running the corporation of the family, keeping it in the black. And in this way, not only was I a child product to be managed, but Father was a product to be managed, too.

"God willing, everything is fine and Dougie doesn't want to press charges," Mother said. "I can assure the police that we are taking this seriously, that you are getting help. They just don't want another, what's it called, *Columbine* on their hands, Spencer. This kind of thing is very serious." She took a deep breath. She was done. She popped her door open. "Be a good kid and help me with the laundry, okay?" Then a big smile, like, *No big whoop.*

"But what are we going to tell Dad? About me?" I gestured to my face and its many throbbing peaks.

LITTLE F—

Mother's face was set into the sort of steely expression you see a mother get on television when they're protecting their children from zombies or wolves. "You were with that friend of yours, Julie—"

"Joy." I only had one friend, and she only had a one-syllable name, but neither of my parents could ever remember.

"Joy." I saw the effort of her thinking, a barely perceptible flinch in her Botox. "You and Joy were hiking a canyon and you tumbled right in. Thank God you're okay, no more hiking in canyons, you're too klutzy! Got it?"

"Sure." I would never hike a canyon. While I enjoy the desert scenery from the comfort of an air-conditioned automobile, I don't really want to go *into* it. I hate hiking, and I *hate* canyons. Canyons are sad, empty, lonely, desperate places where you could starve or freeze or burn to death in an instant. They were the nooks and crannies of hell itself: Arizona.

"Now, laundry?"

"Okay, but just so you know, I'm sort of hurt? I might not be able to carry that much?" My arms, when I moved them, made me think of *The Wizard of Oz*, of the Tin Man when he needed oil.

"Oh, you're fine," Mother said. "Try not to make a big deal about it." Mother had two settings: *hysterical* and *over it*. I followed her to the small room at the back of the garage that smelled like chemical cleanliness, where the laundry chugged along in shaking appliances. Light fanned out from beneath the door.

"I can't believe I would leave that on," she muttered, and she flung the door open to reveal Father, her husband. He was fresh from work, his ducks-playing-golf tie still knotted close to his throat, and he was even sweatier than we were, his face as red as a pepper and shiny. The fluorescent light bounced off the slick pages of the magazine he was holding, revealing a man in the centerfold—*man!*—his you-know curved out like a big banana, so huge you couldn't not see it, even as Father grasped it and snapped it shut. The cover showed a model—*man!*—dressed as some sort of authority figure, with a hat and a badge and dark sunglasses and a moustache. Village People porn. *Hung Up* was the magazine's title. I stared at it so as not to stare at Father, but it was hard to focus because Father was in a sudden rage, shaking it at me.

"What is this, Spencer," he demanded, louder than he needed to, for I was right there and the laundry room is not at all large. *Flap, flap, flap,* the magazine shook in his hand, the pages flipping to reveal the various flesh tones of various men. "Do you want to explain this magazine of yours I just found?"

I recognized his look, that sweaty, bug-eyed face. That was my face right before I sassed Dougie Prine. A trapped and desperate face that says: *OhWellFuckItWhatever*. And you are so scared you do not even care. *Father!*

My parents' eyes were on me expectantly. Would I assume my role in the family lie?

"It's porn," I confirmed flatly. "*Gay* porn." I stared back at Father as I stressed the word *gay* and wished I could make it roll slo-mo out from my mouth: *gaaaaaaaaaaaaaay pooooooorn.* "Right, Dad?"

How did I not know this? How did I not *sense* it? Everything I'd seen on the web insisted gaydar was real. How could I not have it? How could I have known I needed it so badly? As blatant as I was in my walk and talk and poise and tone, Father was none of those things. He was just, like—a guy. A dad. My dad. A man with some gray in his beard, a beard he only trimmed when Mother nagged him. A man who appeared to genuinely appreciate all the stock "Gifts for Dad" we got him every holiday—Old Spice and golf things, grill stuff and neckties.

"This is not funny!" Dad snapped, though no one was laughing. "This is . . . disgusting! Do you *like* this?" He was flapping the magazine awfully close to my head. Everyone knows that self-hating gay people are the worst homophobes, or at least everyone on the internet seems to know. I wondered how big the bus of self-loathing that Father was tossing me under was. Double-decker?

"No," I said truthfully. "I do not like gay porn. I think it is totally stupid."

Mother turned to me slowly, like a ballerina in a jewel box that had run out of juice. "Spencer... are those your magazines?"

There was a stillness in the laundry room that vibrated. It probably was the lights, those awful fluorescent bars, but it all felt otherworldly, like a dream. If I could take the fall for Father— *Father is gay! Ohmygod!*—why not? Why ruin his life, too? He could carry on with Mother here in this neighborhood, swapping out the wind socks as the seasons changed, wearing funny ties. They had a good thing going here; they seemed to like it, they seemed to expect nothing more. I was the weirdo. I was the deviation.

"Yes," I said numbly. "Those are my magazines. I'm sorry."

Father's expression was totally unreadable as he relaxed his hand and dropped the periodical splat on the floor. It opened to a picture of a young man who looked very much like Douglas Prine. Now, I'm not at all suggesting that Douglas Prine was posing for homosexual pornography magazines. What I am suggesting is that Douglas Prine is a type, a common one. There are Douglas Prines everywhere, even in the gay male porn community, looking stupid and blond and hunky. I tried not to stare at it, but the alternative was looking at my parents, which I totally could not deal with. Father's foot entered my line of vision and kicked the magazine behind him. I looked up. "Thank you," I whispered. He narrowed his eyes, as if seeing me for the first time.

"What happened to you," he asked with less concern in his voice than disgust.

"He fell off a cliff," Mother said quickly. "In the canyon, while hiking."

"Actually," I said, "I was pushed."

5

THAT NIGHT I ate canned soup and bread with butter for dinner, propped up in my bed with pillows. Mother insisted on it because of how hurt I was, but really I think they both just wanted me out of sight so they could focus on blaming each other for my condition. I dunked the bread crust into the oily, salty soup. It was delicious, the way even not very good food can be when you're utterly starved.

    I closed my eyes and tried to imagine my parents' rants coming out of the mouths of old Hollywood actors, the living room beyond my door gone black and white, stark orchestral notes highlighting the drama. Father was blaming Mother for cursing me with the name Spencer, which he had never liked, which he had always found a little faggoty. Father's name was Robert. You can't really say anything bad about the name Robert. It's just there. It's like a telephone pole. Spencer had been Mother's favorite character on her soap opera; had I been a girl I would have been named after a character called Sharlene. Some of my earliest memories were watching Mother's soaps with her. I remember Spencer moving stiffly in a tuxedo, and Sharlene with golden hair and smoky makeup that never dribbled its colors down her face no matter how much she cried. I never really understood the ups and downs of the love affairs and betrayals, but I would copy Mother, gasping when she gasped, shaking my head ruefully as she shook her own.

LITTLE F—

Soap opera Spencer *had* been dashing, but these days "Spencer" is best known as a store at the mall where you can buy baseball hats ornamented with three-dimensional women's breasts sculpted from foam, or a black-light poster of Bob Marley.

"I'll tell you one thing right now," Father said. "He is not going to that charlatan therapist anymore. There's too many women around him. He only has that one friend, and she's weird, and then there's you. Plus, he's always in his room on his computer—that has to go." I heard a thunk—Father pounding his hands on something, a real *I-Mean-Business* sort of sound. "He probably found out about all that, that *stuff* on the internet. And it's confusing him. He's confused, and he needs to be monitored. He needs our eyes on him." He sighed. "Maybe we just insist he does soccer. We insist upon it. He's the child here. He doesn't get a say. *We* get the say."

While they made their sinister plans, I called Joy.

"I've been lighting candles for you," she told me. Joy was a witch. It meant she worshipped the earth and loved cats and knew how to mix herbs and light candles. Different colored candles meant different things. "White candles," she elaborated, and I knew from past candle experiences that white is for healing and protection and purity and all-around good vibrations. I wasn't sure if I believed in everything Joy did, but I did believe in Joy, and it was nice to know someone was lighting candles for me somewhere.

I placed my soup bowl on the little tray Mother had brought in for me and shoved it across the floor. Room service. And my room was like a hotel, sort of. It was as beige as the rest of the place; my desk and bed from the big everything store, beige sheets, a puffy beige blanket. Where did one buy things that *weren't* ugly? I've yet to see in real life. But at least it was comfy. I pushed my phone into my pillow and laid my head down on it, pulled the fluffy comforter over me. Like being in a wad of Silly Putty.

"You heard what happened?" I asked. "With Douglas Prine?"

"Yeah, of course. Everyone knows."

Joy wasn't even in my class; she was a grade older, so if she knew about it then everyone really did know.

"What's the word?" I asked.

"Uh, you attacked Douglas Prine. All his friends watched you do it. You, like, lost your mind or something. You were superhumanly strong like in a horror movie. You just kept coming back for more punches. He was protecting himself. You were probably on drugs."

"Wow," I said. I could picture Joy in her bedroom, one of my favorite places. She had beanbag chairs, and it was always smoky from burning bundles of twigs that made her room smell like the woods. It stressed out her parents who didn't know better and feared the smell was marijuana. Joy dealt with her parents by treating them like these kooky little kids who thought they were parents. She humored them but basically did what she wanted. They were mystified by her authority and generally unsure how to challenge it.

Joy had purple hair that lent a lavender sheen to the skin of her temples, and she had pierced her own nose with a sewing needle. She was much cooler than me and in a better school would probably have found other witchy girls to be friends with. Even though I was actually pretty normal, the fact that I was gay made me weird, whether I liked it or not. Even though this is obviously unfair, I was happy that it brought me to Joy. Joy had guessed that I was gay, nodded very seriously when I confirmed it for her, and said, *All the best people are.*

"When I'm done doing this healing spell for you, I'm going to do a curse on Douglas. A mirror spell where all his bad energy comes back to him three times as hard."

"Joy, you know school is going to be really horrible now. Worse than ever."

"I know," Joy said. "And you haven't even had a boyfriend! You have got to get a boyfriend so that all this gaybashing is worth it." Joy was always pestering me to get a boyfriend, but having a boyfriend was such a *public* thing to do. I preferred being gay in this *all the best people* way with Joy—secret and powerful, like her witchcraft.

"There's no one to like," I said, blowing off the question.

"I know some of those nerds are gay," she said, referring to the various useless nerds that went to our school. I say useless because, being historic outcasts, you'd think they'd band together with the one lone persecuted fag—me. But they didn't. They just ran along the walls like scared mice, hoping no one noticed them.

"You're wrong," I said to Joy. "That's the whole point of nerds. You think they're gay, but they're not—they're nerds. They all go home and watch the same internet porn as Douglas Prine."

"Gross," said Joy.

"Speaking of porn," I told her, "my father got busted with gay porn and blamed it on me. Me and my mom walked in on him."

"What? No! No, you are kidding right now!"

"Not kidding," I said.

"What happened, what did you do? Did he have his penis out?"

"God, ugh, no!" I had such a moment of extreme gratitude I briefly considered phoning Peyton with the breakthrough. "I took the blame," I said. "Who cares. I already let my mother tell him I fell off a cliff hiking with you, and that's why I look like I got hit by a truck."

"I *wish* you'd come hiking with me," said Joy. "Spencer, this is crazy! I don't understand. You can't let your parents walk all over you like this."

"Joy," I took a breath. "You know how school is really awful, right?"

"Yes," she said.

"And then, you know how the whole world is really awful too, right?"

"In what way?"

"Oh, like, you know, slavery, for starters. Do you know that basically every culture has had slaves? If that doesn't convince you that humans are basically horrible, what will? There's homophobia, war—I'm being general, but I could go into the details, they're just so horrible. All the dead and persecuted witches," I stressed. "All the torture they did to the witches, the burning and drowning. You know how they tied up the witches and threw them in water, and if they *drowned* they were innocent and if they somehow managed to *live* they were witches and then murdered? That's a *metaphor for life*, Joy."

"Godddddddd," Joy said. "You are bumming me out."

"Women get raped," I told her. "Like, what is the statistic?"

"One out of three? Spencer, I don't want to talk about all this."

"I know, no one does," I said. "Think—if one out of every three girls are raped, then one out of every three guys is a rapist."

"That doesn't account for repeat offenders," she said quickly.

"It also doesn't count for all the rapes that go unreported."

"Spencer, stop," she said. "You need a negativity-absorbing stone, I'm going to bring you one tomorrow."

"Joy, I'm going to kill myself."

The words entered my bedroom and vanished, as words do. I half expected something so enormous to float from my mouth in a banner or to curl out in neon tubes. But I said it, and that was it. It was gone. But the saying it vibrated inside me like I'd hit a tuning fork buried deep within.

"Not funny," Joy said. "You can't even joke about that now with all those gay bully suicides."

"I'm not joking," I said. "What gay bully suicides?"

And so Joy directed me to my computer, where I learned that as I was getting pummeled by Prine, a sort of media explosion had occurred around three teenagers from different parts of the country who all happened to kill themselves at the same time. All of them were gay and getting beat up at school. In the wake of these three deaths, the suicides of other kids no one had previously cared about were suddenly revived, and then a bunch of other kids who had *almost* killed themselves went public, and then a bunch of grown-up gay people who seemed sort of sad and uninspiring made videos telling all us bullied gay kids to wait till we're twenty-one, when we can find some sad and uninspiring gay bar to install ourselves in and drink till we've forgotten all about our terrible childhoods. There it was, all over the internet, a lead on every news site and linked on everyone's pages. Unbelievable. Gay suicides, gay bullying, and the weird, gay grown-ups I was destined to grow into. Even in this, my darkest moment, I was a cliché.

"These videos just went up today?" I asked, incredulous.

"Yeah," Joy said. I could hear her typing as she spoke. "While you were getting gaybashed. Ironic, right?"

"Is that the correct use of ironic?"

"I think so," she said. "I'll check." Another typing flurry clattered through the phone. "Hmmm, maybe not."

"I didn't know about this," I told her.

"You can't make jokes about suicide," she said. "And you really can't commit suicide, either, because you'll just seem like you're trying to be trendy."

"I was going to ask you to help me," I told her. "To fix me a poison, like Socrates." Reading about Socrates's death online, drinking hemlock didn't seem too bad. He drank the poison and walked around till his legs went numb, and then he laid down and died while all his boyfriends gathered close and cried. His last words were something like "Don't forget we owe that guy a chicken." It seemed a smooth way to go.

"You'll be a gay internet martyr," Joy said, stabbing my fantasy in the heart with the dagger of reality. "They'll have a big memorial at school for you and everyone will pretend they care and Douglas Prine will walk around looking fake tormented all day and giving bewildered quotes to the news. Do you want Douglas Prine to have the last word on your life?"

"I don't know what to do," I moaned. "That was my best idea." I realized my once-cozy comforter was starting to suffocate me, and I kicked it onto the floor. It's so hard to be cozy in Phoenix. The air conditioning fanned out over my sweaty, banged-up body.

"Spencer, why don't you just talk to your parents? Be honest with them. Your dad is *gay*. That's *amazing*. The healing potential of that is really incredible."

Joy had crystals in her head. She thought that everything could be healed and fixed and purified and that everyone could live happily ever after.

"I can't go back to school," I said. "And I can't stay here in this house with my horrible gay father and his *wife*. Can I come live with you?"

"And just hang out here all day with my mom?" Joy said uneasily. "I don't think so, Spence."

"Well, I'm running away, then," I said. Running was the second most popular choice made by teens in despair, according to the internet. After suicide.

"That's great harm reduction!" Joy cheered. "Where will you go?"

"Provincetown." It slipped out of my mouth as impulsively as my first plan had. All this time, all my gay googling, my fantasizing about other gay lives I might be living—or ways to maybe not live at all—all the facts and stories that streamed from my computer into my brain, and I hadn't even known I was *planning*. In some deep and desperate way. Waiting for something worse to happen, and then something worse, and then something worse. Something so bad that I really, truly couldn't stay here anymore.

"Provincetown!" she cheered. "Perfect!"

"You come too, Joy!"

"I can't," Joy said. "I have school and stuff."

"Fine," I sulked.

"When will you leave?" she asked.

"I guess tomorrow. When I wake up?"

LITTLE F—

"Come over before you go," she said. "I'll give you stuff. Protections, and money. Okay? I'll wait for you."

"Yes," I said. We got off the phone and I googled *runaway*. It brought up a bunch of music and movie links. I shut off my computer and went to sleep.

6

THE BULLYING SUN woke me in the morning, squeezing between the slats in my shades, jabbing into my eyes like little lasers. It was late. Mother had let me sleep in. I took a look around my bedroom for the last time. I wouldn't miss it. It had always felt like a holding cell, someplace I'd eventually be released from, and now that time had come, sooner than I'd thought. My walls were bland and undecorated. Preventing Mother from trailing her Southwestern motif in here seemed like the biggest act of rebellion I could muster. That my room was boring was the point of my room. But that would change in Provincetown. In Provincetown, I would sleep in a room with *wainscoting*. I'm imagining a decorative little ledge running around the top of my walls. The walls are a pale blue. You could put something, an antique figurine perhaps, on top of the wainscoting, use it like a tiny shelf, but I wouldn't do that, and that's because I'm a bit of a minimalist.

What would I need to run away? I put on a comfortable pair of jeans I had cut to my knees, and I slid my feet into loafers. A polo shirt. I would look so good in Provincetown. I selected a few replicas of that outfit and my softest sweatpants for sleeping. I packed my backpack with deodorant, hair product, and all the money I could scavenge from my room, including my jar of coins. I would need a book. I thought of the "If you were trapped on a desert island, what book would you want with you?" question. My answer was *The Bell Jar*. I grabbed the busted, yellowed paperback with the dramatic lettering and the black rose dying on the cover. I loved that lady, Esther Greenwood. I wished it was another era, one when I could lose my mind gracefully, with elegance and style, and not have it splattered all over the internet like some cheap reality television show. Mental problems are private, or they used to be. Just another thing to hate about my life and times. Just another reason to want not to be here.

The backpack was heavy on my shoulders, which I still worried might be broken. I was one long ache. The bruises on my legs spread out from the hem of my shorts like a stain. I hobbled down the hall past the wide family room that Mother had decorated in shades of maroon and taupe. Dark colors for a dark room, the shades perpetually drawn against the aggressive Phoenix sun. It was a spooky room: too large, too rarely occupied, like staging for a house on the market. Mother sat on the brown leather sectional, smoking.

"Mom!" I gasped. "What are you doing?"

"I'm smoking," she said. The neon cherry of the cigarette was the brightest thing in the room, and the haze of smoke in the gloom made it even harder to see her clearly.

"Mom, your skin," I said. "It's so bad for it."

"Oh, my skin," she said, taking a long drag, the tip glowing brighter with a crackle.

"The money you spend on it," I reasoned. "To then undo the work, it's just—"

"Spencer, baby, I know everything," Mother cut me off. "Okay? Just so you know. I'm not a fool. I know everything."

I felt stuck in some scary old movie. The dim room, the smoke, Mother speaking in a new tone. Not hysterical, but sort of like *over it*, like her denial had dropped and underneath was Joan Crawford, jaded and cloaked in smoke.

"Okay," I said simply. What exactly did Mother know? That I was a little fag, that her husband was a big fag, making her— what, a fag hag? We should string a disco ball from the ceiling and have a dance party. "Okay," I repeated, "Okay, what do you want from me? What do you want me to do?" My voice rose upward, like the tones of a xylophone. I should be drawling something droll, something too wise, too knowing, too cryptic for my simpleton parents. I should be the one smoking and jaded on the couch. Instead I felt small, smaller than I normally felt, and normally I felt pretty small indeed.

"I want you to go to school. I want you to apologize to Douglas Prine for attacking him. Clean up your mess. If you're lucky I will be able to convince your father to keep you in therapy, but don't plan on seeing Peyton ever again."

I shrugged. "I didn't care for Peyton."

"What do you know." She flicked ashes into the palm of her hand like a monster. She breathed smoke. The cigarette glowed shorter, closer to her face, illuminating it like some ghoul at a carnival haunted house. She'd delivered my portion of her plan. I presumed she had a plan for Father as well. Would it stick? I imagined what had happened in the laundry room could be brushed away, tucked away, hidden like the magazine, and life would go on as normal. Father could stay hidden. I—could I stay hidden? Had I ever been hidden? How could this work? It couldn't. I saw this now, starkly. Just by existing, I was going to mess with their whole facade.

"Goodbye," I said to Mother, backing away from her, moving down the hall, heaving the heavy front door open to the relentless, predictable, eternal sun. I had never been so happy to stand in its light.

7

THE WIND SOCK outside Joy's house is a Disney princess wind sock that would make you think a little girl lived there, but in fact it's Joy's mother. She is really into Disney and has a whole room that sparkles with her collection of Disney snow globes. Joy tried to have a sort of Disney intervention with her parents, refusing to go on their annual trip to the Magic Kingdom, but they were all *When-you're-paying-your-own-rent-you-can-go-to-Stonehenge-but-while-you're under-our-roof-you'll-come-on-our-vacations* about it. Joy actually thinks her mother is a repressed witch who can't find any safe cultural outlets for her impulse toward magic and so she gets stuck in Disney fantasies. She's got a whole theory about it.

I walked right into Joy's house, not because they are hippies but because Joy always forgets to lock the door. I walked into the kitchen where her mom was drinking coffee and reading from her computer. "Spencer, how did you get in here?"

"I just—"

"Joy, what did I tell you about locking the door!" Her head was tilted back so she could yell this out into the house. "We're lucky it's Spencer. What if it was a crazy?"

"What if Spencer is a crazy?" Joy said, walking into the room. She wore a long black cotton skirt that grazed the linoleum and a too-small tank top that revealed a roll of belly. Her purple hair sprouted like a pineapple from a messy bun on the top of her skull.

Joy's mom squinted at me as if she were considering it. "Are you all banged up?"

"I fell off a cliff," I said. Joy raised her eyebrows. "In the canyon."

"See?" She turned to Joy. "You think I'm overprotective, but things happen. Canyons are dangerous." She turned to me. "You hear about the man who fell down a canyon and had to saw his own arm off with a jackknife?"

"Yeah, Ma, it's a movie." Joy made a face at me.

"Well, it's a true story. Joy wants to go to something in the canyon where people are playing drums and howling at the moon or something crazy. No way."

Joy adopted an annoyed posture, hand on hip. *Thanks a lot*, she mouthed at me.

"I didn't really fall off a cliff," I said. "That's just a lie I'm telling my father. I actually got beat up by this kid at school."

"You did?" Joy's mom looked alarmed and motioned to her computer screen. "I'm just reading all about bullying, they're calling it an epidemic. Kids can be so cruel." She glanced at her daughter. "You're still not going to that rave, or whatever it is."

"It's a religious ceremony," Joy said gently.

"Try going to church for once in your life if you're feeling so religious. Also, why aren't you at school?"

"No school today," Joy said breezily, bending and kissing her mother on the cheek. "Remember?"

"No, I don't."

"You never do, Mom!" She tugged my wrist. "Let's go hang out in my room."

JOY'S ROOM HAD a poster that illustrated the progress of the moon through the entire year, a moon calendar. There were little red dots where she tracked her period. It's so crazy that women have periods and it has something to do with the moon. I can't tell if it makes the world more or less magical. Like maybe there are supernatural forces and everything is connected, or maybe we're all just animals and there's nothing mysterious about it at all. Joy's room had a lot of fringed shawls tossed over things. Lace curtains hung over the shades that blotted out the sun, and paper flowers sprung from behind an old-fashioned mirror. Joy put on witchy lady music from another time—a high, warbling voice. She lit a clove cigarette, which she got away with by telling her parents it was incense. Joy really did have her parents under her control.

"Spencer, all of this is just temporary." A grape-colored curl sprang loose from her bun, and she tucked it behind her ear. A metal ankh dangled from the lobe. "We'll become adults and do whatever we want. We'll be free."

"Well, until then, I'll be on the run. You can come visit me in Provincetown."

"Provincetown," she mumbled around the cigarette clamped in her teeth as she pulled up a US map on the computer. She inhaled and then exhaled a sweet, spicy stink into the room. "Spen-cer." She shook her head. "How are you going to get there? Look."

There was the mean chunk of Arizona, heavy at the bottom of the map. Way at the other end of the country sat the dignified cluster of New England, a clique of pretty states. The elegant tip of Provincetown was barely visible beneath the crammed text: *Massachusetts, Rhode Island, Connecticut*. It was a magical place, and much like all fairy tales, to get there I would have to find my way through hostile territory. Texas alone is like its own angry nation, one that takes multiple days to get through.

"Do you have any money? Can you fly?"

Flying seemed like a ridiculous way to run away. "I can't fly," I said.

"How will you get there?"

"I don't know... hitchhike."

"You'll get murdered," Joy said, "And you know it. You understand how heinous people are."

I didn't like that Joy was telling me to be responsible, to consider my safety. My plan was to hold onto the whole "letting go" aspect of suicide while actually staying alive to see what happened. To see what happened without caring too much about it, I mean. Although the more I kept imagining a little room in Provincetown—where maybe you didn't even *need* to hang art on your walls because outside your windows was the ocean, with an actual sailboat drifting lazily in the breeze—the more I felt like caring.

"C'est la vie." I shrugged at Joy. Joy only listens when you speak French or talk spiritual. "I'm just going to trust the universe."

"Well, here." She handed me a pouch full of crumbly dry leaves and small pebbles and tight, dried buds and something fine like sand. I pulled open the drawstring and shoved my nose in it. It smelled amazing, like flowers and spices, water and fire. "It will protect you. And here." She handed me a wad of cash. "It's mostly dollars, but there are some twenties in there, too. Don't get mugged."

"If the protection works, I can't get mugged, right?" I asked, shaking the magical pouch. The wonderful smell of it stirred the air. I tied the tiny drawstring to my belt loop and let it bounce jauntily at my thigh. "Cool."

"And my final gift to you—come to the new moon ritual with me tonight, and then I'll drop you off at the bus station in Tempe. You'll be out of Phoenix in case anyone starts looking for you, and you can buy a bus ticket east."

I flung my arms around Joy and got a choky cloud of clove smoke in my face as I squeezed the air from her lungs. "Thank you. I can't believe you'd help me like this."

She pried me off of her. "You are so strong," she said, "for such a sissy."

8

JOY'S MOTHER HAD told her to stop burning incense in her car, so in order to smoke her cloves, Joy unrolled all four windows and smoked with the wind battering the hair from her pineapple bun, wind sucking the smoke from her mouth and pushing it all over everything. The crazed weather in the car slammed my bangs into my eyes again and again until they teared up, until it looked like I was crying.

"What's your favorite part of *The Bell Jar*?" I hollered to Joy over the roar of it.

"Hmmmm." She took a drag off the skinny, dark cigarette and blew it out the window where the wind shoved it back into the car. "I think when she loses her virginity to the translator and can't stop bleeding." She shuddered. "Ugh. Watch. That is totally going to happen to me. I know it."

"I like when she can't read anything but tabloids and then starts tearing them up into little pieces. Or when she's volunteering at the hospital and has to deliver the flowers and starts taking out the stems that aren't perfect, but none of them are perfect, so she ruins all the new mothers' congratulation bouquets."

"Perfectionism." Joy nodded ruefully. "It's a real spiritual sickness."

In the darkened canyon we followed the sound of chanting and drumbeats until a small glow came into focus. With the only light being the presumed bonfire up ahead, it already seemed like I could be anywhere. This was it. I was really doing it. My life. Taking it into my own hands like any hero from television or Greek mythology. The stones all around us lost their rusty color under the stars, bathing in a silvery, pale glow. Inside any of them could be geodes, spiky little castles of crystal. You'd need to break them open to see, and this is what I was doing, I thought proudly, wildly—breaking open my life to find the magic.

Some magical, crystal-harboring rocks rolled under my loafers, twisting my ankles. I held on to Joy for support. "Wouldn't it be so funny if I really did fall off a cliff here, in the canyon, and got even more messed up?"

"Or died," Joy said. "Wouldn't that be ironic?"

We walked slowly, carefully. The sky was perfectly dark, no moon to light our way. That was the point of the ritual, Joy said. The moon had waned until it disappeared, and tonight it would begin its cycle anew, fattening toward fullness. According to Joy and the assembly of shirtless guys with dreadlocks and witchy ladies with long, uncombed hair, it was a good time to make a wish. To have an intention. To start a new chapter of your life. The sun was in Virgo and the moon was in Virgo and I am a Virgo—if you believe that means anything, and I don't—I don't believe in that stuff at all, but there was something orderly about it that I appreciated.

Smoke billowed from fat bundles of burning leaves. Some hippieish people were dancing around, their billowy clothes silhouetted by the light of a small bonfire. We were on a relatively flat area of the rolling landscape, the ground dotted with tufts of scrubby grass. A chain of scrawny utility poles cast skeletal shadows; it seemed like out here, even these human-made markers of civilization turned a little wild. I imagined animals crouching beyond the light of the fire, where the desert turned inky black, observing us, waiting for us to leave so they could return to their world.

Joy pushed her lip against her teeth, chewing a patch of chapped skin. She seemed suddenly self-conscious, stalled at the edge of the gathering.

"You brought me here," I said to her. "Show me what I'm supposed to do."

"I don't know." She wiggled nervously. "If you weren't here I'd probably dance or something, but it feels stupid with you watching me."

"You're the one who wanted me to come."

"Fine."

Joy walked away and started twirling with some shirtless hippie guys whose armpits I swear I could smell from a distance, through the smoke and everything. I'm not saying it was bad, just powerful. I inhaled it deeply, as if that were the purifying vapor, not the magical twigs. Maybe I needed to breathe in the smell of *man* to initiate myself into my new life of rootless faggotry. Weren't there pheromones in BO? I could feel myself becoming bolder and gayer in the smoky stink. I even tipped my hip to the beat of the drum.

When Joy returned to me, she was smiling and her cheeks were pink and shone with sweat by the firelight. "What do you think," she asked, reading my mind because she was my best/only friend and a witch. "Do you like hippie boys?"

Figuring out what kind of boys I liked was a frustrating mystery. It seemed like if I was so gay that I was getting beat up for it in school, I should at least have been in love a couple times, or in lust, or whatever. But no one really did it for me. How do I even know I'm even gay, then? I'd whined that question at Joy, who'd replied, *Have you seen yourself?*

I considered the hippie boys, their dreads like dark tubes snaking around their heads. "What are dreadlocks?" I asked Joy. "Like, are they just long tangles??"

"Maybe on those guys," Joy mused. "For many Black people, it's more like an art. Creating them, styling them. There's a way of thinking like, white people shouldn't even be wearing their hair like that. It's like stealing. *And* they're giving the world the wrong idea about dreadlocks, because they don't know how to take care of them and wind up looking like mangy dogs."

"How do you know so much stuff when you're just here in Phoenix, same as me?"

Joy shrugged. "I just pay attention."

I paid attention, too, I thought. But maybe I mostly paid attention to myself.

WHEN IT WAS time to make our wishes to the moon, I took the scrap of paper I was handed—a torn piece of a paper bag—and numbered it one through ten. Did I even have ten wishes? I didn't really think about wishes, wishes weren't real. But Peyton had talked about intentions. Like a wish, but more practical. I started writing.

1. I want to be safe and protected while I run away.
2. I want to not get arrested by the police for running away.
3. I want to meet a boy and fall in love.
4. I want to not care what anyone thinks of me.
5. I want to totally take care of myself.
6. A boyfriend.
7. A boyfriend for Joy. Or a girlfriend, etc.

I wasn't the only one who didn't know what was going on. Joy didn't know if she liked boys or girls or what kind of either she liked. She wasn't angsty about it like I was, but she wasn't getting beat up at school, either. Every now and then someone would call her a devil worshipper, but she had a good attitude about it.

8. I want to have a good attitude.
9. Detachment.
10. I don't want anyone to get too upset that I'm running away.

That last one was for Mother and Father. It was hard to know how they would take this. Father would probably take a couple days to realize I was gone, unless he had more gay artifacts he was trying to pin on me. Mother would know right away. But would she care right away? I was doing them a favor, I decided. I was giving them space to work on their relationship, whatever that was. Once I got settled in Provincetown I'd call them from a phone booth, just a super brief call to let them know I was okay, hanging up before the cops could trace it, just in case anyone was looking for me. Maybe I could do this a few times a year—holidays, my birthday. Then, on the day I turned eighteen, I'd tell them everything. Who knows what might have happened by then? Maybe Father would be out and proud, wearing baseball hats with little embroidered rainbow flags. Maybe Mother would have gotten remarried to some really great, not-homophobic plastic surgeon who would give her facelifts for free. Maybe we could have a reunion by the sea, sitting out on my patio, drinking lemonade made salty by the air on our lips.

I followed Joy's lead and walked my list of wishes to the bonfire and fed it to the flames. It seemed like a destructive thing to do, but only if you believe in destruction, and none of these witchy-hippie people do, they all believe in transformation—like, we didn't just *ruin* our lists, we transformed their energy and made it easier for the universe to digest. The universe digests ashes easier than large scraps of paper. Everyone's wishes curled up liquid orange and then rose, charred, into the air. Joy put her arm around me. She was crying.

"I'm so sorry you feel so bad," she hiccupped. "So bad that you wanted to kill yourself." She put her other arm around me and stuck her wet face into my neck. I patted her back.

"It's okay," I said.

"It's *not* okay," Joy said intensely, pulling back and looking at me hard, her crystally eyes ringed with muddied mascara. "I am going to put the biggest spell on that asshole, I don't care if it's black magic. I am going to send his energy back to him threefold. He is going to be *fucked*." Harsh words from Joy. They sort of nestled around me like a cozy armor. "Let's get you to Tempe."

9

JOY AND I shared our wishes. "You wished for a boyfriend? For me? That's so sweet!" She stuck another clove between her teeth and lit it with a tiny plastic lighter, her eyes on the road. "I wished for a lot of things for you. A lot of protection. Also I wished to be nicer to my mom, and for her to be protected from my lies." She blew a spicy cloud from her mouth. "She thinks we're studying right now. It's like they're children, parents. You have to protect them from life's harsh realities."

On the radio was some strong-sounding woman with a guitar from the '90s. Joy wished so hard that she had been a teenager then. If not the '90s, then the '70s, or the '20s, or then any time after the turn of the century. The 2010s were so garish. There was hardly any magic, just technology and reality TV. The dried-up landscape was monotonous in the dark, the cacti skinny and stooped, like old, sick smokers. Bye-bye, desert. Somewhere out there in the dark, the Atlantic Ocean was pummeling the edges of the continent. I imagined the drumming of it sending the subtlest vibrations through the land, reaching me, even though I couldn't know I felt it. Joy exited the freeway.

"What if you just hung out in Tempe," Joy said, looking at a sparse cluster of buildings twinkling against the night sky. "It's cooler than Phoenix. I bet you can find some homos. There's a lake."

"A lake is not an ocean," I said. I wasn't going to go from a suicide plan to running to Provincetown to settling in Tempe, not even an hour from home. "I'm trying to do something grand," I explained to Joy. "Something wild and unexpected. I'm even going to hitchhike."

"Spencer, no!"

"Yes," I said. "It will save money. And it will let the universe know I'm trusting it. This is the *first night* of my new life. I should do something I've never done before." I popped open the glove compartment as Joy swung the car into the bus station parking lot. As expected, a stash of mom snacks. Joy's mom was a big snacker. Skittles, Slim Jims, M&M's. I stuffed them all in my backpack and climbed out of the car.

At the edge of the parking lot, I gave Joy a hug. "Everything feels cheesy," I said. "Saying goodbye and everything. Like it's such a big deal."

"I hate that you're hitchhiking," Joy said.

"But I have my bag." I swished my hips so the little pouch swung. Tears returned to Joy's eyes.

"It's witchcraft!" Joy hollered. "It might not even work—I don't know!"

"Come with me," I tugged at her. "It will be fun."

"It won't be fun," Joy shook her head solemnly. "It's going to be hard. Like having a baby or something. I'm going to go home and live in my parent's house and eat their food and use their stuff. But I'll wait with you while you hitchhike. I'm not letting you drive off with a psychopath."

So we waited. Joy was a dark cloud at the edge of the freeway, scowling in a column of clove smoke. It hung in the heavy desert air, the occasional speeding car fanning it out so that it glowed in the lights of the bus station behind us. It felt nerve-racking to be standing there, so close to these hurtling chunks of steel. The heat of the day was sunk into the pavement, radiating up my legs.

Not hot enough to fry an egg on, but maybe hot enough to warm up some leftovers. Lifting my thumb into the air felt dramatic, like I was in a performance, a performance of my ridiculous life. Look, I'm a hitchhiker! Watch me go!

"Limp wrist," Joy noted, and I punched my hand out strongly. My thumb looked commanding. A car even stopped. A busted, old-fashioned station wagon with a bumper sticker reading "One Nuclear Bomb Can Ruin Your Whole ... Life." "Oooh!" Joy cooed, encouraged. "That's a very good sign."

We ran down the road toward the idling vehicle. I smelled them before I saw them. The holy armpits of the dreadlocked boys.

"No way!" I exclaimed.

"Hello," Joy nodded and blushed.

"Hey, little brother," said the guy on the passenger side.

"Whoa," said the driver taking me in, my neatly parted hair and my tasseled brown loafers. He looked at his companion for validation. "Right?"

"I danced with you in the canyon tonight," Joy reminded them.

"Your car break down?" the driver asked, not taking his eyes off me. "Where you going?"

"She's not going anywhere," I said quickly. "But I'm on my way to New England. As close to that region as you're going, please."

"New England," said the driver. "Whoa."

Was it even safe to drive with stoned people? Joy, my telepathic sister soulmate, stuffed her head into the window and sniffed.

"How stoned are you?" she demanded. "Can you drive?"

"We're driving," the passenger grinned. "We don't want any problems, officer."

"Are you guys like psychos or serial killers or anything?" she continued. "Because I am a very powerful witch, and if anything happens to this person, you will spend the rest of your life wishing you were dead. Okay?"

"Jesus," said the driver, shifting in his seat. "Never mind."

"No, no, no, no, no." The passenger touched the driver's naked shoulder gently. "Man, this is love. I honor this." He turned and looked deeply at Joy. "I totally respect that you are leaving this little brother in our care, and I swear to you on the wishes I made tonight that while he is with us, he will be safe."

"Oh," Joy said, disarmed and awkward. She smiled at the passenger. "Well, thank you. I appreciate it."

"You are powerful," the passenger affirmed. "I felt it."

Joy blushed. She turned to me. "I think this is okay. I trust them." She wrapped her arms around me and kissed me on the cheek. "Call me all the time."

"We're wasting gas," said the driver. "Which is wasteful and expensive."

"Okay," I said, folding myself into the back seat. We were both crying when I zoomed away down the highway. I felt alone in the little capsule of the back seat, a place that smelled a little like vitamins and a little like the sweaty bodies of the two guys in the front. I closed my eyes and felt the car pull me further and further away from my life. If I were blindfolded, if I were being kidnapped, there was no way I'd be able to trace my route back to where I began.

10

"THAT YOUR GIRLFRIEND?" the passenger asked me. He was wearing a vest as a shirt, something woven in another country. There were lumpy beads in his dreadlocks. I wanted to touch them, fascinated, but I was also afraid of them and plus did not want to be weird. How did they get their tangles to clump so neatly? They looked like Play-Doh heads, like their skulls were toys that perfect tubes of putty were being pushed through.

"No," I said. "She's my best friend." The driver raised his eyebrows at me in the rearview mirror. He was checking me out in this sneaky way, like an undercover cop expecting me to shoplift.

"We're going to Austin," said the passenger. "Do you drive?"

"Uh, no. I mean, yeah, but I got my license revoked. For reckless driving." I tried to sound proud but not too proud. "That's why I'm not just driving myself to New England."

"Huh," said the passenger. "How about gas money, you got any?"

I thought about this. I did, but if I'd wanted to spend my money I'd have bought a bus ticket and avoided enduring endless small talk with strange, dreadlocked boys who wore dirty pieces of string as necklaces. "No," I said.

"So, how are you going to contribute?" asked the driver, flashing his eyes at me in the rearview mirror.

"I don't know," I said. "I can help navigate? I'm very good with maps."

"Maps," the driver laughed, and knocked at the GPS sucked to the windshield. "Thanks, we've got that covered."

"Well, it's safer to travel in packs," I scrambled. "And I am a good conversationalist. I know a lot about world history, Greek mythology, and the mid-century poet Sylvia Plath."

"It's okay, little brother," said the passenger. "We told your lady we'd take care of you. There's hummus back there if you're hungry." The back seat of the automobile was torn, the ripped faux leather sharp. A Mexican blanket was spread over the seat, and a grocery store bag on the floor held hummus and peanut butter and rice cakes. I was hungry, but it felt wrong to eat their food, especially after being called out as a freeloader by the driver.

"I've got some food, too," I said, digging into my pack for the snacks I swiped from Joy's mom's car. "M&M's, Skittles, and Slim Jims."

"Whoa," said the driver, whom I will just refer to as Whoa. "Slim Jims? They still make that garbage? Do you know what that's made of? Cow lips, man. Cow lips."

"I didn't even know cows had lips," the Passenger said, stunned.

"Of course cows have lips, what are you talking about?" said Whoa.

The Passenger spun around in his seat. "What's your story, little brother?"

I paused. I could tell these guys anything. They were strangers, they were stoned, they were dreadlocked. A scalp-y, unwashed odor kept drifting into the back seat.

"You're not a runaway or anything, are you?" asked Whoa suspiciously. His blue eyes checked mine in the rearview mirror. "I don't want any trouble."

"You're not doing marijuana, are you?" I sassed. "I wouldn't want my life to be in danger."

"Haaaaaa!" The Passenger was delighted by this. "Doing marijuana!" His smile ate up most of his face. Like Whoa, he was very tan, and his eyes were blue and his dreads were blond. But their faces were very different. The Passenger's face had been molded, it seems, by a lifetime of laughing, while Whoa's had been trained by a lifetime of sulks. The Passenger's face was pleasant, but it was all right there—you got it in an instant. Whoa's face was more interesting. It seemed to hold a code you could crack. It was challenging. What would it take to make him smile? I imagined it illuminating his face like lightning.

"We don't have anything in the car," Passenger assured me. "The forfeiture laws in this state are whack; they'll take your whole car for a roach. We can't risk it. We live in this thing."

"You live here in this car?"

"Sure do." Passenger grinned. "I mean, it's too small to sleep in, so we pull over and sleep outside, but this is it, man. Home sweet home."

"Wow," I said. They were like grown-up runaways. They were choosing a runaway lifestyle. "What's in Austin?"

"Barton Springs," Whoa said. "We're gonna go swimming. Stay in our friend's yard for a while."

"He's got geese," Passenger said brightly. "And a dog, this little schnauzer that's messing with the geese, we're gonna take him. He's such a little scamp, am I right?" he asked the driver.

"I'd rather get a bigger dog," Whoa said. "But whatever."

"How old are you guys?" I asked.

"Twenty-three," said the passenger. "How old are you, little brother?"

"Eighteen," I said.

Whoa laughed. "My man, you are not eighteen," he said, and he caught my eyes in the rearview again. I always thought of eyes as thing that took things *in*. But his eyes seemed to be shooting some sort of energy straight at me, as if scanning me with an invisible ray. And in the shock of being looked at—being *seen* by his eyes, both hard and sparkly—guess what happened? A chill ran down my spine! Not like the kind of chill I get when I'm watching horror movies late at night with Joy and something creepy happens. Instead, it was a nice, warm shiver that didn't scare me until it dissipated and I realized what had happened. I looked away from the mirror.

"Fine, man." Whoa lifted his hands from the wheel. "Better you tell me you're eighteen. You're totally eighteen. Even though you look like you're twelve."

Twelve! I'm thirteen! I wanted to snap, but as my chauffeur requested I remain within my lie, I did not correct him.

"What are you gonna do in New England?" asked the Passenger. "Oh, I'm Travis." He stuck his hand out and I inserted my own into it. "That's Jackson." Jackson looked at me in the rearview again, and a strange spear shot into my chest. A stirring in the loins. No. I clutched my backpack to my lap.

"Dude, we're not going to steal your Skittles," Travis laughed at me. "Loosen up!"

"Oh, no," I said nervously, suddenly shuffling through my pack. The jar of change caught the shine of passing headlights. I covered it with my cardigan and pulled out the bag of Skittles. I was barely breathing. I promised myself I'd never look at the rearview ever again.

"Just looking for my Skittles," I said stupidly, pouring some in my hand and inspecting them intently, as if they were rare jewels. I popped them in my mouth, one by one.

"We mainly eat a raw food diet," Travis explained. "I don't think we can eat Skittles. Something was probably cooked, right? To get the sugar in there?"

"You don't eat cooked food?" I asked.

"We try not to. It's better for you. Healthier. What's your name? Damn, those Skittles smell good. I can smell them from here."

I could have just said, Spencer. It's a fine name, in spite of everything my father had to say about it. It *did* have a refined air about it, if only due to its association with Diana Spencer, RIP, an actual *princess*. But something about the night zooming around us, me inside this bubble of energy with these two strangers, one sweet and one salty, the *zing* that had rang in my body a bit ago, the absolute freedom I was confronting, a freedom so free I could barely look at it head-on. Something about all this newness seemed to call for a celebratory new name. Of course, optimally, the selection of a new name should be given serious thought; one should take their time. But right then, with the flash of Jackson's eyes in the rearview mirror distracting me, and Travis's expectant, golden retriever energy turned my way, I did not have time to think. I was a runaway, on the lam, living by my wits.

"Austin," I said quickly. I resisted the urge to say it aloud again, and again, familiarizing myself with my brand-new name. That would have been weird. Still, it rang inside me: *Austin, Austin, Austin.*

Jackson shifted his head in a way that I knew his eyes were in the mirror. I gazed out the window at the dark freeway. The sickly cacti had faded out. We were entering a new region.

"Your name isn't Austin," Jackson said. "And you're not eighteen years old. I just want you to know you're not fooling me."

It was like Travis and Jackson were playing good hippie/bad hippie.

I bit my tongue, because when I get annoyed or upset I get even faggier. Joy has told me this. She's done imitations of me ranting, her arms akimbo, her head waggling, one hand on hip and one limp wrist slapping the air in front of me. And the voice. I hope my voice doesn't sound like that, but I'm pretty sure it does. So I sat tight, all balled up like a little clam. Just because these guys are hippies and we saw them at the moon ceremony doesn't mean they don't hate gay people. Joy once met these hippies that seemed really cool, and then it turned out they thought women should be pregnant all the time. Sometimes people who are really into nature have stupid ideas about what nature is. What was the chill that shuddered my spine at the sight of Jackson's eyes, if not nature? But I would keep my nature to myself. Assuming they hadn't already figured it out when they saw me skipping toward their car.

"What's in New England?" Travis asked. "Pilgrims?"

"That's where it all started," Jackson said darkly. "America. Killing the natives, Thanksgiving, all that bullshit."

"True," Travis concurred. "True dat."

"I have an uncle there," I said. Of course I didn't, but I'd imagined this dream uncle so many times I sometimes feared I had begun to believe in him. Tall, well-groomed, wearing a crisp, pink button-up shirt, an expensive pink shirt, because he lived in a place where a man could wear a pink shirt and no one would accuse him of being a fag because lots of men wore pink shirts and also lots of men were fags and it was no big deal. It would be like going up to a redhead and being like, "You redhead!" as if there were anything wrong with that. "He's an antiques dealer," I continued the story of my uncle. "A retired professor. From Harvard. He lives on the Cape."

"Must be nice," Jackson said.

"Yeah, I heard about the Cape," Travis nodded. I could feel Jackson's eyes on me. I kept my eyes on Travis. It was weird how they looked so much alike, but I could stare at Travis forever without worrying about anything horrifying happening to my body.

"Yes, it's lovely," I said, and felt a red bolt of panic at the sound of the word *lovely*. Who says *lovely*? Old women and faggots. I tried to play it like I was being sarcastic. "Sooo lovely. Ha."

"The ocean's cool," Travis said sincerely. "The Atlantic Ocean. Epic."

"We were just in the ocean in California," Jackson said. "San Diego."

"Beach babes," Travis grinned and wiggled his bushy eyebrows. They were like little dreads over each blue eye. "Bikini girls."

"We're moving on to Western babes, now. Texas babes. Cowgirls." Jackson was finally smiling. I know because I looked. His words sounded different, being pushed out from grinning lips. The promise of Texan cowgirl babes was bringing him joy. "Bitches who ride the bull!" He smacked Travis on the shoulder.

"Austin," Travis began, "if that is your real name. Have you yet to experience the pleasure of a female?"

Was it even worth it to lie here? Three strikes and you're out. They were letting me slide with my name and age, but I didn't want to push it with stories of an improbable heterosexual sex life. I shook my head.

"Finally," Jackson said. "The little man speaks the truth."

"Lucky you, dog," Travis swatted my arm. "Lucky you. It's gonna blow your mind." He looked at Jackson. "Don't you wish you could go back and lose it all over again? It's the best."

"I'd pick some older chick," Jackson said. "Not old, just, like, older. Not some girl who just lies there all freaked out, you know? You feel like a fucking rapist even though you're like, *Is this cool, Is this cool?* And she's all, *Yeah it's cool*, and I'm like, *Really? Cause you seem fucking bummed.*"

"Who, Julie Atherton?"

"Yeah."

"She was cute, bro."

"Yeah, but that doesn't even matter when it's happening, you know? Better get it on with some ugly chick who likes it than some fucking Snow White who just lies there like a dead fish."

The conversation felt homophobic adjacent, like speaking about girls in this private, straight-man way was just around the corner from talking about gay men, *faggots*, like my dream uncle and me. It made me feel jittery even as I pushed myself to pay attention. It was probably good for me to get a sense of how such men spoke, lest I be forced to portray one in my ongoing adventures.

Travis looked at me. "You're getting an education, little brother. Think of us as your mentors."

"Thanks," I said, and I dumped the rest of the Skittles into my mouth.

11

SPRAWLED IN THE back seat as we hauled through first New Mexico and then Texas, I fell over time into dreamy thoughts of being a kid asleep in the back of my parents' car, coming home from a late night at my grandmother's or an evening movie. In this sleepy state I found myself missing both of them with a sadness so sharp it kept me awake. Mother tried so hard to bring the cheer—that's all she wanted, just to bring harmony to life, and if she had to lie and scheme to get it, well, it just showed how dedicated she was to our familial happiness.

And Father. How could I, still battered (from my battering), blame Father for hiding so desperately? How had he made it so far? Why hadn't he killed himself or run away or something? He had figured out a way to survive, and he was so committed to it he was ready to sacrifice me, his only son. It was sort of biblical.

What did Father think when he looked at me, a little faggot? Was he angry that I hadn't managed to cover it up like he did? Did he think I deserved what I got? That I should have copped steroids from the jocks and bulked out and joined the wrestling team to sublimate my urges?

The longer I thought of it, the less sad I felt. More perplexed and pissed off.

And hungry. I was out of candy, and slowly, like a mouse, I began nibbling into Travis and Jackson's food supply. When we stopped for gas, my rumbling stomach begged me to buy it anything: chips, a yogurt, lunch meat, more candy. I couldn't let Travis and Jackson know I had money. When we got to Austin, I would take myself out for real food in a real restaurant. I would order whatever I wanted; I would even get dessert. Meanwhile, I finished off their hummus and a strange baggy of crumbly crackers and what I think was seaweed. It tasted very fishy, but not in a bad way. Or maybe I was just starving and could have eaten torn shreds of the paper grocery bag and found it savory.

I was half sleeping when Travis shook me awake.

"Are we there?"

"Almost," he said. "But we can't keep driving; we're hallucinating. Give Jackson the back seat. Me and you will go sleep under the stars."

I tumbled out and onto the bank of a river. An overpass hummed above, but it was still a river, with tall green grasses swaying alongside it. The water was wide and dark, and everything smelled of its wetness. It was cooler outside the car, which was still hot from absorbing the Texas sun all day. The swaying grasses felt like a caress where they brushed my legs—nothing like the stiff, dry grass of home.

I wanted to lie down in it, and that was what I did. I didn't even care about bugs, about there maybe being spiders in the grass, or the crickets I could hear fiddling their legs. I didn't think about ants getting lost in my hair or fat, slimy worms turning in the dirt under my head. Everything felt lovely and cool, and I felt a gratitude toward all of it; the river like the source of all the water in the world, endlessly flowing, a miracle after a life in the desert. I wanted to weep, to salute its water with my own.

Travis, close to me but obscured by the grass, began to snore. I bundled a bunch of grass beneath my head like a pillow and fell into a sleep like honey, like cool water, a wood nymph asleep on a tender leaf.

12

I STAYED THAT way until morning, when Jackson woke me up by throwing my empty backpack onto my stomach and kicking a spray of dirt into my face.

"You fucking phony liar, wake the fuck up." He loomed above me like a monster, his dreads wild around his angry face. His face wore the universal look of I'm Going To Fucking Kill You; it looked like Douglas Prine's face.

I sat up and scooted backward on my butt, away from him. This wasn't supposed to happen here, in the sweet grasses that had held me like a fairy. Faces like that were for the desert, for the hot dust, the hate-criming sun, the strips of identical houses where people's souls were buried.

Jackson shook my glass jar of coins in one hand and clutched my wallet in the other. His anger pumped through his arms; I could see it plumping the veins in his muscles. He looked about to hurl the jar at me like a Molotov cocktail.

"*Hi, my name's Austin, I have no money*," Jackson spoke in a horrible, lisping voice. That was what I sounded like. That's what he heard when I spoke.

Travis rose from the grass beside me. "Dude, why are you so aggro? What is going on?"

"This fucking kid's name is Spencer, and he's got a shit ton of money stashed in his fucking backpack," Jackson said. "And it seems like he's in fucking junior high or something, so he's totally a runaway, and guess what? I am not going to go to prison for taking some little runaway bitch over state lines. We're in Texas. You know what they do to you here for shit like that?"

"We're almost in Austin," Travis said reasonably, as if Austin were not Texas.

"Look at this," Jackson held the jar of coins up to the sky, filling it with sunlight. It looked like the Holy Grail or something. "There's, like, a lot of money in here. And this." He dropped the jar into the earth with a thud and whipped open my wallet. It was stuffed with all the money Joy had given me, plus some of my own. He pulled out the wad of it.

"Damn," Travis said.

"It's mostly ones," I defended my abundance. "My friend gave it to me."

"We picked you up," Jackson said, "Out of good karma. Wanting to do a good karma thing. And you mooch off us, you don't help with gas, you eat our fucking food, you eat all my raw food crackers—which are *not* cheap, plus very hard to find—and you lie. That's the worst part." He looked at Travis. "He's got, like, credit cards in here."

"Those aren't mine," I said. "My parents let me have one of theirs."

"Parents," Jackson said bitterly. "Must be nice. I don't know what kind of fight you had with your mommy that made you run away, but you're not getting back in my car. And I will take this"—he stuffed my cash into the front pocket of his cutoffs—"to reimburse me for gas, for my fucking food, and for the danger you put me in with your lies. You can keep your piggy bank." He kicked my jar with his sandaled foot.

"Jackson, Jesus." Travis rubbed his sleepy face with a big, tanned hand.

"I'm not tugging some fucking freeloading trust fund kid around with me. I didn't want to pick up a fucking hitchhiker in

LITTLE F—

the first place, that's your thing. Let's go." He slid my wallet into his back pocket. I sprang from the ground.

"Give me my wallet," I demanded. "Come on."

"Dude, we promised that witchy chick we'd take care of him." Travis's brow was crinkled; he rubbed the back of his neck like he'd suddenly gotten a cramp.

"You did that. I didn't promise shit."

I advanced on Jackson. I could smell him. I could smell heat and sleep coming off his skin. "Give me my wallet."

"I was trying to use your backpack as a pillow," he told me. "And I was like, what the fuck is in this thing?" He kicked the jar.

"Yo, he's a kid," Travis said.

"Give me my wallet." I thought about Douglas Prine's story about how I had attacked him, come at him again and again, crazy, like some horror movie monster that wouldn't die. My hands shot out and shoved Jackson in the chest. My fingers made contact with his skin. I felt the scribble of hair on my fingertips. I'd never touched a man's chest before. I'd never shoved someone before. I did it again. He barely moved, his face half amused, half infuriated. When I went in for a third shove, he reached out and snagged my limp wrists. He walked me backward through the grass, roughly, toward the river.

"What the fuck is wrong with you, huh?" I was tripping over my feet, my loafers filling with dirt as I scuffed backward, trying to stop. But he kept moving. His red face was all I could see, sweat beading at his hairline where the intricate root system of his dreadlocks began. My heels scudded down a slope.

"Jackson, come on!" Travis yelled, and I was falling backward into nothing, and then the water rushed over me, tumbled me and dragged me. It had looked so gentle from the banks, but inside was a current. The river was all business; it had someplace to be, and it was bringing me with it. I struggled against it, tried to stand up, but my loafers twisted under me in the gravel. It wasn't over my head but I couldn't get footing, kept falling and sliding, taking a mouthful of water and coming up sputtering. Crying? Probably. My face was wet and red with the river anyway.

"Can you swim, little brother?" Travis called to me from the bank. The water pushed me toward a low-hanging branch on the other side, and I grabbed it, hung there like a fool. I swam in bright blue swimming pools. Safe squares of chemical water, anything wild skimmed out with a net. Not in rivers, living things with their own agendas, stones scattered under their waters to trip you up and stub your toe.

"Yes," I called weakly to Travis. "I can swim."

"He has a fucking swimming pool at home with mommy and daddy," Jackson spit bitterly, out of sight. "He probably plays water polo. Must be nice. Come on." He kept talking, but I couldn't hear him over the choking rev of his car's engine. Travis looked behind him, then at me, then behind him.

"Little brother," he said. "I am sorry for this bad scene. I wish you hadn't lied to us. You need help getting out?"

I just wanted them to leave. I hated them, Travis especially, who acted like such a cool dude but just wanted to hop in the car with his asshole bestie and forget I ever happened. The only way I could like Travis was if he got my wallet back from Jackson, and he wasn't trying to do that at all.

"Just leave!" I screamed from my branch, holding on like a kitten in a *Hang in There!* poster. "Leave me alone!"

Jackson looked somber, pained. He brought his hands together like praying and brought them up to his face, bowed.

"Namaste," he said, and he backed away out of sight.

13

I MADE IT out of the river, crawling on my hands and knees. It took forever. Each time I tried to stand, the river threatened to knock me over, and I flung myself to its bed and clung there. I almost lost my loafers, but I didn't. I breathed slowly, deliberately, like I was meditating. Isn't that what meditators do, breathe? *Namaste.* That was a spiritual word. Joy would know what it meant.

When I got to my backpack, I called her. I was shaking and wet, half worried that I was breaking my phone with all the water streaming from my hair, but I didn't care. I lay on my back and cried. The sun dried me. It was growing strong; its warmth would soon grow fierce and mean, like the hippies. I imagined the sun as Jackson, its rays like dreadlocks. It would dry the river water soaked in my clothes; it would dry the sweat from the car and the mud from the banks to a crust on me, and maybe that would all be for the best. Maybe I needed a little armor.

"Namaste—the divine in me recognizes the divine in you," Joy said. "It's like a way to remember we're all spirits or gods."

"Well, he recognized that," I said. "And then he got in the car with all the money you gave me and left."

"He is going to pay," Joy said sharply. "I wasn't kidding. I am going to lay a curse on them."

"Fine," I said weakly. I needed food, real food, beef lips. Those expensive raw crackers felt like nothing in my system. No wonder Jackson was so crazy. He probably had low blood sugar all the time, like really low blood sugar. He was living a low blood sugar lifestyle.

"Where are you?" Joy asked.

"I don't know. Outside Austin."

"Just get to Austin. Figure it out, you're smart. You can do it. Watch out for cops. People are looking for you. I got questioned. I don't want to make this about me, but I'm in a bunch of trouble."

"What do you mean?" It was hard not to get excited by the drama.

"Well, everyone knew I was with you, and the cops put out this search, and I got in trouble saying we were at the library because then people said they saw us at the moon ritual. So now I'm super grounded and the cops are acting like they could put me on death row or something."

"Wow," I said.

"I told them I thought you were heading to San Francisco. They totally bought it."

"No one even knows about Provincetown," I said happily. "It's kind of obscure."

"It's a big deal at school," Joy said. "The news picked it up and everything. Everyone feels really bad for you. It's kind of like you killed yourself but better because the story isn't over, right?"

I thought about everyone at school feeling bad for me. It was hard to imagine any of them having feelings, so I couldn't get a good visual of it. Was my picture on posters taped to the rough bark of palm trees? Were kids who never spoke a word to me bragging about sitting by me in Civics, just to see themselves on the news that night?

"Are you popular now?" I asked. "For being my friend?"

"Sort of," she admitted. "It's weird, but now that you're gone, I don't have anyone to hang out with, so I'm kind of into it. Brenna Solis had me do a love spell for her."

"Wow." I felt really far away. It was like I'd thrown a party and got run out of town. Everything was carrying on without me, because of me. "I should go," I said sulkily. "I don't have a charger. I should save my battery."

"Do you want me to tell your parents I heard from you?"

"No," I said. "Are they worried?"

"Yeah, duh."

I felt a stab of an ugly feeling. "Good," I said. "Let them worry."

"You still have your pouch?"

"Yeah, lots of good it's doing me."

"Are you kidding?" Joy demanded. "It probably saved your life! Got that goon away from you before he killed you! Got you across the river safely!"

"Thanks," I said sarcastically.

"Thank me later," Joy said. "When you mean it."

ON THE BANKS of the river, I let the sun dry me out. I could feel my extra-super-pale skin prickling pink at its violence, but I did it anyway. I needed to toughen up. I wrung out my magic pouch, and it dripped its potion into the dirt. "You're welcome," I told the plants.

I felt very close to the river. I did not hold it responsible for almost killing me; as Joy suggested, it was all perspective. If it wasn't there to receive me, perhaps I would have gotten another beating. I had started it, after all.

That was incredible. Had I told that to Joy, that I had started the fight? Who cared that I'd lost? This was a major triumph of fearless living. The more I thought about it, the greater I felt about it. I decided to walk to Austin. The hippies had said it wasn't far. I left the river bank, sad to say goodbye. It still felt special to me, and I took that as a sign I was on the right track, somehow.

14

I WAS IN a little town called New Braunfels. It was oddly Germanic for Texas, not cowboys and longhorns but Fräuleins and sweet rivers. My jar of coins rattled heavily in my backpack. In what appeared to be the town square—a quaint place with ye olde buildings and fake wagons on the side of the road—there was what appeared to be a parade, or a rally. Hundreds of sweaty, happy people in matching shirts. I slunk up into the mix. I sort of stood out; I sort of didn't. I was sweaty, too.

"Want some?" An elderly lady with a wrinkled tan and a sun visor offered me a giant jug of water.

"Thank you," I said, and chugged it.

"Careful, careful," she ordered. "Don't make yourself sick. You know you can die from drinking too much water."

"No," I gasped. "I didn't know that."

"My friend's friend's cousin. She was trying to win something on a radio program. They were giving away a video game to whoever drank the most water without going to the bathroom. She won, too. Such a sin."

"God," I said. "Did anyone get in trouble?"

"Nope." She brushed her hand cynically. "They all have insurance, these companies. They can get away with murder." She regarded me. "You're a little thing. You been with us since the base? Your dad work there? How come I don't know you?"

I stuttered, sorting around for a lie, but I didn't know what the situation was so it was hard to come up with something.

"Are you just hanging around New Braunfels, or you walking to Austin with us?"

"Oh," I said quickly. "I'm walking to Austin with y'all." *Y'all! Can you believe it? I am so fast.* I took a conservative gulp of the lady's water. That water-death story hurt my heart. I hated this stupid world.

The lady looked skeptically at my loafers. "In those? You don't think you're gonna get a blister? You need running shoes, hon."

I shrugged. She took back her water.

"Something not right about you," she observed. I nodded. It was true.

THE PEOPLE HAD been walking from some air force base miles away from New Braunfels all the way to Austin. It was called *I Walked To Austin*. They weren't doing it for cancer or diabetes, just for something to do. I guess it gets boring living on an air force base. It's probably a lot like Phoenix. Mostly it was women walking, and mostly they were older, around Sophie's age, Sophie being the woman who'd shared her water, the person I had decided to mooch off next. In spite of thinking there was something not right about me, or perhaps because of it, she allowed me to shuffle alongside her, accepting the bits of PowerBar and Vitaminwater she offered.

"You're like my little Mokie," she laughed and reached out to scruff my head. She called out to a woman trudging along in front of her. "Phyllis, wasn't I just saying how much I missed my Mokie?"

"Yeah," Phyllis yelled over her shoulder.

"That's my cocker spaniel. She likes when I give her people food. I miss her, but she's too old to do something like this. And now I got you. What's your name?"

"Brendan," I said. There was nothing wrong with Spencer except that Spencer was wanted by the cops. Older women often commented on the elegance of my name and I would have liked to have impressed my new friend with it, but oh well.

"I'm Sophie," she said, and frowned. "You're too young to do this alone, Brandon. How old are you?"

"My folks wrote me a note," I said quickly. "It was approved. I'm older than I look. And I am very mature."

She laughed and scruffed my head again as if I were a cocker spaniel. Sophie was satisfied. "So, what, are you staying all by yourself in the motels, then?" I nodded. "Oh, you have to stay with me and Phyllis tonight, then. We'll keep an eye on you."

AND SO IT was that I walked to Austin, slumbering with a couple of old ladies in the sorts of worn motels with swimming pools wrapped in chain-link fences and free waffles in the morning, the sweet batter pre-poured into Styrofoam cups. I enjoyed it all immensely. I enjoyed watching Sophie and Phyllis apply their face creams before bed. I enjoyed watching them tuck their hair around curlers and in the morning mist their heads with hair spray. I enjoyed watching them pat foundation onto their faces only to sweat it off along the road. They wouldn't hear of me *not* eating their food, using their sunscreen. They were mothers and grandmothers, and this was what they did: They shared their food with children, they took care of them. I shared a bed with Sophie and she cuddled me like I was a stuffed animal. It was sweet until it wasn't, with her breath annoying the back of my neck. I squirmed away.

Sophie and Phyllis both had grandsons, and they both noted how much more polite I was, how well-mannered, how I'm not a roughneck. I kept their company easily, as if we were all the same. You know why? Because old ladies love little faggots. I didn't know what these women thought about gays, and I didn't want to. They certainly had opinions: Their husbands were military guys, they were probably Republicans who voted to make sure nothing good or fair ever happened to a gay person. But they liked me, they were sweet to me, and the reason they liked me was because I was a fag. *That's* how I wasn't like their grandsons. *That's* why I laughed at their jokes and enjoyed their gossip. Phyllis gave me Band-Aids for the blisters at my heel, and Sophie clucked and said I told you so.

When we arrived in Austin there was a party in a park with picnic food: platters of rolls and pink curls of meat, aluminum casserole dishes heaped with various salads held together by mayonnaise. I fixed a wobbly paper plate for myself, then stuffed a bunch of little bags of potato chips and pretzels into my backpack for later.

I gave Sophie a hug goodbye, filling my nose with her drugstore grandmother perfume, the dry smell of her hair spray. She frowned, confused. "Aren't you coming back with us on the bus?"

"I'm meeting my uncle here," I said, transporting my imaginary uncle from Provincetown to Texas. "He's a professor at the university."

"Well, where is he, then?" Sophie looked around. "You walk all the way here and he doesn't show up to meet you?"

"He's teaching," I said.

"On Saturday?"

"Yeah," I nodded, like that was normal. Sophie kept looking at me. I felt a rush in my chest.

"You aren't from the base, are you? Who are you? You some kind of runaway?"

I didn't say anything. I wanted to flee, but that seemed dramatic. Sophie sighed. She stretched her hand out to my head one last time.

"You didn't take nothing from my purse. I checked. Phyllis did, too. Not to insult you, just, there wasn't something right about you from the start. I called it, I did." I would have nodded, but her hand on my head felt nice, and I figured it was the last bit of human contact I'd have for a while. "I noticed the bruises, too. I figured something happened to you, but you don't know. Boys, they're always getting banged up." She removed her hand from my head. "All right then, Brandon, you better skedaddle. Get on with yourself. I'll tell Phyllis you said bye."

Phyllis was over at the potato salad station, testing the limits of a paper plate with a heaping, wet mound of it. Sophie shooed at me with her hands. I wasn't Mokie anymore. I was some sort of stray.

"My name isn't Brandon," I told her. "It's Spencer."

"Spencer." She smiled. "Is that so? I had a beau named Spencer. I always liked that name."

And I headed off in the direction of the buildings in the distance.

15

THE SUN WAS almost gone from the sky by the time I found my way to the bus station. At the ticket counter I cleared my throat and conjured the dignity of a thousand proud women in distress, black-and-white-movie women with wide-brimmed hats and slim skirts. I arranged my face in an earnest yet proud expression. My eyes would connect deeply, hopefully, with the ticket seller, a woman who was ignoring me. She was a little jowly, her hair slicked back with a palmful of discount hair gel, a shuddering green mound of Dippity Do, Jell-O for hair. Her lips were very pink. They looked like a sticker of lips on the tan of her face. I cleared my throat once more.

"I see you," she said. "I see you there with the coughing. You'll have to hold on a minute." I placed my hands on the countertop primly. I was channeling innocence. My bruises were fading, but if one looked close enough, one could see the jaundiced patches. I hoped the woman would look closely. I hoped her eyes would open wide with concern and benevolence. I straightened my posture, imagining silver screen heroines resting on sensible pumps.

Why a woman, you ask? Why not a man? Because a man wouldn't be in this situation. A man would find some way to man his way around it. Men are not vulnerable, do not rely on the kindness of strangers. That is something women do. Women, and also little faggots.

Dippity Do raised her face. "Now I am ready for you," she said, barely glancing at me, readying her computer screen for a sale. "Where you going?"

"Well, madam—"

Her face cut up at me in a scowl. Whoops.

"I would like to speak with you about a conundrum I have found myself in," I continued.

"Are you buying a ticket or aren't you?"

"I most surely *was* buying a ticket, that most surely was my intention. But I seem to have lost my—" I almost said *purse*, but I didn't; I did not say *purse*. "—billfold. And so I find myself stranded. I was hoping that you and your employer could kindly provide me with a ticket to New England, and upon arrival my uncle, a Harvard law professor, will reimburse you for your kindness." I paused, a smile on my face. I am someone people say yes to. That's what I was channeling.

"There's nothing direct to New England. We have a bus that goes as far as New York. It's two hundred and fifty-four dollars." She looked at me blankly. She did not understand a word I said. She did not speak the elegant language of a proud women in distress. Could I be a kid instead? I assembled my face into something more *gee whiz*. But then if I was too much of a kid, she might call the cops. I put my face down on the counter. Now she'd think I was a drug addict.

"I don't have any money," I said frankly. "I need a free ticket. I can get the money to you later. Okay?"

She laughed at me outright. "We don't give free tickets, sorry."

"But I'm stranded. I don't have the money. I've been in an accident, see?" I angled my face at the light, urging her to see the greenish-yellow tint to my cheekbones. "I need your help."

"Join the club." She motioned outward at the waiting area, the various people slumped in chairs or against walls. Some were watching me. Shady looking adults, adult men. A kid, a boy, someone my age, maybe a teenager. He was by himself. He had dark skin and slippery black hair in need of a haircut. I looked away, embarrassed at being a spectacle.

"You think I should give all of them tickets, too? Huh?"

"Yes!" shouted an old man with a crinkly white beard. "Praise the Lord!"

"See?" she demanded. "Come back when you can pay for your ticket like everyone else. Next!" There wasn't anyone behind me in line. That was my dismissal. She bent her head of crunchy hair back down toward the computer and hit some keys. My heart hammered in my chest, I felt the eyes of a roomful of bored people on my back, and this lady, this terrible lady acting like I was a piece of trash that had blown onto her windshield.

"Good day!" I huffed, and turned my back to her, facing the people. All their eyes really were on me; feeling it, I felt tears start to prickle. I searched wildly for a place to hide, spotted a bathroom, aimed myself into it.

The bathroom was a dank cave, one that seemed attached not to the shiny and relatively clean bus station but to an abandoned building in a bad part of town. Like someone would pop out of a stall and try to sell you drugs. The dim yellow light flickered, and the mirror over the sink was a polished piece of metal that warped your reflection. The stalls, amazingly, had no doors on them. How beastly! Were men expected to defecate publicly, like animals at the zoo? The whole scene was so abjectly fascinating that I, for a moment, forgot my humiliation, but then it returned, and my face began to run with snot and tears. I tugged rough paper towels from a dispenser on the wall and mopped my face.

I was huffing and sniffling when a man came into the room. One of the guys from the waiting room. He was maybe thirty and looked like nothing. Sandy hair, white face, a T-shirt, pants. He could have been homeless or had a home. He could be poor or he could be okay. He could be upstanding or he could be a menace.

"There you are," he said. "I saw that, at the counter. That bitch is a real bitch, ain't she?"

Of course she was, but I didn't want to sink to the level of this bus station culture, calling a pathetic lady a *bitch* while chatting in a rancid bathroom with some strange man who says *ain't*. But you're a runway, I reminded myself. This is what runaways *do*. I looked up at the guy, toughening my face, flicking my crumpled paper towel into the overflowing wastebasket. Being a woman hadn't worked. Maybe I'd try being a man.

"Totally," I said. "Total fucking bitch."

"You need money?" he asked. "You're going to see your uncle. Where does your uncle live?"

"Massachusetts," I said. "Provincetown."

He wrinkled his face, which was already wrinkled. His face had spent its life in Texas, never using sunscreen. Tanned creases. He had gray in his hair, but his hair was sort of light, so it blended in. He didn't have any luggage. "Provincetown. Never heard of it."

"It's wonderful," I promised him.

"You really got in a car accident?" he asked. "Or did your dad do that to you?"

I blanched. "No! My dad—no. He would never do that. He's never hit me."

"Uh-huh." The guy nodded like I was boring him to tears. He wasn't very exciting either, but at least the encounter had prompted me to pull myself together.

"I can give you money for your ticket if you help me out," he said.

Oh boy. As if I needed further evidence that every bad thing you hear about the world is true. If I tried to dash out of the bathroom, the man could easily block me. He had positioned himself in that way. Like everyone, he was considerably larger than me.

"Gee," I said. "Let me guess what you want me to help you with." I sounded smart, but my heart was pounding. I could scream, but if I made a scene the police could become involved. Who knows what this man would tell them? I was a street kid trying to scam a bus ticket. I was wanted for attacking a popular kid like a rabid pit bull. I was an unreliable witness to my own experience.

"You've helped out men before?" he asked.

"No!" I snapped.

"You don't really have an uncle," he said, studying me. "And you weren't really in an accident. I'm not going to touch you, but if you come in the back stall with me, I'll buy you a bus ticket."

"Can I come, too?"

The long-haired boy from the lobby was suddenly with us, sliding around the man and into the bathroom. His voice was loud, and there was something colorful about him, a boundingness, as if he was a small rubber ball that had ricocheted into the room.

"Hey," he said. "I heard all that. I need some money. Me, too."

The man looked annoyed. "Calm down," he said to the kid. "What, do you think I'm a bank? I'm making an arrangement with this boy right here. Don't try to horn in on his game, it's rude."

The boy looked at me. His eyes were dark and wide. "Am I?" he asked. "Am I cutting in on your game?"

"No, no," I said quickly. "I don't have a game, you can have him."

The man reached out and cuffed my arm up by my shoulder, squeezed me there, like a snake choking a rat.

"I want you, not him," he said.

"Hey, you said you wouldn't touch me," I struggled.

"You did, man, I heard you say that. No touching," the kid chimed in.

The guy let go. "Jesus," he sighed. He couldn't take his eyes off me. Great, so I learn I am irresistible to perverts. Why didn't he want the other kid? The other kid was sort of beautiful. He looked like a shard of desert stone, a slice of canyon. He wore baggy skater shorts he'd maybe just chopped from a wide pair of pants and some sort of army shirt with the sleeves cut off. He wore a rope around his neck with nothing on it. When his long bangs flopped around his face, I could sometimes see something, a speck on his cheek beneath his eye. A star.

"Listen, I am not a rich man," said the pervert. "I have enough for a bus ticket. One bus ticket. You two want to split that money, figure it out together. Now. I don't have all night. There are other boys I could be helping if you don't need my help."

I did. I did need help. Enough to do this? If he didn't touch me, I couldn't be hurt, right? It would be easier with someone else there, even this kid, a stranger. His sneakers were filthy old high-tops with zebra stripes. He had zebra stripes on his arm, too. White lines, little scars that glowed pale on his skin.

"Sure," I said. "You can come. I'll split it with you." Because wasn't this all my punishment—my karma, Joy would say—for not having been generous with the hippies? For lying, for not sharing what I had, for taking so much from them? Now I needed help, and this was what I got. Should I be grateful? I'd have a hundred and twenty-five dollars, half a ticket.

"After you," said the kid, gesturing.

The man led us into the wide, piss-y handicap stall at the rear of the room. I turned around to make sure the kid was really coming. He was. He winked at me, or perhaps it was the light. It was dim and slightly strobed with the flickering of a half-dead bulb. In the stall, by the toilet where the man leaned, it was even darker.

"Come here, come close," said the pervert. "Let me see you. Both of you."

He unzipped. I didn't want to look. I didn't want that one to be the first one I'd ever seen. I guess I felt like there was something inside me that needed to be protected, even if I didn't know what it was. The kid was looking straight at it. I know because I had decided to look at the kid. His bangs fell down his face and, peering in, I could see the smudge of that star. Did he draw it on his face? I wondered. What would I look like with a star drawn on my face? Ridiculous. Like a clown.

"You can touch yourselves if you like," the pervert generously offered. "Or each other. Just relax. Do whatever you like."

The kid looked at me, and I looked away quickly, scared to have been caught staring at him. I looked at the man, not meaning to. Ugh. *Dogs, cow lips, Slim Jims.*

"Want me to come closer?" asked the kid.

The man nodded and made a noise. He was losing his verbal skills. The kid slunk away from me, alongside the wall, like a cat. He slid up to the man. He unzipped his pants. His hand disappeared, but not there, not into his zipper. Into his pocket. He pulled out a dark handle, and with a barely audible flick a sharp blade sprung from it. It caught all the light in the lightless room and glowed like a magic wand. It was at the pervert's throat in an instant.

"I don't care about you, man, *at all*," the kid said into his face. "You get it, right? You get it? I will push this into your fucking throat and flush your head down the toilet."

I stopped breathing. I felt dizzy, like I was someplace very high and had suddenly looked down. I reached out and touched the cool cinder block wall of the bathroom. I did not care that it was filthy, that I was maybe touching excrement or who knows what. The cinder block wall felt solid. I watched the kid's slender arm muscle flex.

"Feel that?"

"Yes," the pervert said in a very small voice, afraid to move his vocal cords against the knife.

"Reach into your pocket and give me your wallet. Fucking *slowly*."

The kid's muscle flexed again and the guy whimpered.

"It's sharp, right?" said the kid. "It's real. This is fucking real."

The guy shifted, and a wallet was in his hand.

"Throw it on the floor. Throw it to him."

To me? The wallet skidded like a puck on the floor, hitting my loafers.

"Pick it up!" the kid ordered. Was he robbing me, too? Was I his helper or was I under his command, or both? I picked up the wallet. It was leather, worn and smooth, warm from being so close to the pervert's body. And it was fat.

"Open it, quick."

I did. There was a lot of money shoved in there. It was way more than two hundred. He could have bought bus tickets for me and the kid and the old man praising the Lord out there in the lobby.

"Check his ID."

I did.

"What's his name."

I squinted in the dark. It was a Texas ID. There was the man, maybe a few years back. A little less wrinkled, a little less tan. That's what he looks like when he smiles.

"Darren McDaniels," I said.

"Darren McDaniels," the kid said into his face. "Darren McDaniels, Darren McDaniels. I bet you're on the registry, huh? It would be so easy to bust you. If you fucking try anything, we will bust you. I'm going to give you just a little cut, just so you have something to take care of, and we'll get the fuck out of here. Okay?"

"Okay," said the pervert, who had a name. Darren.

The kid drew the knife across Darren's neck. I gasped. So did Darren.

"You fucking—" The pervert named Darren clutched his neck.

"Chill out," said the kid. "I didn't kill you." There was blood on the knife.

The man roared like something shot but not fatally, just enough to make it charge you, to make it want revenge. His hands shot out and shoved the kid against the wall. I heard his head hit the cinder block. I screamed. The kid still had the knife. He jabbed out with it, getting Darren in the arm. The knife was in the arm, then out of the arm, and there was blood, and Darren clutched his arm, roaring.

"Run!" yelled the kid, and I did.

16

I STILL HAD the wallet, right in my hands, like a thief. I was running with a stolen wallet. I could not stop to put it in my backpack or my pants—I just ran with it out into the terrible brightness of the bus station where people had heard the commotion, heard Darren's roar and my scream through their sad daze.

"You go," cheered Praise the Lord man. "You go, you go, praise the Lord."

Dippity Do stood up from her swivel chair and looked around, upset. The kid was behind me, his sneakers smacking the floor. His knife was still open, covered in blood.

"Call the cops!" Darren McDaniels hollered. "Help me! Stop them! Call the cops!"

The glass door flung open and I hit the warm hot night like a wall.

"Go!" the kid urged me. "Go, go, go!" He drew ahead. "Follow me!"

And I did; I followed him, tripping over my loafers, holding on to the wallet as if it was keeping me alive.

IN THE DARK I lost sight of the kid and then found him again, a bobbing dark form in the distance. My body's many injuries sounded their alarm at this sudden rough motion. I can't run. How I hate to run! How I hate to break a sweat! How jealous I was of Joy and all the girls, with their womanly excuses to skip gym class once a month. I huffed and puffed while the kid flew.

LITTLE F—

We were moving over rocks that jumped up as my feet hit them, slowing me down. And then I tripped over a bar on the ground and did a face-plant into a bed of chunky gravel. We were on train tracks, I realized. I still clutched the wallet. I did not let go of the wallet.

I looked behind me, waiting for Darren McDaniels or one of his pervert friends. I was that girl in the horror movie, the fallen one, looking back in a red-mouthed scream. But no one was there. All was silent, all but the sound of the kid jogging back to me, his feet light on the gravel. He still had his blade out.

"You okay?" he asked. Then, "You still got the wallet?"

I waved it at him.

"Give it to me," he said, and I obeyed. He was holding a bloody knife.

He slid the wallet into one pocket, then kneeled down and stabbed his knife into the ground, pushing the blade back into the handle. "It opens good, but it's hard to close."

"Aren't you going to clean it?" I asked.

"Naw. It's scarier that way. Like, I've killed and I'll kill again!"

"Have you?"

"Naw," he said. "But I would if I had to. My dad told me if you carry a weapon, you've got to be ready to use it."

"Your fly is still down," I said helpfully.

"Thanks." He zipped it. "Listen, I have a boxcar down here I'm staying in. Do you need a place to stay? Or if you just want to come by, I can pay you out. I don't want to do it here on the tracks. Someone could still be coming."

"Pay out?" I scampered back on my feet.

"Your cut." He smacked his thigh, where the pervert's wallet lay.

"Right," I said. I had been part of that, a robbery and assault. An assault with a deadly weapon.

I crunched alongside the kid through the darkness of the tracks until we reached a disabled car tilting off to the side against a stand of trees. It wasn't easy to get into. It was big, heavy, and rusty. The rust coated my hands as I clutched at some bars and hoisted myself up on my belly, sliding along the floor like a seal. The kid was more like a monkey. He swung himself in expertly, but it was his house.

And it really was a house! He had a little oil lamp, which he lit, and a lousy blanket, and a plastic bag of scavenged food. Around the lamp were some rocks, including one that looked like a geode—sparkly. And a feather and a little black-and-white picture, like from a photo booth. It felt cozy, like a clubhouse.

"Wow," I said. "How long have you lived here?"

"Just a couple nights," he said. "Tonight is the last one."

"It looks like you live here," I said, noticing the trashy garland of ribbons stuck on the metal above our heads.

"I like to make a home everywhere I go," he said. "I bring my light and my blanket, but everything else I leave. I always find new decorations wherever I land." The kid slid onto his butt and dug the perv's wallet out of his pants. He flipped it open. "Man, this feels good," he said. He pulled out the bills: a mix of tens, twenties, fives, and ones. He counted it and put it in piles. "Three hundred, even," he said. "For both of us."

"Three hundred each?"

"Yes," he affirmed. "That gets me to New Orleans with cash to spare. And it gets you straight to the other side of the country."

The car was warm. He pulled up his shirt and wiped his face on it, leaving me there with his stomach. It was a nice stomach. I guess you would call it ripped. As if all he did was eat scraps and swing on boxcars and run from people he stabbed. His belly button was an outie, plopped there like a bead of putty.

"That was great," he said. "You picked it up great. It's like you knew what I was doing—you were right there."

"I didn't," I said. "I didn't know what you were doing."

"Well, you were right on the ball. That was a great job. Do you feel good?"

Good? I thought about times I'd felt *good*. Acing a test, sure. Lounging with Joy in her bedroom with a tray full of snacks and the knowledge that no one would bother us, yes, very good, very relaxing. Getting accosted by an actual child molester, then helping a beautiful stranger rip him off at knifepoint? My stomach lurched. No, I didn't feel *good*. But I shrugged. "I don't know."

"Have you eaten?"

"Not so much."

The kid untied the knot in the plastic bag and pulled out a bruised apple and half a loaf of bread. "The bread's moldy, but you can eat around it," he said.

I did, happily. I was hungry, and that run had taken it out of me. The run and the panic and what I'd seen and what I'd done, what I'd done that I didn't even know I was doing.

"You mugged guys before?" he asked.

"No."

"What do you do, just get with them? Turn tricks?"

"No." I shook my head, speaking over the glutinous blob of bread in my mouth.

"Really?" The kid was surprised. "What do you do, what's your hustle? How're you getting along?"

I shrugged, and something dawned on him. "How long have you been out here?"

"A few days," I said.

"Oh," he said. "Oh, okay. Have you run away before?"

"No."

"So, this is like your first everything?" he asked.

"Yeah, I guess."

"Well, you're a natural." He pulled his shirt straight off his body and balled it up like a pillow for his head. He had more white stripes on his chest, around his heart. He was part zebra, I thought. What are those animals? Okapi. Part zebra, part not. "What's your name?"

"Spencer," I said. "That's my real name, but police are looking for me so I keep using different names."

"I'm Velvet," said the kid. He didn't ask me why the cops were after me. I guess that was normal around here. "Where you headed?"

"Provincetown. It's in Massachusetts."

"How come?"

"I have an uncle there," I said. "He's so great, he's, like, a professor, and he collects antiques. And the ocean is there. It's sort of old-fashioned. It's a small town."

"Sounds awful," Velvet said. "I'm going to New Orleans. My sister Stacia lives there, she's a dancer. I'm going to stay with her."

"She knows you're coming?" I asked.

"Nope," said Velvet, rolling onto his side. "It's a surprise." He looked so comfortable there on the floor, as if it were a real bed. Curled like a kitten, a tabby.

"I can really stay here?"

"Sure," he mumbled. "You can even come to New Orleans with me. It's on the way to that place you're going, right?"

"It might be," I said. "Is it easier traveling with someone else?"

"Depends," said Velvet. "Sometimes. If they pull their own weight."

"I do pull my own weight," I said.

"I figured, or I wouldn't have asked you."

"Well, thank you for letting me stay here," I said awkwardly.

"Yeah, just blow out the lamp and stop talking, okay? Talking time is over." He rolled over and pushed his face into his T-shirt. His back was sort of amazing. Why? I asked myself. Why is it amazing? I studied it, trying to understand its pull. It was just a back. But its shape was pleasing. The width of his shoulders and the way it all tapered down, a strip of grimy underwear rising out of his too-big shorts. His skin looked like it got along with the sun, like it didn't have my abusive relationship with it. If I put my hand on his back I would feel the sun there, inside him, warming him.

Ugh, I would never do that! I was just looking. Just like the pervert. I shuddered and felt sick and quickly blew out the little glass lamp. A dark, oily smell floated up into the car. I took off my shirt and rolled it under my head like Velvet. I curled fetal with my back to him, but our butts were slightly touching, butt to butt.

He snored. I did not sleep, everything that happened that night still vibrating inside me, and there, in the quiet, too loud not to notice. I tried to steady my breathing, like Joy would tell me if she were there, long and smooth in, long and smooth out.

After a little bit of this, I realized I had synced my breath with Velvet's, and his little snores turned faintly hypnotic. My eyes were closed, not clenched. I fell asleep.

17

I WOKE TO a banging, clanging cacophony.

"Hey there boy, hey boy—boys? Ya multiplying in there?"

A man was smacking the dense metal of our clubhouse, his voice close. Something grabbed my ankle, and I jumped up. My limp wrists shot out and started clobbering at this blur of a human.

"Don't touch me!" My heart was beating. My hand throbbed. That clobber had hurt me more than it did him, for sure. The man rubbed the glinting scruff of his face with a grubby hand, chuckling in the morning sun.

"Well, pleased to meet you, too!" He had let go of my foot, though. Velvet sat up.

"Harlon, Spencer. Spencer, Harlon."

"Spencer, Spencer Tracy," the guy grinned, a smile with no teeth. "I'm not gonna hurt you. Hey, boy, your friend thought I was gonna hurt him."

Velvet looked at me and made a face like, *This guy's crackers.* It was an insider-to-insider sort of exchange, and I felt special to have caught it, to be this person called Velvet's confidant. "What do you want, Harlon?"

"Well, I was wondering." He was leaning so far into our car he might as well join us, and he did. He hauled himself up on his scarecrow body and folded himself before us, a pile of bones in some dingy work clothes. He came with his own smell: part dust, part swill. His long black hair was streaked with gray. "Did you eat all that food we scored the other night?"

"Practically," Velvet said, annoyed. "What happened to your own?"

"Well, I ate it!" he exclaimed. "I'm a full-grown man with a full-grown appetite."

"I'm not giving you my food," Velvet said. Then he did this thing that I'd only ever seen on old Westerns screened on obscure television channels that no one but me and a few elderly insomniacs watched: Velvet rolled his own cigarette. He had a pouch not unlike my own magical one, but it was filled with rusty crumbles of tobacco and a little packet of tissue-thin paper. He rolled one up, concentrating hard, licking the paper, twisting it into origami. A regular plastic lighter lit one end on fire. A bubble of smoke floated toward Harlon, who sat there, a dog begging for scraps.

"But you gave *him* food, didn't cha?" Harlon pouted. "And he didn't help with nothing."

"It's none of your business," Velvet said. "You don't know anything, anyway. You don't know what he did."

"I know he can't hit worth shit," Harlon said. "That's not gonna help you out very much."

"You woke me up," I said in my own defense, though had I been awake, I surely would have been too scared to hit Harlon at all.

"You caught him off guard," Velvet dismissed him. "Anyway, you know I'm leaving. Today's the day."

"The least you can do is leave me some food," Harlon begged. "After all I've done for you."

"There's a heel of bread, you want it?" Velvet snapped. He flung the plastic bag at Harlon's head. "There, have a feast."

Harlon took the bag without looking at it and shoved it in his back pocket, where another man might keep a wallet. "Thought you were leaving yesterday," he said.

"Well, it didn't work out like that. I'll leave today."

"You and Spencer Tracy," he huffed. "That trouble over at the bus station prevent your departure?"

"You heard of it?"

"Oh, yeah," Harlon nodded. "That vagrant Johnny Cornflakes told me about it. A couple boys and a bloody knife and some fool pederast yelling and crying. He said it was a good show. Made his night."

"The cops come?" Velvet sounded disinterested, making conversation.

"Nah, don't think so. You should be cool. Really taking off, huh?"

"Yeah, and we said goodbye already." Velvet stubbed out his skinny cigarette on the wall of the car. He started rolling things up and shoving them in a pack.

Harlon turned his attention back to me. "Look at you," he said. "You're like this." He did a poor imitation, his mouth in a prim, nervous grimace, his eyes a bit bugged. I felt my lip curl up, repulsed. I might not succeed in comporting myself with the grace and dignity of old-time movie ladies who live in my head, but I didn't look like *that*, either.

"You can't say boo to a goose," Harlon went on. "You gonna run with this one?" He shook his head. "Hey there. He can't say boo to a goose, your friend."

"I heard you," Velvet said.

"What does that even mean?" I said. "Why are you even here? Maybe it's time to go."

"Oh, is it?" Harlon put on some airs, sat there with his hand on his hip and his eyebrows up high on his face. "Your friend thinks I should go. Well then, as you said, we've had our goodbye. May the road rise up to meet you." He scuffled sideways like a rickety crab-man and hopped down from the car.

"For fuck's sake." Velvet followed him. "Wait here."

LITTLE F—

AND SO I did. The car was still dark except for the gash of blinding sunlight cutting in the gaping door. I packed my scant belongings, wishing Velvet hadn't given the bum that bag of bread. I didn't have much of a claim to it, but it would have been nice. Today I would eat in a restaurant. Somehow. What had Velvet said? I could go straight to the other side of the country with three hundred dollars. The horror of the previous night felt far away, like I'd dreamed it. But didn't this boxcar feel like a dream, too? Didn't Velvet? Joy would never believe it.

I lifted Velvet's shirt, the one he'd slept on, and lifted it quickly to my nose. *Pervert.* He smelled like the bum, but better. There was dust and food gone bad, but there was something sweet. There was his hair, his cigarettes, which didn't smell like normal cigarettes but like something Joy would burn at her altar. Velvet was beautiful, and his smell sort of was, too.

I put the T-shirt down just in time. Velvet swung back up into the car by one ropey arm, landing with a thud of bad vibes.

"Fucking fuck," he said, continuing where he had left off.

"Yes?" I asked politely. "Is there something wrong? Can I help?"

Velvet grabbed his shirt from where I'd just been huffing it, considering the odors like a French perfumer or something. He didn't put it on; he pushed it into his face. His shoulders did a single heave and he breathed in deep and rubbed the fabric from his forehead to his chin. He pulled it over his shoulders.

"Harlon's got my money," he said.

"What?" I squeaked. "That bum? Let's go get him! You have your knife, I bet you can just scare him." Look at me, one exposure to crime, and I make it my lifestyle. But I'd watched this kid take on an actual menace; he could knock over that toothpick Harlon with a kick in the shins.

Velvet was shaking his head. "I gave it to him."

"The money from last night? The child-molester money? The money from the wallet?"

Velvet nodded. "Yeah, that money. The only money."

I felt frantic. "Well, why did you do that? That's crazy—let's go get it back!"

"Just leave it, okay? Leave it alone. Harlon's my dad."

18

WITH MY CUT of the child-molester money, I bought two tickets to Houston: one for Velvet, one for me. That was as far as my cut would take us. I didn't have to do it. Velvet said as much. "This is my problem, not yours," he said. "You don't owe me anything. That's your money, fair and square." He seemed to have a code he lived by, like a long-ago thief or a prince. It made me trust him, and the thought of leaving him behind sent a parachute fluttering sadly in my chest. It would be good for me to have Velvet, and if it weren't for him, I wouldn't even have this money at all, would I?

The bus station was the same, but the woman behind the counter was different. A familiar old man leaned against the window with his eyes closed and a smile on his face.

"What up, Cornflakes?" Velvet broke his reverie.

"Praise the Lord," he said serenely. "You two. God bless you two."

"Give him a dollar," Velvet said, nudging him. I did. "Give him another." I looked at Velvet, like, really? He stared back. I gave the man Cornflakes another dollar.

"Bless you boys," he nodded.

"THEY'RE FUCKED," Velvet said outside on the curb, squinting against the sun, having just rolled a cigarette and begun the consumption of it. Nearby our bus idled, preparing to take us to

Houston. "Those old guys, Cornflakes and Harlon and the others. That's it. What are they gonna do, scam a child molester? They got no games left. They're just waiting to die."

"Well," I started slowly. "Can't they—"

"Even this," he said, lifting the plastic bag of slowly molding hamburgers he'd scavenged from a giant trash bin behind a fast-food joint that morning. When he'd first emerged from the dumpster, the bag in his raised fist like a trophy, the smell of them had pulled my belly into a tide of hungry growls. Having eaten some of them, the smell now had the opposite effect. I angled my nose away from the catch. "They can't do this. Their bodies are all messed up from life. It takes a toll, living like this."

"You seem good at it," I observed admiringly.

"I'm sixteen," he shrugged. "I could live anywhere, I can do anything. For now. I stay out here, though, and I'm going to end up like Harlon. Sick, sleeping in bushes, no scams left, can't even get it together to dumpster a loaf of bread on his own."

"Well," I tried again, "can't they get jobs?"

Velvet looked at me like he was trying to figure out whether I was joking, and then whether my question should make him angry or sad. He hit his skinny cigarette again and spit stray tobacco from his lip. "No," he said. "They can't."

"How come?"

"I don't know," Velvet shook his head. "They just can't. It's too hard for them. Like, it's easier for Harlon to be out here than have a job and all that. He just can't keep it together. He had jobs when I was a kid. He worked at an auto shop and did odd jobs. But he just couldn't hack it. I mean, think about it."

Velvet looked thoughtfully at the sky, into the sun. I had my backpack spread over me like a weird cape or turtle shell. If I looked at the sky, it would render me blind for a half hour. Velvet was like a solar-powered battery.

"This world is set up in a certain way," he continued. "And then you get born into it, and what if it's just not your way to live like that? And you're stuck in this prefabricated civilization, right? And you just can't hack it? Harlon just wants to live on his own. He don't want to work, play that role. He's like an animal, in a good way. He wants to be free."

I thought about Harlon, this guy who couldn't hack it. I mean, that was kind of my story, too, in a weird way. Born into Phoenix and that family and that school, and yet I guess I couldn't hack it. Suddenly, running away didn't feel as triumphant, like a wild escape or an insistence upon my own destiny. Suddenly it felt sad. I didn't want to be like Harlon and Cornflakes, these guys who couldn't make their lives work.

Or was I like Velvet? Velvet knocked the burning tip off the end of his cigarette and slid it behind his ear. I could only hope I was like Velvet. Somehow, I could tell, Velvet would be fine.

THE BUS TO Houston was plush and air-conditioned. It smelled like cleaning products, and I hoped, sliding into my giant upholstered chair, that the cleanliness would rub off on me. I was grimy. I had never in my life been so grimy! I wasn't as filthy as Velvet, but he wore it better. He looked like a fashion model who'd been sexily dirtied up before his shoot. I looked like a starved rat that fell down a chimney.

"Yeeeeeah," Velvet said, settling into his throne grandly. "Good-fucking-bye to this place. I hope I never see this town again."

"What about your dad?" I asked. He flinched.

"He'll probably die out there without me." The casualness of this statement shocked me. "He's one of those people who needs someone else to take care of him."

"Can't you help him?" I asked.

Velvet glowed with a sudden anger, like a coal someone had blown on. It rose into his face and quickly cooled. "And die with him? No thanks. I didn't ask to be born, you know?" He studied me intently, which made me very self-conscious of my appearance. I felt both too neat and too dirty. The style of my collared shirt still unmistakably transmitted *preppy*, despite its grimy smudges and overall stink. My loafers had dried into a sort of leather crust on my feet, but they were still loafers. I couldn't tell how I wanted Velvet to see me, but I knew I wasn't hitting the mark. My embarrassment made me blush, which made me more embarrassed, which made me blush even more.

"You got a really nice home you're running from, huh?" he asked. "Are you rich? I bet you've never met a single homeless person in your life, have you? Or even a poor person. Do you know a poor person?"

WE WEREN'T RICH. Of course I didn't know any homeless people—who knew homeless people? The whole point of homeless people was that they were outside of society, right? It's not like I ran into them at school or the library or whatever. Actually, there were homeless people at the library sometimes, but they weren't there for books, were they? They were just there to hang out and be homeless. And *were* there homeless people at school? Would I even know? I thought about the tons of kids above me and below me, vaguely familiar faces that blurred past me as I moved around, trying not to call attention to myself. How would I know if any of them didn't have a place to live?

When I was a kid, I saw a woman I guess was poor at the supermarket. Mother and I were behind her, watching her remove item after item from the conveyor belt. The bored cashier droned, *Sixty-three, fifty-nine*, as her total dropped. Mother shifted, doing the impatience shuffle. The lady got her total down and scurried off. *What happened*, I'd asked.

"She didn't have enough money."

I know I sound like such a horrid child to say this, but it had never occurred to me that you could not have enough money. Mother and I breezed in and out of shops, Mother swiping her cards behind her. Of course this was never a problem. Of course I could have whatever I wanted, unless Mother suddenly decided

LITTLE F—

I was eating too poorly and cut off my Cocoa Pebbles supply or made me eat Fruit Roll-Ups instead of Hershey's Kisses. It was as if the supermarket was an extension of our home, where I could take anything I wanted, and there was always more.

"Why doesn't she have enough money?" I asked.

"How am I supposed to know?" Mother asked back. "But if you don't have a lot of money, you should keep track of what you're buying so you don't hold everyone up like that."

"Do we have enough money?" I asked, now mystified by life.

"For what?" Mother was annoyed.

"For, I don't know. Just, do we have enough money?"

"Yes," she said. "We do."

"How come we have enough money and that woman didn't?"

"How come you ask so many questions?" Mother asked.

"Because I'm a child," I said, offended. "This is how I learn. If you didn't like answering questions all day, you shouldn't have had me." I thought of something my teacher had said. "There are no stupid questions."

"Help me," Mother said.

We were in the hot parking lot then, loading the bags into the trunk before the monstrous sun turned everything rancid. I lifted the crinkly plastic bags and slid them into the car.

"We have money because your father has a good job," she finally said. "And also because his father had a good job, and my father had a good job."

"And that lady doesn't have a husband with a good job?" I asked.

"Probably not. Who knows? I don't know her story. Maybe she's on drugs, did you ever think of that?" Mother slammed the trunk. "Get in. This heat is killing me."

VELVET'S FATHER DIDN'T have a good job.

"I don't know if we're rich," I said. "Do you have grandparents?"

"Maybe," he said. "My family is kind of a mess." He was

speaking with his eyes closed, his head leaning on the window. His long hair smeared its dirt around the glass.

"Where's your mom?" I asked.

"I don't know, she's kind of crazy. I mean, she hooked up with Harlon, right? Had a baby with him? That's pretty crazy. I think she's in LA."

"Oh," I said. This was unfathomable, having a baby and taking off, or not having a job and expecting your child to support you. Here's Velvet acting like it's no big deal, like it's normal even. "But you have a sister," I kept pushing. "And she's a dancer. Is she in a company? Like ballet? Or is she in a modern company?" I acted like I knew all about dance, but I didn't so much. Velvet opened his eyes and grinned at me, a grin that shot me up with such feeling I hardly noticed when he reached out and hit my shoulder, my head was so abuzz.

"No, she's, you know, a dancer." He laughed. "She dances in the French Quarter, at a place called Big Daddy's."

"Big Daddy's?"

"Yeah, it looks crazy." Velvet smiled. "It looks cool."

"How come she doesn't know you're coming?"

"We had a fight," Velvet admitted. "I want to give her time to like, cool off. If I talk to her I'm just a voice on the phone, you know? But if I show up, it's like, I'm her little brother! What's she gonna do? Besides"—he rapped his knuckles on the wide glass window—"she won't accept my calls. Collect."

I thought about offering Velvet my phone, but I thought better of it. I didn't want him to think I was a person with a phone. I didn't want him to think I was who I actually was. "What did you guys fight about?"

"I was staying with her," he said. "And I fooled around with her boyfriend."

The air around us both seemed to shimmer like a hot highway. Velvet was speaking incredible words. *I fooled around with her*

LITTLE F—

boyfriend. Velvet liked to fool around with boyfriends! Velvet was gay!

"Oh my God!" I gasped, and clutched at his arm like a little monkey, abandoning all decorum. "Oh my God—you're gay! I'm gay, too!"

"No shit," Velvet said, nonplussed. "Why do you think I asked you to come with me? You are so gay. You're gonna get killed out there by your lonesome."

"I'm so gay," I repeated, a little stunned. "I'm so gay?"

Velvet nodded. "I mean, you know that, right?"

"Well, yes," I said, trying to get control of my fluster. "I got beat up. Maybe you can tell."

"A little," Velvet said.

And so I told him my story, all of it. I told him about Douglas; I told him about Father, about the pornographic magazine. I told him about Joy and how the hippies took my money. I told him how I walked with the old women. He listened closely, laughing and shaking his head, his dark eyes stuck to me so that it made me feel famous. My telling became bigger, wilder; my hands gestured and my eyes rolled. Velvet pushed his bangs from his face to see me better; his star shone on me. I told him everything—I hardly left out a detail. Just the cell phone in my backpack. And that I had never, ever kissed a boy, or even seen one I thought I'd want to kiss.

"Man, that's a crazy story," he shook his head when I was done. I leaned, breathless, back into my seat. "I guess it's really true. Everyone's got problems, even rich people."

I cocked my head at him like a little dog. That was what he'd gotten from my story? That I was rich? That my life was supposed to be perfect because I lived in a big, ugly house that had a bunch of food in it? Well, what did I know. Maybe my life had been perfect, and I was too messed up in my head to know it. I thought of my dad clutching the porno mag, and a big angry NO rose up in me. And then I thought of Harlon, taking all Velvet's money. My head swam.

"I'm not rich," I said weakly, the bravura of my moment gone.

"Well," Velvet said, his eyes closed once more. "You're rich to me."

I dug a cold burger out of the burger bag, ate it, and fell asleep on my seat, the jostling of the bus tossing me closer and closer until I was snuggled up against him.

19

THE SHUFFLING OF energy as the bus pulled into Houston woke me up. I was horrified to see that I'd drooled on Velvet. A smear of saliva glistened on his arm. I tried to dab it off gently, but I woke him up, and so I pretended to be shaking him awake while I was really rubbing my spit into his arm like a vile lotion.

"We're here," I said. He had left his own spit drooled on the window, and his cheek had lain against it. We were both a mess. Messy and hungry and broke.

"I was tired," Velvet said as we climbed off the bus. He seemed like he was still in a dream, peering through the slats of his bangs, not bothering to brush them from his face. We pushed through the throngs of people shuffling out into the city. Immediately, Houston felt like Phoenix: you could tell it was too big, and you could feel the city energy radiating around you infinitely. It was hot and barren and built up. We weren't supposed to live here. Even at night it was a wall of dark heat.

I couldn't wait to get to Massachusetts, where cool ocean breezes would soothe my hot mind. I would think differently. I wouldn't feel like a matted tangle on the inside. Things, life, would feel simple. Currently, life was not simple. We needed to eat, and we needed money.

"If I hadn't been so wiped out I could have grabbed someone's wallet," Velvet said regretfully. "Everyone asleep, with their bags all over the place. God."

"Don't be so hard on yourself," I said, secretly glad he hadn't stolen anything from anyone. "Even thieves need to rest."

We headed toward illuminated golden arches like explorers following the North Star. It was closed.

"Perfect," Velvet said. He jogged toward a bulky hunk on the edge of the parking lot. "Help me," he said, and I helped him pull back the heavy lid of the dumpster, rattling on its hinge. "We're going in."

As I felt a sort of blah dread at the thought of another meal of congealed cheeseburgers, the phrase *beggars can't be choosers* boomeranged in my head, and I stifled a laugh. I felt fizzy and light, and I knew I needed food—protein—period. Even if I did make a note to suggest ransacking a Taco Bell dumpster next time.

Velvet seemed to relish this particular lifestyle: hopping into dumpsters, plotting, stabbing, running. In another life he could have been some amazing high school athlete, tackling and catching, sprinting and sliding. Perhaps Velvet just enjoyed life, period, whether he was fishing old burgers out of the trash or, like, cruising around in a Lexus with his pals. Maybe it was all the same to Velvet. I couldn't tell if this was wise or foolish, but there was something beautiful about it.

"Come on, help me," he called from inside the giant bin. He'd pulled himself up by his arms and swung his legs over, disappearing with a soft thud.

I did not want to go into the garbage. I just really didn't want to.

"How about I do lookout?" I offered, scanning the empty parking lot and the empty night beyond.

Velvet popped out his head. "There's no one out there, Spence. I need you in here, come on."

I scrambled clumsily up the side of the dumpster, my loafers finding little footholds. Everything was obviously covered in germs, and there were many rust patches. I moved slow as a mime, fearful of cutting myself and getting blood poisoning and dying, dying on the streets of Texas like a starved dog, never making it to Provincetown, never meeting up with my uncle, my pink-shirted gay uncle, so completely true to me as I plunged into the trash. Even so terribly far from him, I could picture the exact cut of his wavy hair, his high cheekbones, how he was both manly and fey, a perfect gay, hair buzzed neatly at the nape of his neck, his smooth face, his kind eyes. How nice it felt to stroll beside him, each of us holding a perfect cone of ice cream in the perfect summer evening, the tang of salt forever in the air, in our mouths. Had I lost touch with reality, or was I becoming psychic? Maybe this man was waiting for me on the other side of the country, a lonely Geppetto, and I, a puppet turned real boy, was headed toward him. We would become a family.

The bed of leftover hamburgers under me was soft and greasy. The wrapping tufted around me. Velvet was unwrapping them, lifting them to the street lights for inspection. If they were good, he wrapped them back up and piled them on the dumpster's door. If they were bad, he flung them into the street.

"Do we have to litter?" I asked uneasily.

"I don't want to keep checking out the same rotten hamburger," he said. "We aren't coming back here; I don't care about this parking lot. I don't fucking care about Houston."

Well, I didn't either, but I didn't like littering. "Give me the bad ones," I said. "I'll stack them in the corner."

Walking in the dumpster was very strange, like walking on a waterbed. Velvet scanned the burgers quickly, handing me some lousy ones. I wedged them in the far corner, which came alive with squeaks. I screamed. It was a nest of baby mice—or, more likely, rats.

"Oh my God, oh my God, oh my God, oh my God," I chanted hysterically.

"It's cool. Leave them alone. They'll leave you alone." Velvet squinted at a cheeseburger. He plucked a pickle from it and tossed it in his mouth. "I'm fucking starved. Let's get out of here and eat."

I was already clambering out of there. I was on my belly on the edge of the dumpster, legs kicking. I knew I looked stupid, and I didn't want to, I didn't want to look stupid in front of Velvet, who was the opposite of stupid, who was like every wonderful, impossible thing in the world stuffed into the body of a beautiful boy. I didn't want him to see me flailing like some weird drowning spaz on the edge of a dumpster. He didn't want to see me like that, either. He took me by my loafers and tossed me onto the pavement, where I belly flopped. It was interesting to be treated so roughly by someone who wasn't a foe. Who was really just trying to help. Who maybe even presumed I was tough enough to take it.

But my face was bleeding. My face! It wasn't the best face ever—it was no Velvet—but it was good enough, and I'd had every hope that it would get better as I aged. My bruises had only just gone away, and now here was this pebbly road rash down my right cheek. Velvet hopped down, landing beside me in a shirtless crouch. His T-shirt was bundled with burgers. He cupped my chin in his hand. The fall—or push—was maybe worth it for that moment. I remembered Jackson's eyes in the rearview mirror of the hippie mobile. I kept my own eyes closed and felt Velvet inspecting my face.

"Nice," he complimented. "You needed something extra, something to toughen you up. You kind of look like you got lost on the way back from the mall or something."

"But my bruises," I defended.

"They're pretty much gone. We got to make sure you always have a black eye or something to make you more fearsome. You're like a little lamb."

My raw face stung. I didn't want to be disfigured. "You didn't need to push me," I said.

"I did," Velvet nodded. "You were just lying there. And you

really didn't pull your weight with the burgers. You kind of freaked out. You're going to see a lot of fucking rats, okay? Just deal with it."

I took a breath. "Okay, sure," I said. I should be grateful to Velvet. He was showing me the ropes, thinking of things I would never be able to think of.

"We are rats," he said. "Remember that when you see them, if they scare you. We are rats."

WE WALKED TO the bus station, and I washed up in the bathroom. Velvet picked bits of gravel from my face, and his breath was warm on my cheek as he focused his fingers on my skin. We washed our hands, went back into the lobby, ate dumpster-salvaged hamburgers, and cruised for child molesters.

"Go—sit over there." Velvet pointed to a lone seat across the room bathed in an overhead light. "That's the seat. Go there and look super sad. Look like your best friend just died."

I shuffled to the seat and pouted. I felt silly. I kicked my feet in a forlorn manner. I let my head loll on my neck like it couldn't bear the weight of the pain inside it. I chewed my lip and sighed so big it shook my shoulders. I grimaced. There were some men inside the lobby, but not many, and they appeared not to be perverts, or else ones who preferred molesting happier teens. I shuffled back to Velvet, my frown authentic.

"No one's biting," he said, nodding. "That was good, though, that was a good show. You'll pull your weight one way or another. If a pervert asks you what happened to your face, tell them your dad did it."

It felt like a sadness to blame it on my dad. For all the misery he'd wrought on my life, he had never put a hand on me, and never could I imagine him doing such a thing. "Did Harlon hit you?" I asked Velvet.

"When I was a kid," he said. "Till I could hit him back, and then he stopped quick."

THE CLOCK ON the bus station wall said 11:30. I practiced looking morose. Or should I look tough? Velvet had said fearsome. I tried to walk like someone else, someone heavier, someone who left a stronger mark on the world. Not swishing like a little faggot whose busted face was the result of a common high school gaybashing.

"I got an idea," Velvet said. I didn't ask, I just followed as he grabbed a free newspaper and flicked through it, then led me over to where some cabs loitered at the curb. "Be ready to run," he said, and we climbed into the taxi. The space smelled sickly and warm, like the cherry-colored scented tree dangling from the rearview mirror.

"2898 Pacific," Velvet said. "The Flamingo Club."

The cab took off, giving us a tour of Houston. I liked not knowing where we were going. I had made this epic decision to run away, and from there everything had its own momentum. The cab paused at a red light a block away from a throbbing, lit-up building with the word *FLAMINGO* glowing on its roof. I could see people clogging the sidewalk outside it.

Velvet pushed the car door open. "Run!"

He slid out, but I couldn't shimmy behind him fast enough, and my loafers twisted together on the rubbery mat. Then the light turned green and the driver screeched off, the taxi door hanging open like Velvet's mouth as he watched us zoom away.

"I don't think so!" the cabbie hollered back at me. "No way, no way, I do not think so!" He was about my dad's age, his hair thick and receding, a moustache. He looked full of murder. His head kept spinning wildly between me, clinging to the one closed door, and the street ahead of us. "I do not think so!"

I dug, panicked, into my backpack for the jar of change. "I have it, I have the fare!" I yelled. I shook the jar, streetlights glinting off the coins. "Please, stop!"

"You think you're going to pay me in pennies?" he shouted. "I don't think so!"

"It's not pennies! It's quarters! There's dollar coins in here, I swear!"

He didn't slow the cab. "I'm taking you to the police," he said, and quickly I began to weep. Who knew my tears were so close to the surface? I couldn't go to the police. This couldn't be over so soon, my escape. I couldn't be thrown back to Phoenix. I couldn't never see Velvet again.

What would Velvet do, if he were me?

"Please don't!" I sobbed, inspired. "My dad did this to me!" I tilted my face at him, the raw gore of it speckled across my cheek. "Look! Please!"

The man looked in the rearview, and his face went sour, like my wound had offended him. "Jesus, what'd he do, take a rake across your face?"

"Yes!" I shouted. "Does it really look like that? That's incredible. Because that's what he did. A rake!" I burst into a fresh torrent of tears. My nerves were frayed. I'd eaten but a few half-rotten hamburgers. I'd climbed in and out of dumpsters, I'd run through parking lots, had my face half skinned. I'd seen a man get stabbed and befriended the hoodlum who'd stabbed him. I'd seen a penis. I'd forded a river. It was all too much. I needed to call Joy. I needed to work this cab driver and then make a phone call.

The driver pulled the cab over to the curb. He kept it running. He switched on the overhead light and leaned toward me. I pulled my cardigan from the mouth of my backpack and mopped my tears. "I'm sorry," I said, and my voice was sincere. I was sorry. A sorry little thing. I didn't like lying to people. The man's face was upset. "Your dad did that to you?" he asked again. "With a rake?"

"Yes," I nodded. I made a claw out of my hand and sort of raked it in the air above my cheek. "Like that. I couldn't take it, I had to leave. I just grabbed this—" I shook my jar of coins. "But I'm trying not to spend it. It's all I have." Lies work best when there is a thread of truth inside them.

"What about that kid with you," he asked.

"My brother," I said. "My half brother. Our dad hits him, too. We just took off. I'm sorry, we don't know what to do."

"Why you going to The Flamingo? That's a fag club." The man shook his head. "You can't even get into that place. No business, a couple of boys around all those men."

"Our aunt bartends there," I said quickly. "Maybe she can help us."

"They let women in there?" He laughed. "Real women?"

I didn't want to have a conversation with this person. "Please, can I just get out?" I begged, wondering why I was asking permission. The car was at the curb, the door open. Velvet probably would have stabbed him, robbed him, slashed his tires and been in another city by now. Oh well. That just wasn't my style.

"I'll drive you," the man said, wearily. "Jesus. Shut the door."

He swung the taxi in a U-turn and headed back toward the glowing building that leaked its party onto the street. When we stopped, I unscrewed my jar and scooped out a handful of change. "How much do I owe you?" I asked, hoping he wasn't going to charge me for the time we'd spent gabbing at the curb.

He waved away my offer. "Please," he said. "Don't make me laugh. Here." He dug a wad of bills from his pants and peeled off a twenty. "My dad used to get a little crazy," he said. "When he drank. Your dad a drinker?" I nodded. "Lay low but go home, okay? You don't want to be out on the streets. And trust me, you don't want to hang around that place." He nodded to The Flamingo.

I took the twenty and shoved it into my pocket.

"Thank you, sir," I said. The man's face looked like a big pile of hurt, folds of sad cheeks and eyes. It looked like a big rubber mask, and if you pulled it off, you'd find a boy, a boy whose father used to beat him. I pushed the cab door open. "Thanks so much." I wandered into the throng of sidewalk revelers, and the taxi peeled off from the curb.

20

I HUNG AROUND for a bit, awkwardly staring at faggots. I'd never seen so many in my life. Actually, I'd never seen any in my life, my father notwithstanding. There were big ones and little ones, bald ones and ones with tufts of hair gelled up to the sky. Skinny, faggoty fags and muscled ones that looked like they'd stepped out of the pages of *Hung Up*. Mostly they were smoking, or they were fanning themselves and gulping air. It was hard to imagine what the inside of the club was like if the hot Texas air felt refreshing to them. Some of the fags were feminine and some were masculine. A couple were schlumpy with potbellies and beards like regular dudes. A couple silver-haired men were well groomed and had pleasant faces. Occasionally one would catch me staring and give me a tender little smile, and it shook my heart. They made me think of my imaginary uncle. So many of these men were just like my uncle. It thrilled me. I would go to Provincetown, and it would be just like this but better because there would be ocean and no Texas, and I would find a man who was a conglomeration of all these men, some wonderful gay Frankenstein, and he would take care of me.

I was so enraptured by what I was seeing that I didn't even see Velvet come out of the club until he screamed "My boo!" It was kind of a showy exclamation for Velvet, but with Velvet, everything has a purpose. He hurled himself at me, practically knocking me over with his embrace.

"Oh, my boo, my boo!" He clutched me tightly to him, and it was horrible and wonderful and confusing. "Kiss me," he hissed in my ear, and then he kissed me, violently. Maybe it wasn't completely violent; maybe if I'd been prepared I could have withstood it. But I was flabbergasted, and so my mouth remained in a shocked O while Velvet plumbed it with his tongue. "Kiss me back," he spoke into my teeth, and so I tried, I tried to kiss him back, but I couldn't catch it, his kiss was like a train that had pulled off from the station and I was some poor sucker running alongside, making half-hearted grabs at the door as it gained speed.

He pulled away and gave me a look of undeniable disappointment. We had gained a tiny group of fans, gay men who were swooning and cooing over our cuteness. From the doorway, the bouncer watched us. His skepticism was a like a glacier, but our kiss, even our little failure of a kiss, was global warming. Velvet folded his hand into mine and tugged me toward The Flamingo.

"See?" he whined, thrusting me at the bouncer. "Look at his face!" The bouncer did.

"That's awful," he said gravely. "Where did this happen?"

"Down by the Greyhound station. There were two of them calling us faggots. We tried to run, but they grabbed my boo." Velvet gave me a squeeze. His hand around my waist felt so nice; I'd never had someone put their arm around me like that. I rested against his ribs. I could smell his terrible, excellent smell.

"You gotta report this," the bouncer said. "You really have to."

"We will," Velvet whined again. Velvet didn't whine. Usually, his voice was serious and steady, sort of low. He must have thought that whining would get him somewhere with this guy, make him seem younger, more vulnerable and harmless. He leaned on me, cuddled into me. We were cuddling into each other. The bouncer grinned.

"Y'all are cute, that's for sure," he shook his head. We were puppies in a pet-store window. His admiration made me bold: I turned my head and kissed Velvet's cheek. It felt like actual velvet against my mouth. Was that how he got his name? My heart got hot at the understanding that someone must have given it to him. Maybe someone else who'd kissed his face. The bouncer took off his baseball hat, smoothed his hair, and pushed it back down. I couldn't believe this guy was gay. He looked like he could be any guy from anyplace. There wasn't anything faggoty about him except the kindness in his eyes as he watched us canoodle.

"You can come in," he said. "But I didn't let you, okay? Anything happens, you snuck right past me, you hear? Here."

He turned his back to us and faced the throng of happy smokers. We stared at him.

"Go on, idiots, go!" And we ran behind him into the dark of the club.

THE FLAMINGO CLUB was huge. It had three floors, and each floor had different rooms, and all of it was a dark purple-y black that spun with lights. Maybe it was like being inside a Magic 8 Ball, or maybe it was like being underwater at night, swimming with tropical fish. There were gay people everywhere, gay men, though maybe there were some women, it was hard to tell, they looked like gay men, too; and then there were the drag queens, which I had only ever seen on the internet, and so up until that point they may as well have been cryptids, urban legends. But there they were, like a herd of unicorns. They were in a room on the second floor, lip-synching to music. That room had a little stage hung with shredded Mylar curtains, and Christmas lights were wound around the speakers. The woman onstage was a flash of gold from head to toe: gold wig, gold lips, and her eyelids spackled with chunky gold glitter. Gold shoes poked out from the hem of her gold lamé dress. *Goldfingerrrrrrrr*, she lip-synched, pulling her hands into the shape of a gun. Her nails were golden acrylic claws. She stretched her mouth wide around the words.

"Here," Velvet said, and he gave my lower back a gentle push into the room. Were we still pretending we were boyfriends? A chill rolled up me, vertebra by vertebra. We moved to a row of empty tables, and Velvet scanned the cocktail glasses, sweating and abandoned. He found two that had some watery liquor and handed me one. I sipped. I'd never had alcohol before. It tasted like melted ice cubes with a kick. Velvet knocked his back and had emptied another by the time the busboy came in to swipe the rest of them.

The golden woman left the stage, and a voice from the DJ booth brought out another queen, and that's how it went. They looked like carnival rides, each one a new configuration of makeup and sparkle, eyebrows arched like bridges over eyes that shimmered vivid blue, green, purple. Blush cut up the sides of their faces like spray paint; their faces looked like murals of faces. Their mouths were luscious and muscular, working around the songs like they were eating them, and their hair looked like bird's nests or war helmets, like Marie Antoinette or Dolly Parton. Their clothes were robes of sequins, lamé, rhinestones, and, in some cases, glitter paint. They were a race of Amazon fairies that haunted makeup boxes, come alive on this night to whoosh Aretha Franklin at you through their intricate and dazzling faces.

I was very excited. Being at The Flamingo was like being at the gay zoo, and now we had reached something grand, the lions, perhaps. "Drag queens!" I squealed up at Velvet, who was about a head taller than me. An angular, tattooed fox face of a head taller. He pushed his slippery bangs to the side and they fell back into his face. In a moment he'd do it again; he swiped his hair out of his face as regularly as breathing. His hand wasn't on my back, but we stood close, and I was deeply, cellularly aware of our closeness. I felt like I was standing beside an electrified fence.

"How'd you get out of that cab?" he hollered over Lady Gaga. The drag queen on stage was a dark diva, slithering over the floor, her body cut with silver slashes of disco ball, a black mask somehow obscuring her vision as she whipped herself around and mouthed the words.

"I told him we were brothers and were running away from our abusive father," I said, hardly believing my words. "He felt so bad he gave me twenty dollars and told me about his own abusive father."

"Nice." Velvet nodded his head, impressed. When he swiped at his hair, I saw the star beneath his eye, and then the bangs fell over it like a cloud in the night sky.

"Why were we boyfriends out there?" I asked super casually. "Or whatever."

"Gay people love gay teenagers in love. They go fucking bonkers over it. And the story I gave them, you being my gaybashed boyfriend, forget it. It breaks their hearts worse than a rom-com. It's a great act. We can get practically anything with it." Velvet seemed proud of his diabolical genius. I felt slightly weird about it. I didn't want to scam off gay people, right? Gay people were good. Probably we could just tell them the truth and they'd help us. Probably Velvet was so used to being a lying, knife-wielding, scamming homeless kid that he'd forgotten sometimes he could just be honest.

It felt so great to be at the gay bar. I mean, it was a cacophony, and a lot of people were drunk in a way that seemed scary, but you could dodge them pretty easily; they lumbered without grace and were so loud you could hear them coming over the music. The little drag room seemed like a magical theater. "Let's sit up front," Velvet said—a great idea. There was a table at the foot of the stage with a mostly empty beer that he grabbed and pounded. He'd stopped trying to find any for me, and that was fine. I felt strange, like everything was extra, and I didn't know if it was the little bit of liquor I'd already drank or if it was Velvet's woozing effect on me. Or the overstimulation of The Flamingo, or hunger, or sleep deprivation, or all of it: the totality of my life itself.

The drag queen scooped a tiny pile of balled-up dollars from the stage, pushed them into her cleavage, and was gone. The stage was a dark pause, like the end of a breath before another is taken.

Then a voice came out from the DJ booth, one that sounded like how I imagined whiskey tasted.

"Ladies and gentlemen, drag kings and queens, faggots and lesbians and even bisexuals, welcome The Flamingo's prima diva—The Lady."

Rather than a performer coming through the heavy red curtains, the lush fabric was raised, tier by tier, like at a real theater. A sort of backdrop was leaned against the wall, twinkling darkly, black glitter catching the light. It was a mural of a cemetery with great ornate mausoleums, their swirls painted elegantly and the sky above doused with sparkling clouds. Bare trees, their branches twirling forward. And in the center of it, on a wooden stool, a female creature with black hair that hung in glittered banana curls. Her face had a perfect mask of white on its natural brown, like a doll. Her eyebrows were spare parentheses high on her forehead. Her dress was made of night itself! Cobwebs and dreams! I gasped aloud. I waited for the song to come on, but it didn't. Instead, the Lady began to sing! Her own voice came out from her dazzling mouth, and it was lovely, and French! The Lady sang in French, a few warbling lines, and then music swelled in behind her, but her voice continued, her eerie French song riding the waves of a melody like something bobbing helplessly in a churning sea.

I was enchanted! I looked to Velvet to see if he'd been transported, too. He was nodding, checking the rain of dollars that had begun pelting the stage like a hailstorm. The Lady raised her gloved—gloved!—hand, and as if magically commanding money toward her, money came. Admirers even dared approach the stage, and in humble gestures raised their bills. The Lady plucked them from the admirers' fingers with a quick nod, never breaking her song, and she let the bills float to the floor with the rest of her bounty.

"Yes," Velvet said. "That's the one."

The Lady trilled her French, and it grew terribly fast, the

words an undulating train, and then it slowly pulled apart like a sugary wad of gum. In the end they twirled upward in a spire, a crescendo, until at last she slid from her seat and took a deep bow, her ringlets bobbing perfectly around her cool face. The applause was so loud it drowned out the constant *um-cha, um-cha, um-cha* of the endless dance music outside. The DJ announced the end of the show. Of course—who would be able to top that?

"Please stick around and meet your performers! They work hard for the money—buy them a drink!"

From the back room a parade of performers strutted onstage, the gold lady and the fake Aretha and the mysterious queen who could somehow see through the mask that covered her eyes. The Lady collected her pile of money, gathering it in a scarf she'd had around her waist. She dashed backstage. A few moments later, she returned, greeting her admirers.

"Follow me," Velvet whispered, and grabbed my hand. His hand in mine felt bony and strong. Why was he holding my hand? Were we still fake boyfriends? I'd never felt a boy's hand in my own. I held it tight as the crowd banged and bumped around us, everyone jostling toward the queens.

Suddenly I understood why they were called queens: they really were like royalty, something rare, something not normal. Their *not normal* was extraordinary, precious. I had to find a way to make my own *not normal* special, not an unfortunate loser's *not normal*, but a *not normal* that was better than normal, extra amazing, bigger than life, singular. And then it occurred to me, like the tiniest chime in the back of my brain stirred by all the winds this night had kicked up, that maybe it already was, always had been. It was just that those really normal people didn't know what to do in the face of my magnificence.

I thought Velvet was tugging us toward the Lady, but at the last moment he veered, tightened his grip on my hand, and dragged us backstage. A perfect dream of a backstage. A mirror—round and wide and ringed with circles of light. A counter scattered with makeup and sleek brushes. There were piles of jewelry and sequined everything, and a mess of costumes exploded from a rack in the corner.

"Oh wow," I breathed, but Velvet was already upon the Lady's scarf, the treasure of cash visible beneath the lace.

"Velvet, no!" I snapped, like I was scolding a dog. Velvet's head snapped up at me, puzzled.

"Excuse me?" He laughed at me, deftly untying the loose knot in the scarf. "Get over here; I need your backpack."

I walked slowly toward him, apparently unable to not do what he told me to. "Velvet, we can't steal from drag queens," I said. I tried to steady my voice, conjure a tone of authority. "They're like, our family or something." As I said this, I remembered Harlon, Velvet's dad, and realized *family* probably wasn't the most convincing word.

Velvet ignored me, dumping handfuls of cash into my backpack, which I helpfully held open for him, even as I pleaded. "I'm doing what I do, what I always do," he hissed, his dark eyes giving me a shock. "This is how I get by. You want to go figure out some other way, go off on your own, good fucking luck to you. You want to stay with me, don't get in the way of my game." He nodded quick, flinging the scarf into a dark corner. "Zip it."

I didn't know if he meant my mouth or the bag. But there I was, standing with them both open, just as the Lady came into the room.

21

I SMELLED THE Lady as I saw her, a breeze of something that smelled similar to dark, orange flowers. She filled the room like something supernatural: You saw her, you smelled the flowers of her, and then you felt her.

"Oh no," she said, but it wasn't like, *Oh no, oh no, help!* It was like, *Oh, no you don't.* I screamed—the same scream I'd screamed at the baby rats. Velvet shot me a look and tried to bolt past the Lady, but forget it. The Lady's legs were long and ended in fat, shiny platform boots. Something a normal person would need intense circus training to learn to walk in. The Lady's leg shot out in a sideways kick, and with the effortlessness of a showgirl and the impact of a ninja, her platform boot smashed Velvet in the stomach. He keeled over and flew backward, flying into the rack of costumes, pulling the whole spangled mess of it down on top of him.

"And you," the Lady aimed herself at me as if to stop or block me, but I was paralyzed, my hands white-knuckled around my backpack filled with her money. Before I could speak to her, tell her I was sorry, that she was amazing, a star—a real star—she had the acrylic tips of her nails in my hair, gripping my scalp while her other hand snatched my pack easily from my limp wrist. Her dollars spilled out as she yanked it. "Very nice, boys." She shoved me backward and I tripped over the pile of tulle and beads that was Velvet. My feet tangled, my loafers came off as I went down.

"Fuck!" Velvet yelled, muffled.

"Pardon your French," the Lady said, shaking her head at us. "Oh my Lord." Her accent was Texan, a surprising twang. I'd expected European. "Divine, Georgie, get in here!" Her voice was booming. A shuffling sound brought Goldfinger and Black Mask into the tight space.

"Mary, what is happening in here!" Goldfinger crowed.

"Little thieves stealing my monies," Lady clucked, shaking her head. The shimmering eyes of the queen were upon me.

"That little thing, Mary?" Mask laughed.

"Oh, he has an accomplice, Mary." Lady walked toward the pile and kicked away a swath of velvet, revealing Velvet.

"Ooh, Mary!" Goldfinger cooed. "They look like some real hooligans."

"What are you, Spider-Woman?" Mask pulled a snarl of tulle off Velvet's head. "Did you shoot a web of lace from your palms?" She laughed and struck a pose, flashing her palm at Velvet, who scowled. She still had a mask covering her eyes.

"They weren't hard to catch," Lady said. "They're a couple of starved rats. Look at them."

"You want me to get Don to throw their asses out of here?" Goldfinger asked. She sounded like a cigarette was caught somewhere in her throat.

"Naw, naw, naw," Lady smiled. "I got it. I just wanted you to witness."

"What are you gonna do with them?" Goldfinger demanded.

"Oh, I'll figure something out," Lady nodded.

"Well, make it hurt," Goldfinger growled. "Nothing skeezier than a couple of little babies stealing from their mommas."

"You're not my fucking mother!" Velvet growled back, his voice muffled by the fabric tugging his mouth.

"Did that motherfucker just say we're not his fucking mothers?" Mask gasped.

"Oooh, I'm getting out of here before I start child abusing."

LITTLE F—

Goldfinger walked out with her hands held in front of her, where she could keep an eye on them. Her hands shone like a temple. Mask stomped out behind her. "Holler if you need me, Mary!" The room had a door, and Mask slammed it.

The Lady exhaled a long, low breath. She kicked a chair in front of the door and sat on it, trapping us. My backpack was on her lap. My regular, nothing, not-that-great backpack on the shimmering lap of the Lady. Velvet squirmed behind me, still trying to free himself of the glittering booby trap. Booby trap—I thought briefly of making a joke, but thought better. The Lady's hands dipped into my pack, pulling out her dollars, smoothing them between her long fingers.

"So what do you call yourselves? How old are you, where are you from? Give me the story." The cash was rising in a wrinkled stack on the countertop. Velvet made a harrumphing sound, like he wasn't going to go along with this degradation; but I wasn't so bold beneath the Lady's stare.

"I-I-I'm Spencer," I said. "I'm—" I wanted to tell the Lady the truth, I really did. I thought if I came clean, told her all of it, she'd see how contrite I was at pocketing her hard-earned tips. But I didn't want Velvet to know I was thirteen. It was too young—ugh, just the sound of it in my ears: thirteen. I wondered how old I could pretend to be without insulting the Lady's intelligence. Sixteen seemed edgy; I would go for fifteen. I didn't want Velvet to think I was too young to kiss if he wanted to try again.

"Fifteen," I said to the Lady.

"Fifteen!" she said. "Girl, what's wrong with you? You have that disease where you get younger as you get older? You look twelve. What about you, Romeo?"

Velvet replied with a scowl. The Lady raised an eyebrow, a perfect arch above her eye that slid elegantly up her forehead.

"That's Velvet," I said, and Velvet kicked me, but the blow was softened by velvet bunting.

"Velvet..." the Lady breathed. "How old is Velvet?"

I didn't know that Velvet wanted the Lady to know how old he was. I hesitated. The Lady looked at me expectantly. At that moment, Velvet was like a celebrity who didn't address his public, and I was his personal assistant.

"I think—"

"Thirteen," Velvet said sulkily. My head spun toward him. The Lady's one eyebrow joined her other way up on her brow.

"Thirteen!" the Lady exclaimed. "You children are just full of lies. That's okay, though. The Lady has told a lie or two, she understands. I won't even bother asking you anything, how's that? Though I am dying to know if you are lovers, if you are runaways—runaway lovers—if you live here in Houston, if you are street kids, how you got that grisly thing on your face, dear one. But I won't waste our time." Her money was stacked, and she rustled through my bag and pulled out the jar of coins. "Rustic," she commented, and she dropped the jar back in my bag. She removed my phone and flashed it at us. "Guess times aren't too tough."

Velvet sat up. "You don't know," he snapped. "You don't know our story."

Sorry to keep referring to my heart, but it was like I hadn't had one previously. Velvet kept doing things to make it stop, or start, like he was a magnetic field disrupting my energy. Had he just defended me? "You're not mad?" I blurted. "About the cell phone?"

"What do I care if you have a fucking cell phone? You probably have a credit card, too." Velvet glanced at the Lady. "Spencer's rich."

"I'm not!" I cried. I looked at the Lady. "I'm really not."

"You tell me," she said, looking at me hard. She could tell I was the weak link. I guess it wasn't hard. "You be real with me. Do you two have a place to stay tonight?" I shook my head. "All right then, you're coming with the Lady." And that was how we came to stay with the Lady.

22

THE FIRST STUPID thing that happened was that the doorman stopped us on the way out.

"Hey, how'd you kids get in there," he said with a swat and a wink. The Lady faced him sternly, with her hand on her hip.

"Yes, how did these little thieves get in here, Larry? You know I found them backstage stealing my dollars!"

Larry looked at us, Velvet and me, with a look of betrayal so pained I felt it in my stomach like a bad meal. He seemed to begin to speak to us, then swallowed and looked at the Lady.

"I don't know," he said flatly. "I don't know how they got in. They must have just gotten by me." He stared at me. Velvet was looking at the ground; I was the one all splayed open in the face, my big, dumb, guilty eyes ready for connection. "That's probably how that one got beat in the face," he said bitterly. "Probably got busted stealing from someone. Is that right?"

"No," I mumbled, but it didn't matter anyway. He was essentially right, I was essentially a liar, and it hadn't been a bashing. But I had been bashed. I wished I could explain myself, but it was all too much of a mess. My insides pulsed and roiled with my troubles. But Velvet: He breathed easy.

"You want me to call the cops?" Larry asked the Lady. His eyes were big and brown, what people call puppy dog eyes. Larry seemed really nice. I felt a quick sting of tears.

"No, no need to involve the man when you got the Lady," she said. "I got it. You better try doing your job, though."

With one hand tight around my wimpy arm and the other gripping Velvet's slender muscle, she hustled us into the street and summoned a taxi with a whistle that ripped through the night air. A taxi slid to the curb. The driver stuck his head out the window, locked eyes with me. No, I thought. What were the chances? What kind of crazy night was this? The taxi idled as the driver wrinkled his face at me, focusing his stare.

"No," I said aloud.

"Open the door," the Lady directed. Her hands were full—full with us.

"I can't," I said. The taxi driver stared at me.

"You all right?" he yelled out his window.

"Yeah," I said weakly.

"That your aunt?" he said skeptically.

"Your aunt!" the Lady cried. "Indeed." She jostled me roughly. "Open it."

I did. The three of us slid across the back seat and the Lady gave the driver an address. Velvet shut the door and laid his head on the Lady's shoulder. The Lady looked down at Velvet and gave a sort of snort laugh, then regarded the driver. She repeated her address.

"I need to know that you know these kids," he said solemnly. "Are you their aunt? Is there some way you can prove it?"

The Lady shook her head. "I'm sorry. Should I get another cab?"

"Kid," he looked at me, "this is your aunt? Really?"

"It's our fucking aunt!" Velvet erupted. "Drive the cab!"

"You don't talk to me like that! You think you're gonna fuck me over again?"

"Whoa, whoa, whoa, whoa . . ." The Lady waved her hands. "Why you think you can talk to people like that?" She was looking at Velvet. "I don't care how bad a hand you think you got dealt,

LITTLE F—

you do not talk like that to a person. To a worker. This man driving a cab. You might try getting a job rather than robbing and sassing hard-working people."

The driver seemed satisfied by this, though not wholly. Velvet peeked up quickly behind his bangs. "Sorry," he mumbled. It didn't warrant a pushing away of the bangs. It wasn't that level of an apology.

"I'm gonna need the money up front," the driver said, in a kinder tone. "I'm sorry, it's just—I already dealt with these kids today."

"I bet you have," the Lady said. She dug into her purse and handed the driver a twenty. "Let's get on with it."

23

"SPENCER AND VELVET," the Lady said. She carefully peeled the wig from her head, the banana curls sending a dust of glitter onto the Persian carpet that lined her bedroom. The room held lots of carpet and lots of wigs propped on lots of little heads—some Styrofoam, some plastic and vintage looking—the faces of bygone ladies painted onto them. The glitter glinted soft color throughout the room, the candles the Lady lit making it shine. There were old flyers hung all over the walls, and dangling from the tacks that held the flyers were flowers: fake flowers, plastic and paper, real flowers, shriveled and crispy.

The Lady's hair beneath her wig was a small afro that glowed like a halo in the light. With all the white on her face, she looked less like a doll now and more like a mime. She pumped liquid from a glass bottle and smeared it across her face, and the mask of her makeup moved beneath her hand. With a handkerchief she wiped it all away. She removed her eyelashes slowly—they looked like leeches. She cracked her nails from her fingertips, revealing other nails, still longish and painted but not those dazzling claws.

"Whew," she said. She sat at a vanity strewn with makeup, balled-up handkerchiefs, and scraps of paper. She pulled open the bottom drawer and removed a crystal decanter. "I am having a drink. You boys. What to do with you. You drink, I suppose?"

"Yes," Velvet nodded. "Please." The Lady spilled a splash of liquor into a tiny crystal glass and handed it to him. He knocked it back and held it out again.

LITTLE F—

"You done used it all up," the Lady said. "You think this is a bar? That was your drink. You chose to drink it like a vulgar American. You're out of luck."

She sighed and handed me a tiny glass as well. I pressed my lips to it and licked the terrible liquid from my mouth. Bitter and warm with an unfriendly sweetness.

"Look," she gestured to me. "You should have done like your friend here. But what would you know, being thirteen?"

"I'm not thirteen," Velvet confessed.

"I know you're not thirteen," the Lady laughed, sipping her own tiny glass. "But I'm not gonna believe anything you tell me tonight, so don't bother trying to come clean." She inspected us. "Though I do so want to hear your stories. I don't want you to bore me. I brought you here to liven my night. My little baby Genets. You know him, the writer Genet?"

We looked at her dumbly.

"Oh, loves." She rose from her chair, a wooden chair carved with roses, its seat embroidered with more flowers. She moved over to a wall stacked with books. Shelves and shelves of raw wood planks and concrete bricks, the wood sagging slightly under the weight of them. She pulled out a book that looked old. The jacket was torn, and it held a black-and-white photo of a handsome, sort of sad-looking man staring straight into the camera.

"Genet," she said, "was a Frenchman. A faggot, a criminal. He was a thief. He went to prison and wrote about drag queens. He is your ancestor." She shook the book at me. "You are his children. He would love you. Stealing from other queers. He had no morals. Criminality was his morality."

"I didn't want to steal from you!" I blurted. "I loved your act!"

"You loved my act," the Lady chuckled. She tossed the book at Velvet. "Velveteen," she said. "I know you are going to leave this house with some of my belongings—"

"No!" I jumped in. The Lady had brought us to her home, which looked the way a home should look, full of decor that held meaning and stories, wise little objects that carried on a mystical relationship with the dweller, the way a rusty anchor would in a cozy house in Provincetown. I spied a crystal ball and a Barbie doll and a doll of a Black woman in a gingham dress and turban. A wooden chest with iron hinges. A whip, curled on a nail upon the wall. It wouldn't be possible to take any of these things. It would be like taking the Lady. They would come alive and strangle us in the night. "We won't take anything, I swear."

"Who picked up who, here?" The Lady wiggled the book back and forth between me and Velvet. "What is the nature of this relationship? Who is holding the power?" She squinted, flung the book at Velvet. "You steal this, okay? You steal my books. Steal as many as you like."

"Is this, like, reverse psychology?" I asked. "We're really not going to—"

"Shut up, Spencer!" Velvet roared. "Jesus! I like you, but you're so—ugh! Jesus!" He looked at the Lady, and the Lady looked back at him. "I thought it would be good for both of us, but . . ."

"You're a long way from home, ain't you, baby?" the Lady asked, and smiled at me kindly. She folded her arms. Her dress hung in shreds around her body, and it was as if I was seeing it for the first time. It was tattered. It was so torn the tears became their own pattern, a pattern that disguised. If you had asked me, I would have told you the dress was beautiful, from some beautiful place, that it had cost so much money. But it was trash. It was magical trash, and it shook around the Lady, perfectly lovely, as she spoke.

"Just Phoenix," I shrugged. "Not that far."

"That's not what I meant," she said. "You a long way from home with this one. You watch yourself."

"I'm not gonna do anything," Velvet said. "I fucking saved him. He was about to get raped."

"I told you, I won't believe a word you say to me tonight, either of you. But I can feel certain truths, you dig? And I feel you're gonna rob me cause you don't know no better, and that's okay. You take what you want. You take books. You take the food I got in the fridge." She moved back to her vanity and lifted the wood-and-iron box under her arms like a tiny dog. She held her purse, a clutch, in her fist. "I'm sleeping out there on the couch, and I have my purse, and if you mess with *that* while I sleep, I will wake up and kill you. Believe it. But you take whatever else. Take my liquor. Enjoy yourselves, boys." Her lips puckered into a kiss, and she slinked from the room like a shadow, a perfume of wet orange trees behind her. I looked at Velvet, at where he was seated on the carpet, twirling his tiny, empty glass between his fingers, staring at the Lady's vanity, where her stack of tips sat tufted in the candlelight.

I SAID I wasn't going to steal from the Lady, and I wasn't.

"This?" Velvet dangled things before my eyes. A little hat with a veil that would sit upon your head like a decoration on a cupcake. A bracelet set with a chunk of turquoise. An umbrella. "Practical," Velvet said, twirling it like a cane in the hands of a Broadway dancer. I shook my head.

I had nested myself on the Lady's bed. It was enough to steal this—the Lady's bed for a night. A bed! I wanted to cry, it felt so good. The sheets and the pillows smelled like flowers, like the Lady. I imagined white blossoms growing up from her lungs, blooming at the back of her throat, perfuming the world with her words . . . I was drowsy. My little glass of whatever that was had made my body feel like a big fur coat. I rolled luxuriously onto my side, facing her little bedside table, where there sat an almanac of sorts, a leather book filled with old maps, their colors the colors of time gone past—sepia, an aged color.

"Oh," I said, reaching toward it, flipping open the antique pages. "Look, Velvet. We should bring this with us. An almanac. For our journey." I tried to dig deeper into the pages, looking for Massachusetts, the little part of it that curled out into the sea,

Provincetown. But Velvet took it in his hands and let it thump onto the ground.

"You would want that," Velvet scoffed and joined me in the bed, rolling into me with his body, nudging me over. "It weighs ten fucking pounds. You gonna run to hop a train with a fucking almanac in your bag?" He laughed, but he brushed his hair from his face so I could see his eyes. They were soft. He stretched out on the bed. "Damn," he said.

"I know," I said.

"Spencer, you can't fuck up my game. You really can't. You gotta get it. Fast."

"Okay," I said, looking into his eyes, like my own were stuck there with magnets. "I won't fuck up your game."

Velvet stared back, like my eyes were magnets, too, holding his steady. It was like that for just a second, a second that felt like a million years, and then Velvet broke the spell; he scowled and pulled his hair in front of his face, closed the curtains. *The End*. He curled himself into a fetal knot, his head pushed against my chest.

"I'm going to fucking steal from everyone, okay?" he said. "Like ... everyone. Cause if I don't, I'm over. You don't get it. You're going to go back to your rich family."

"They're not—"

"They *are*, Spencer. Or—fine, I don't fucking care. But Spencer, you're *fine*." Velvet sighed and raised his head, looking at me through wisps of hair. "There are people looking for you. I got people looking *not* to see me, you know? That's all I got."

"Your sister?" I asked, hesitant. Velvet sighed.

"I got me," he said. "That's all I got."

"You got me, too," I said, boldly. "Now you got me." I took my hand, and I placed it on his head. My palm on his crown, my fingers splayed in his locks. I looked at my hand, resting there like a starfish.

"For now I got you," Velvet said. "For now." But he didn't move. He didn't shake my hand away.

LITTLE F—

I'M NOT GOING to feel bad about stealing from the Lady because she said that we could, which doesn't make it stealing at all. Still, it is true that I had to further alter my consciousness with gulps from the crystal decanter. The shining mouth of it became globbed with thick red and purple, the color and texture of our mouths layered in the Lady's lipsticks. At her vanity, we lifted pencils and drew eyebrows on top of our eyebrows, arches so wild you couldn't even see our boring normal eyebrows underneath. Our mouths, dry, dehydrated, became creamy with color. When I muddied the space beneath my eyes with a pencil, coloring outside the lines, poking my soft pupils, Velvet grabbed the pencil from my hand.

"Let me," he said. With his fingers he pulled down the bottom of my eye. How gruesome! I pulled back, imagining the teary, bloodshot pinkness.

"Don't," I said. "I'll look like a ghoul."

"You'll look like a *girl*," he corrected. "Come on."

He grabbed my face and again tugged the skin beneath my eye. Tugged the pencil across it. An obscure part of my body that had never been touched, now touched. By Velvet.

My eyes rolling this way and that, my eyes pinched closed, I couldn't see him; I rested into the feeling of being seen by him. It felt nice, to be so fully beneath his gaze, not to have to feel the horror of returning it. I let him tickle my cheeks with a fat brush. I let him clean the edges of my mouth where I had been sloppy.

"I used to love doing Stacia's makeup," Velvet said with something like wistfulness.

"Are you excited to see her?" I kept my eyes closed as Velvet's fingers moved from my face to my hair. He ran his hands over it, mussing it horribly, then began pulling and poking here and there.

"You don't really have enough hair for me to do anything with," he said. "You should grow it out. You'll have more options."

I opened my eyes and saw what looked like some new wave, punk rock lesbian looking back at me. Short hair a mess, my face like a coloring book. We both gazed at me in the mirror and burst into laughter.

"I think I like you better as a boy," Velvet said, and a hot flush scampered through me. Liked me how? Liked me how? "I was thinking maybe there was some sort of scam we could do with you looking like a girl." He sounded a little disappointed.

He lifted the decanter and took another swig, passed it to me. I was starting to understand how to drink this stuff. You sort of had to hold your breath. When I am with my uncle in Provincetown, I bet I will be given small cups of champagne on special occasions, a tiny cup not unlike the one the Lady had presented me with, but it will be filled with this light and bubbly drink, liquid bonhomie, and we will clink our glasses elegantly and take dainty, appreciative sips. We will not *glug glug* it like people predisposed to alcoholism. I tried taking a dainty sip from the decanter, but the fiery liquid ran down the side of my chin. Some liquor, I am learning, is meant to be swigged. When I am in Provincetown with my uncle, we will not drink that liquor.

And then, as I think this thought, Velvet catches my eye in the mirror and smiles a real smile at me, and I feel terrible for thinking of my uncle. It feels like I am somehow cheating on Velvet, and I guess I am. *For now*, he had said, back in his glum mood on the bed. I didn't want to be a *for now* with Velvet. There in the Lady's bedroom, with the candles and flowers and the makeup and the terrible liquor, I wanted to be a *forever*. I gazed at Velvet in the mirror with an audacity I couldn't normally manage. Maybe because it wasn't him but his reflection, maybe that's why he stared at me so curiously, too, both of us turned forward, our faces a smeared mess. But he, to be truthful, did look like a beautiful person in the makeup, a maybe-boy, maybe-girl creature, and you wouldn't even care to find out, only the most boring person would need such information. Maybe it was the makeup working like masks to change who we were, and almost certainly it was that cheap liquor all dressed up in crystal, but when I leaned back in my chair, Velvet caught me and we kissed again, and I did it better this time, much better, anticipating the violence of his sticky, perfumed mouth and meeting it boldly with a gusto that was new to me, that I hadn't known I'd had.

After spending a moment in the buzzing darkness of that kiss and opening my eyes, the stillness of the Lady's room felt loud. I felt like I *was* the kiss, a mushy, buzzing spectacle. I gave a laugh, like the kiss was something silly, a joke. I didn't want it to mean as much as it did, enough to send my heart tearing off across my body. More than it meant to Velvet, this I knew from the way he yawned, lifted a lace doily from the Lady's vanity, and casually rubbed the makeup from his mouth. He snapped off the light.

"Good night," he exhaled, and he flung himself back into the Lady's perfumed bed. I crept beside him, and my body could not hold any tension in the luxurious softness. I melted.

"That the first time you ever kissed a person?" Velvet spoke into the darkness. I opened my mouth to speak and it hung that way, like a fish caught on a hook.

"I'm the first person you ever kissed," Velvet said, a statement now, not a question. I felt him roll toward me in the bed, felt his hand reach out for me, land on my hand and grab it. He rolled me around him like a cloak, clutching my hand to his chest. He wriggled the knot of our fingers up beneath his shirt and sighed into sleep. Slowly, my body relaxed around his. He was so warm. I remembered looking at his back in the train car, how I thought it would feel like it contained the sun. I was right. We fell asleep, our bodies drifting up and down like an ocean.

24

SO THE JEAN GENET book turned out to be kind of boring. Which is a weird thing to say about a book with a lot of criminals and drag queens in it. It just didn't move along the way I think a story ought to move along, but what do I know? Jean Genet was a French person, and everyone knows they have more class than Americans, especially Americans from Phoenix. I'm probably just not cultured enough to get it. That's why I decided to hold on to it. I plan to grow to appreciate it—it will be a measure of my sophistication. Plus, it smells exactly like the Lady's flowery bed, like she slept with it under her pillow, and I don't ever want to forget the smell of that bed, that room, that night.

Velvet took some items as well. Rings and other jewels that caught the light briefly as he dumped them into the chasm of his pockets. I watched them swing against his leg as he took his long, loping strides down the street, eyes darting around the run-down neighborhood the Lady lived in, widening in delight when they landed on a pawnshop tucked into a strip mall.

"Called it." He raised his hand in the air, and I dutifully slapped it. Velvet was not psychic; his knowledge was as learned as anything that came from a book. If he knew the Lady's neighborhood would hold a pawnshop, it was because such neighborhoods inevitably held pawnshops. He knew this, and now I did, too. I was learning.

The pawnshop person did not want to buy the Lady's jewelry. He veritably laughed at it.

LITTLE F—

"Test it," Velvet pushed, defensive. "How do you know? You don't know."

"I know," the man said with a not-unfriendly smile nestled in a bushy white beard-and-moustache combo. He had long, bushy white hair, too. A sort of hippie Santa. He tossed the tangle of chains and rings back toward Velvet. "It's my job to know. Believe me, if you walked in here with something valuable, I'd want it. Go return this to whoever you swiped it from."

"I beg your pardon," I said, stepping in front of Velvet. "That is quite a rude presumption. These were gifts." It was true, sort of. Right?

"Well, go find someone who gives you better gifts and then come see me." He gave a wink, a little flash beneath a bushy white eyebrow, and nodded to the door.

"Wait," I said. I unzipped my backpack and started rifling through it, landing on the cool plastic square. I slapped my cell phone down on the scratched glass countertop. A cool plastic square of Joy. My umbilical cord to her and my old life. *My old life.* When did I start thinking of it like that? "How much for this?" I asked. "The battery died, but I swear it's good. You can charge it."

For a moment, I hesitated; I imagined it turning on, the infinite string of messages from Joy. But I could always call her when we got to Velvet's sister. She'd be so jealous when she learned I was in New Orleans. Voodoo, fried food, liberated mayhem. A place famous for some of her favorite things.

Velvet raised his eyebrows at me. I shrugged. I was all in, and Velvet needed to know it. Needed to know I wouldn't hamper his game, maybe I could even add something to it. Maybe I had my *own* game; maybe I was valuable; maybe he'd come to need me as much as I found myself, so suddenly, needing him to get through this world.

"I'll give you a hundred bucks for it," the pawnshop man said.

"One ten," I replied, staring hard into his eyes without blinking.

"You drive a hard bargain, kid," smiled the guy. "Lemme see some ID."

"Don't have any," I clipped, and arched an eyebrow, just one. How grateful am I that Mother passed that gene down to me, the one-arched-eyebrow gene. It goes hand in hand with the gay gene I now know I got from Father. "I'm sure I'm not the first," I said airily, and fluttered my hand about, like, let's not make a fuss. "Do whatever you do in such situations."

The pawnshop man grumbled a grumble that I think was his native language and disappeared into a back room. I spun to Velvet, perhaps a tad too eager.

"Good price, huh?" I crowed excitedly. "I mean, we don't really need a phone, do we?"

"I've gotten along pretty good without one," Velvet shrugged. "I'm always gonna choose cash."

"Right," I nodded at this teachable moment. "Always choose cash."

It was at that moment that we both heard the word *gay* enter the pawnshop, and both swiveled our heads instinctively toward the source of the sound, the blocky television set mounted high in the corner of the room. I once read an article that said any person can recognize their own name over any kind of din and distraction, that it hits some place in your brain, and you wake up to it. I guess the same goes for the word *gay* if you're a gay person.

"Spencer," Velvet said. "That's you."

My body felt like it was doused in some sort of nauseating hot sauce as I looked up to see my last class picture being flashed across the screen. My smile was too wide, too stiff, trying too hard to be happy when there was nothing to be happy about. *Obedient.* That was my smile. And my perfect hair, and the perfect baby blue of my shirt. It was, I realized, the same shirt I was currently wearing, but I wore it different now. It was dusted with a kind of dirt I didn't think Mother would find it easy to suds away.

The newscaster returned and continued to talk about the plague of bullying and how my running away was inspiring copycat runaways. More photos of boys, all little faggots like myself, flashed across the screen, along with a couple pictures of short-haired girls who looked like lesbians. Say what you want to say, but sometimes lesbians look like lesbians. An adult gay guy flashed onto the screen, talking about an epidemic of homophobic violence against young people. He looked sort of like my uncle in Provincetown. He looked like he was... okay.

"That *is* you," the pawnshop man spoke, snapping us out of our television haze. "I thought there was something. You been in the paper the past two days. You're a long way from home."

"That's not me," I chuckled falsely, my glance nervously shifting from the man to the television to Velvet. My cell phone lay on the counter. And then the TV was filled with the ruddy, animated face of Douglas Prine. Someone had made him wear a rainbow pin on his T-shirt. *Alleged Attacker*, read the text beneath his horrible face. A spark of something like joy shot through me, ricocheted inside my body. *Alleged Attacker!* Maybe it was worth being on television in this very inconvenient way if it meant I got to see the truth about Dougie Prine blasted like that, for the whole country to see.

"My parents raised me to, uh, celebrate diversity," Douglas spoke into the reporter's microphone. "I would never hurt a gay or lesbian. Spencer actually attacked me. I, uh, just want him to come home and get the help he needs."

"Ugh!" I yelled into the pawnshop, my words bouncing off the glass cases, rattling the snare of a sparkly drum set in the window. "He is such a liar! He beat me up! He—he fag bashed me!"

"Listen, son," said the pawnshop guy. "You don't have to call yourself names like that."

"There's nothing wrong with being a fag," Velvet said casually. "I'm a fag, too. Maybe you're a fag."

The pawnshop guy laughed a wheezy laugh that turned into a cough. When he recovered, he spoke. "I'm no fag," he said. "But if I *was* a fag, and someone *called* me a fag, I'd bust their ass."

"Anyway," I said, breathing down an anxious fury. "Are you going to buy my phone or not?"

"Nope," he said. "Not with the American public all looking for you. The minute you turn that thing on, it's going to communicate with all the cell towers in the region, and the police are going to be hot on your tail. I suggest you take it and get out of here."

It made sense, but I was pissed. I just scored a hundred and ten bucks for me and Velvet and just like that it vanished, all because of stupid Douglas Prine, still ruining my life here, miles from home in a Texas pawnshop.

"Yeah, well, thanks for nothing," I snapped, palming the Lady's worthless jewels and stuffing them into my bag. If they weren't going to pay our way, the least I could do was return them to her, someday. As we moved toward the door, I stopped and turned. "Are you going to report us?" I asked. I hated the begging tone in my voice, the desperate tinge.

"Lucky you, no one has offered a reward," he shrugged, and waved us out.

And we did get out of town without incident, moving along the barren highway, the rumble of the bus soothing Velvet into sleep upon my shoulder while I sat pretending to read Jean Genet, all the while just savoring the scent of the pages and the weight of Velvet's head, the soft brush of his long hair against my neck.

25

IF PHOENIX HAD an opposite, it would be New Orleans. Where Phoenix was dry enough to give a child the parched voice of a chain-smoker, the air in New Orleans was wet enough to drown you as you walked along its uneven streets. The desert dryness produced ornery plants that sprouted weapons, knife-wielding gangs of cacti. In New Orleans, the trees were big and bountiful, bent with the weight of their lushness, leaning as if to embrace you. New Orleans even had a river, the fat Mississippi, a very famous river that ran right through town. It was where Velvet and I sat, right at its banks, eating the chomped rinds of beignets tourists left abandoned in sugary plates at the Café du Monde. I was a quick table-surfing study, remembering how Velvet had swiped drinks back at the Texas gay bar. I shimmied through the maze of café tables, collecting nubs of dough, adding the dregs of multiple café au laits to my cup until it was full. I always got good grades in school, so I knew I was smart. But often, as I measured the angles of a rhombus or conjugated a verb, I thought, *But why?* To get into a good school, to fulfill Mother and Father's dreams for me. Here, in the wild, swiping beignet bits, my wits belonged to me. No old people were harnessing whatever intelligence I might possess to make themselves feel better about the shabby state of their lives. I was, I realized, free. Freedom smelled like grease and sugar and the slightly dirty smell of the muscular Mississippi.

"So, here's the thing," Velvet said, wiping a grit of sugar and sweat from his mouth with the back of his hand. "My sister is great. But she might be super pissed at me."

"For stealing her boyfriend," I suggested.

"Dude, people don't *steal* other people. That's ridiculous. And anyway, I didn't *want* him. Not like that. I just wanted, like, a kiss. It was nothing."

People always said such things about kisses in movies and on television. *It was nothing.* Prior to this current adventure I would just shrug. What did I know? But now, I did know. I knew that kisses could be so many things—terrifying and euphoric and squishy and hot and overwhelming and delicious—but never could a kiss be *nothing*. To have your face so impossibly close to another that your faces merge, you breathe the other's breath, and your vision is all but obscured, save for the super-extra-close-up of whoever you're kissing's eyelashes and pores—that's not nothing.

But apparently, Velvet wished it was. I wondered what he thought of our kisses, watching him pop another chewed-off bit of beignet into his mouth, seeing the way it landed gently on the pink of his tongue, the way his pointy chin jutted out as his jaw began to grind the dough's sweetness. Was he making it nothing in his mind? Or did, would he allow it to be what it was—a sweet, mysterious *something*?

VELVET'S SISTER STACIA, who may or may not want to kill him, worked in an actual strip bar called Big Daddy's. Something about New Orleans made it seem okay to be a stripper. Like, if you were a stripper in Phoenix, you'd have to work at one of those windowless places on the side of the freeway, where maybe the employees have drug problems or fatherless children. Though when I talked about this with Joy once, she told me I didn't know what I was talking about, and that thinking like that about strippers is no different than Dougie Prine calling me a *little faggot*. I think Joy is being extreme, but that is generally what I like about her. My point, however, is that being a stripper in New Orleans doesn't seem sad. It seems like a sort of daring and fun thing to do, like we've gone back in time to the Wild West, where saloon girls do a cancan on a bar top. I guess it's because the whole city felt like a movie set, or like we fell through a fairy ring to arrive here.

Take Big Daddy's itself. Through a hole in the facade, a pair of lady's shoes flew in and out, in and out, as if on a swing. *That's* fun. Inside it was as dark as you'd imagine, but once my eyes adjusted I could make out a woman, a naked one, lying on a long swing hung above the bar. She was on her belly with her head in her folded arms, smiling a peaceful smile with her eyes closed. She kicked her legs back and forth, like the fake pair coming through the wall outside. The heels on her shoes were so big that I thought they must be made for people to wear while they lie in swings above bars. Surely no one could walk in them.

On the stage was a little platform that spun like a record player. A girl with a silvery-pink wig knelt upon it in a pair of too-small ruffled underwear. She stretched out a leg, and I could see she was wearing the same crazy heels. Then she stretched her other leg out, and suddenly she was holding herself up by her arms. With a silly smile on her face, she flipped her legs straight over her head like a freak show contortionist and just spun there, her head peeking out above her shiny heels. It made me dizzy to watch her.

"Did you see that?" I demanded of Velvet. "Did you see what that girl did?" But my voice was lost beneath the raging metal pouring from the sound system. Velvet had already swiped a watery drink from an empty table, and he knocked it back as he dragged me into a shadowy booth in the corner.

"What is this place," I whispered, but Velvet didn't answer. His eyes were locked on another dancer whose strong legs had her hovering over the lap of some frat bro. She was thick and powerful looking, and her skimpy outfit didn't so much read "stripper" as it did "warrior princess who can't let proper clothing get in the way of kicking and sword fighting and ninja leaping over her enemies." She hung her head and whipped it around to the jarringly loud music, her long, dark hair swinging this way and that. When the song ended, she lifted her face, and with a flash of her eyes I saw Velvet. His eyes inside her eyes, his mouth inside her mouth, his skin no different than hers.

"That's your sister," I said.

Velvet nodded. "Yup." His eyes stayed stuck on her. "That's her."

You hear all sorts of interesting things about siblings, and maybe they do have a type of psychic link to one another, because as Velvet sat hidden in the shadows of the darkened booth, I watched Stacia accept some bills from the frat dude, patting him on the head distractedly as a thank-you, not looking at him but looking around the club as if to see where a smell was coming from. Her nose tipped into the air, like a cat, as she approached our table.

"Oh my God," she said, and she reached out to pull Velvet from the torn plastic seat. "Oh my God!" It was a smile on her face, a big, shiny crimson smile. She smothered Velvet in a hug, pushed him away so she could eat him up with her heavily lashed eyes, and then smothered him in a giant hug once more. And then pushed him away. And then smacked him roughly across his face.

"That was for Manny," she said. "I never got to before. So we're good now. Okay?"

"Okay," Velvet said, rubbing his cheek, immediately red with the ghost of her hand. "Okay, fine, but that is really it. Like, for reals, it."

Stacia squealed a loud squeal and did a little dance in her insanely high shoes, which were clearly part of the Big Daddy's uniform. She opened a small clutch purse that had been shoved under her arm and dug around the mass of bills until she found a small piece of black cloth, which she stretched over her enormous breasts. Which I forgot to mention had been naked—naked and staring me in the face. Just because I am a little faggot does not mean I don't have any feelings at the sight of a set of extra-large, extra-naked ta-tas jiggling in my face. I have a lot of feelings. Fear, for starters, though what I'm afraid of is quite mysterious. I know they're not going to hurt me. Perhaps I just know, with every fiber of my being, that if I am in an establishment where I am greeted by a pair of large, unclothed breasts, then I have taken a strange turn somewhere and something is very much amiss. I recognize this thought is some mental residue left over from the *old* Spencer, not the new runaway Spencer who expertly table-surfs pastries and dumpster dives among rodents. *That* Spencer is completely at ease in an establishment such as Big Daddy's. That Spencer simply feels wonder at the sight of naked breasts belonging to the sister of his, um—boyfriend? No, no, certainly not; I cannot imagine Velvet being anyone's boyfriend. But whoever Velvet is, there I was, regarding his sister's naked breasts. And once I swatted away my embarrassing fear, I felt only wonder, as well as a deep curiosity as to whether or not she'd purchased them.

Both of them, I realize, had been watching me stare at her.

"This is Spencer," Velvet introduced. "He's never seen tits before."

"Stacia," his sister said, smiling and extending a hand tipped with nails as impractical as her shoes.

"It's true," I confessed. "I haven't."

The contortionist, whose name is Ivy, brought us drinks the same silvery-pink color as her hair, and the four of us crammed into a booth to sip them. They looked like something a Care Bear would drink, but they tasted like something a cowboy would drink. I tried not to choke. The good thing about this sudden exposure to alcohol is that when I am sipping holiday wine or participating in the champagne toast at my uncle's, I will not blanch at all.

Velvet told Stacia and Ivy all about the pervert and how he felled him, how we dashed off with his wallet, and how I kindly shared the contents, winning Velvet's trust like Charlie returning the Gobstopper to Willy Wonka. Stacia looked at me, her big, red lips twisting up.

"I worry so much about this guy out there on his own," she said. "Thank you for taking care of him."

I started to push away her gratitude; Velvet helped *me*. Without him, who knows what would have happened in that bus-station bathroom? I shuddered to think where that encounter could have led me. Surely not to this happy New Orleans strip bar, drinking pink cocktails with jubilant exotic dancers.

But Velvet smiled at me then, a soft smile, not his cynical smirk, his chuckling scoff. A real sweet smile. And he said, "Yeah, we look out for each other pretty good."

Ivy got called away to swap places with the girl on the swing, who took to the stage, marching right for the pole and climbing it with the muscles of her thighs. Stacia brought her hand lightly to my chin, closing my mouth. "Come on, now," she chided. I watched as the woman heaved herself to the top and spun gracefully back down, twirling like a one-woman maypole. I jumped when she brought the heels of her shoes together with an ungodly *clack*. So that was what those shoes were for. They were noisemakers. The Care Bear cocktail was having a fuzzy effect that I did not really mind, and I lost myself in the dancer's movements as if I was at the ballet. I wished I had money to throw at her feet, but I did not. The sparkling lights, shining and flashing, were slightly disorienting, but not in an unpleasant way. I leaned into Velvet to ground myself, but his body was not the soft place I'd felt in the Lady's bed or on the Greyhound bus. It was tensed and angular, all bones. I sat back up.

"*Manhattan?*" Velvet was saying to Stacia.

"Oh, I'm going to Manhattan," I interrupted with a hiccup. "I mean, I was before I met Velvet—it's on the way to my uncle's in Provincetown. You should come, too, Stacia. I don't think they have strip bars because it's a gay town, but I bet there is something else fun you could do?"

They both ignored me. I realized that Stacia was showing her hand to Velvet, displaying a shimmery little ring that was, frankly, overshadowed by her magnificent claws.

"*Manhattan?*" Velvet repeated in that same voice, and Stacia drew back her hand, a little angry now. She placed it on her belly, which swelled slightly and was crisscrossed with the black straps of her intricate stripper outfit.

"Yes, Manhattan," she snapped. "Everything has been great between us since you left, and if you fuck anything up for me, I will kick you out of Louisiana with my own two feet. I got pregnant, and we got married, and I don't care about whatever foolish kissy-kissy happened between the both of you, that is over now. You can crash with us until you get a job and find your own way, but that's gotta happen before this baby comes, you got that?" Stacia's voice was firm but not unkind.

Velvet rose up and knocked against her in a way that made me catch my breath, shoving his way around her and out of the booth, through the swinging doors and back out onto Bourbon Street.

"Velvet!" I croaked, but the only one who heard me was Stacia, who gave me a sad smile. She took her cocktail and poured it into my empty glass.

"Take it, hon," she said. "You're going to need it."

26

MANHATTAN, ALSO KNOWN as Manny, is a mover by day. By night he plays the tuba in a band. The band plays in bars, and because most bars are not like Big Daddy's, meaning places where teenagers can saunter in and have cocktails hand delivered to them by corrupting adults, Velvet and I can't see them play.

But we can hear them. We stand together outside on the corner and bump our hips around to the gigantic jazzy sound they make. I have never in my life heard anything so wild and squealing, as if any particular noise—a horn, a drum—could just spin off on its own, spiraling into the gutter, but somehow it all sticks together, moving quickly and joyously. If there was music that sounded like laughing—the big, crazy laughing I sometimes get if I stay up way too late and sneak phone calls to Joy, both of us chattering and getting delirious until we basically collapse in guffaws, tears streaming down our face—if music could sound that way, it would be this music that Manhattan is helping to make, pushing his breath into the tuba so hard his cheeks puff up and his face—a normally handsome face, I will give him that—bulges and looks distressed. I don't want to like Manhattan's music, but you literally can't help it. I guess it's jazz, but not like the boring tinkle-y jazz Mother used to play to try to feel sophisticated. It's this whole other energized jazz, and in that style with those exact instruments they will suddenly play,

LITTLE F—

like, a Beyoncé song, or Justin Bieber, and everything becomes even more weird and wonderful.

Velvet does not know when Manhattan's band changes to something from the radio because Velvet has not listened to the radio, in, like, three years. He is very proud of this, perhaps a bit disdainful that I get a bit excited about these recognizable tunes. I accept and understand his disdain. I myself had believed my enjoyment of pop music was a sort of garbage-y weakness, something I should culture myself away from, but Joy, too, likes these silly songs, even as she enjoys the warbling voices of witchy folk singers, the brooding voices of spooky Englishmen, and even classical music. "Enjoy everything," she recommended with a shrug, and it is hard not to take Joy's advice, since it usually leads to fun times.

New Orleans is a wonderful place because you can dance on the street and nobody thinks you should be arrested like they would in Phoenix. No one wants to lock you in the mental hospital for enjoying life. As we dance, passersby nod and smile, and I nod and smile back, and this is amazing—*amazing*—because never in my life have people nodded and smiled at me with such happy regularity. It seems like in New Orleans, I am not quite so weird. Or rather, New Orleans itself is so weird, maybe it makes me a little bit normal.

Listening to Manny's music, I continue to dance on the street while Velvet sits down with his back against a deli that sells po'boys. He holds his hat and singsongs *Spare change, spare change* to the same passersby who smile at my dancing, and a lot of them reach into their pockets and jangle some coins down at him. Po'boys, by the way, are these giant stuffed sandwiches everyone here loves, but to me they seem like waaaaay too much food, thank you very much. I could literally live off a po'boy for five days. That's what I've been eating since I got here, the po'boy Stacia bought me. I keep it in my bag, and whenever my stomach rumbles, I pull out a chunk. It makes me feel resourceful to ration my food this way. And it makes me feel tough and hardy and very *un*-faggoty to be so fearless in the face of food poisoning. But New Orleans is not the modern world. It is the old world, somehow, and all kinds of rules feel fussy and unnecessary here. Things like underage drinking and refrigeration.

Stacia has told us that we must get jobs in order to hasten our departure from her house so that she and Manny can start prepping the little side room for their eventual baby. Manny had told us we could work with him moving furniture, but Stacia had literally burst out laughing and dared me to lift the old-fashioned treasure trunk she used as a coffee table, a clunky metal thing filled with all her dancing costumes and crazy shoes. And it is true that I could not lift it. And it is true that Velvet could, and did, and then slammed it down and stormed out of the room. Manny then retracted his generous offer to employ us. That was earlier today.

If I stand on my tiptoes outside the bar window I can peek under the heavy red curtain and see Stacia in a tight black dress, her lips a shiny red, her hair held to the top of her head with elastics and bobby pins, twisted and plump as a French pastry. She holds a glass of water in one hand and the other rests on her belly, it always does, as if she's constantly reassuring the baby that she's right here and thinking about it. Her eyes are fixed on the stage and filled with such awe and delight that you know she's looking at Manny and the musicians pumping out this golden, glorious music. Her eyes are filled with such wonder and devotion that you know she loves Manny more than anything in the whole world, expect maybe of course the baby beneath her hand.

Stacia and Manny are both eighteen years old. Velvet is sixteen. I am thirteen. Stacia and Manny's house is what you call a *shotgun house*. A shotgun shack, Velvet corrects me, but *shack* sounds so pejorative. And even though the house does appear beaten up by the passage of time, even though it needs a paint job it will surely never get, even though it is home to cockroaches so big that the old me would have hyperventilated at the sight of them, I can see that Stacia tries to keep it nice. She sewed the curtains on all the windows all by herself, and she hung the walls with funny paintings she found at thrift stores. She has pretty blankets and shawls draped over the various holes in the furniture, and she keeps all her makeup organized in little wooden boxes in the bathroom. So I would feel bad calling it a *shack*, especially since Stacia has taken us in and is keeping us off the streets. For now.

THE FIRST NIGHT we arrived, after I stumbled into the humid night air of the French Quarter, air that sits on your skin like a feathery cloak, following Stacia who was following Velvet, after coming up short against that shocking wet wall of air and vomiting my cocktails all over the sidewalk, vaguely hearing the actual *cheering* of passerby as I upchucked, because this was Bourbon Street and vomiting in the gutter is simply what one *does* here—after Stacia bought me a po'boy to settle my stomach, after she guided us to her car, ignoring the catcalls men hurled at her in her skimpy clothes, ignoring them because they clearly happen *all the time*—after she assured us she was not drunk because she is not really drinking because there is a baby Manhattan growing inside her belly—she drove us through the winding old streets, past drunk people and drag queens and magicians, past kids tap-dancing for coins on the street and psychics set up at little tables telling fortunes. The world whizzed by, this new and magic world, sparkling in the darkness. Shops that sell everything you need to have a voodoo lifestyle. Cemeteries where the dead are buried aboveground so they don't float away next time the earth becomes flooded. Vampires live there, Stacia said seriously, or at least people who believe themselves to be vampires. Velvet turned his head back and told me to take a good look because that's where we'll be living once Stacia kicks us out.

"*Victor*," Stacia said in this annoyed yet motherly voice.

Apparently, Victor is Velvet's real name. This is a surprise, though I had figured Velvet wasn't the name he entered the earth with. But Velvet is so totally and completely who he is. The thought that Stacia might not really know Velvet, the Velvet he'd built himself into, makes me feel shaky. I can't explain it. But every time Stacia slips and calls him Victor, something in my heart tightens a little.

Stacia assured us she wasn't going to make us go sleep in the cemetery, but to be honest, I wouldn't have cared. The cemetery was in New Orleans, and as long as I was in New Orleans, I knew I would be fine. This was a surprise. I had located Provincetown as perhaps the only American city where a person such as I could live without trouble, but now here was this other city that made me feel like my insides could safely flow outward and commune with the world around me and all would be okay. Maybe the old me would have blanched at the thought of sleeping in a cemetery, but dead people don't hurt you like living people do, and I felt in my heart that if I were forced to sleep on the hard stones of the New Orleans cemeteries, New Orleans would protect me.

"*Thank you*," I whispered at the car window, my breath fogging the glass. Velvet kept his neck craned, looking at me deeply.

"You're very drunk," he said.

Back at the shotgun house, Stacia sat with Manhattan on the couch, his one hand on his knee and the other on her belly, and looked at Velvet as he apologized for the famous kiss, the one Velvet had run from and the one Stacia had slapped him for. It had been a foolish, fun moment, but he saw now that it had been unfair to everyone, careless and disrespectful. He hoped that Velvet could forgive him as his sister had.

"Jesus, talk about making a big deal about something," Velvet complained. "Yeah, sure. Where do you want us to sleep?"

Manhattan kept his eyes on Velvet for a minute. He looked truly sad, and like he wanted some kind of forgiveness Velvet wasn't going to give him. The whole scene made me queasy, or perhaps it was the cocktails. Or maybe it was how I couldn't not think about Velvet and Manhattan making out. It made my stomach lurch, sending chills down my arms, and I couldn't tell whether I liked it or not. I mean, I absolutely hated it, but then I had to think about it again right away. I'd hoped that once I was away from Manhattan and his strong face with his stubbly chin and narrow, intelligent eyes, I would stop having these imaginative flashes, but no. In the dark, laying on a heap of blankets next to Velvet—blankets as warm and damp as a swamp thanks to the no-air-conditioning of the shotgun, blankets that I *hope hope hope hope hoped* were not harboring those tremendous, flying cockroaches—there the imagined kiss spooled out into more, a little of this, a little of that, some touching, some grabbing, until I was in a terrible pain, mental and emotional and physical, and so restless that Velvet snapped at me in a groggy voice to please stay still. I flushed red in the darkness, catching my breath, my head spinn-y from the drinks.

"Sorry," I croaked. "I feel unwell."

Velvet's hand slid toward me, landing on my belly. My heart stopped beating, briefly, then started up again.

"I'm sorry," he said. "I'm sorry I brought us here. I don't know what I was thinking."

I thought of Velvet, living in a train car with his dad. "You had nowhere else to go."

His hand moved off my belly, rummaged around my body until it found my hand. "It's true," he said. "But now I have you, and you have Provincetown and your uncle. We've got to go, okay? We've got to get out of here—this shack and my sister and Manny and the baby, ugh." His hand gave my hand a squeeze. "We've got to go. Okay?"

"Okay," I whispered in the dark.

THE THING IS, having taken so strongly to this strange place, New Orleans, I had been reconsidering my Provincetown plan. Had been starting to begin to maybe think about how bona fide crazy it was to have taken off across the country heading for a town I imagined housed a fictional dream gay who would take me under his wing and give me a better life. That was a fine fantasy for the old me, back when I was desperate and dumb and had never even kissed a person. That was an acceptable fantasy for someone who couldn't know that a person like Velvet existed. But now that I knew this, and now that this person had taken me under *his* wing and modeled skills I hadn't even known I needed, my gay Provincetown uncle felt like some ridiculous Mr. Rogers. I'd been hoping that Velvet had perhaps forgotten all about him, that the two of us would continue to make our way through New Orleans, exploring the river bank, swiping beignets, maybe getting a job at a hot dog cart or reading the palms of tourists. Kissing in cemeteries while the vampires slept the day away.

"OKAY," I SAID, "But it might be better for us to stay here. You know? It gets really cold in Massachusetts. Like, blizzards. We wouldn't be able to sleep in trains or cemeteries or anything. We could literally die."

"Your uncle," Velvet murmured. "Your uncle won't let anything happen to us." And he tumbled into a sleep deep enough for my restless rolling not to bother him as I lay there in a haze of nothingness, falling.

27

IT IS UNLIKELY that anyone surveying the individuals hawking psychic services along the cracked flagstones of Jackson Square would select me. For starters, I don't have a sign. Some of the folks out here have paid a professional to craft them a wooden sandwich board sign with decorative, bright lettering that advertises their expertise in *tarot, palm-reading, clairvoyance*. Not I. Nor do I have, as all my competitors do, a simple table and some chairs for paying guests to sit on. Nope. I have a wide, worn scarf filched from Stacia's trunk and a chunk of sparkly rock I snatched from the window ledge above the sink. She hasn't seemed to notice. Probably the biggest strike against me, more prohibitive even than my age—for how could a *child* know enough about the world to advise a stranger?—is my lack of umbrella to keep the brutal Louisiana sun off my would-be customers' shoulders.

All in all, the tarot-reading business I have set up in the Square is not exactly competitive. And yet the customers arrive, they hand over the twenty dollars, they close their eyes as they touch the cards, they shuffle reverently. I feel equally reverent toward them, for it is their hopefulness, their optimism that fattens our nest of cash, bringing us ever closer to our departure to Provincetown. Even with our occasional splurge on beignets. We always bring some back to Stacia, as Velvet insists his sister's twin love languages are food and gifts, and her squeals of delight reassure us that we haven't outstayed our welcome. Yet.

Maybe some individuals prefer to have their fortunes told by young people. Maybe they believe we're somehow purer vessels than adults, full of corruption and lies. Others feel like having to squat on a scarf adds something authentic to the experience: a deeper adventure, a better photo opportunity. I can feel the hostile stares of my fellow readers, adults all, cool in the shade of their wide sun umbrellas, their butts sinking into their folding chairs, idly shuffling and reshuffling their tarot decks as they give me the evil eye. I wonder how long it will take before some of the snootier ones stop seeing me as a trespasser. In the two weeks I've been stationed here, most of the readers have stopped looking askance at me, and one woman, Penny, who wears a big fake flower in her hair and does readings with a little bag of animal bones and seashells, has even smiled at me, asking how my day is going and if I'm doing okay, do I need anything. But there are still a few who greet me with a scowl each time I smooth my scarf across the cobblestones. Personally, I worry about the bad energy they are putting into their cards, handling them while indulging such malicious thoughts. They should know better than me how objects pick up energies, given the millions of years they've been plying their trade. They advertise it on their signs: *Miss Cindy, Since 1989*. But what do I care? I'll be gone soon enough, and all of their lives—Miss Cindy with her hot pink hair, the Amazing Zilly with his gold lamé muumuus and head wraps, the really, really old guy with the beard that drags upon the stones, and the woman whose card table bulges beneath the weight of so many sparkling crystal balls—will return to normal. Whatever normal is for a New Orleans tarot reader.

I'll tell you what normal is for me. I wake up on a mattress on the floor in the room of a baby yet to be born, sweaty and tangled in Velvet. Are we tangled because we are two bodies squished into a single bed, or does love pull our bodies together while we sleep? Is it the relentless humidity that makes our skin stick together, or our quiet longing emerging while we dream? I for one could spend all day pondering these puzzles, but who has the time? Ever since Velvet slunk into one of the voodoo stores in the French Quarter and emerged with a deck of tarot cards stuffed down his pants, my days have been spent studying. *Wheel of Fortune* means a change of fortune, for the better. *The Sun* means the sun is shining on you, good times. Same with *The World*, worldly success, all your dreams come true. These are the sorts of cards I *hope hope hope* come up when I flip them over. I don't like delivering bad news. It's too much, watching hope on a stranger's face evaporate, and it's all your fault. I've actually thought of removing all the scary-looking cards from the deck, but Velvet thinks bad readings are good for business.

"People don't want to know their fortunes when things are going great," he reasoned. "It's when everything is shit that they need help. Keep giving them problems, and they'll keep coming back."

Velvet is probably right, but the real reason I didn't remove bony *Death* with his curving scythe and *The Tower* with people jumping to their deaths from the toppling building is that tarot readings are *real*. I sort of knew this getting into it. Having Joy as my best friend functioned as a crash course in the mystical arts, and what I have found is that the more you pay attention to things such as horoscopes and lucky charms, the more they seem to work. Take that list I made the last time I saw Joy, at that bonfire in the canyon. I can't remember every single wish I fed to the fire that night, but I know that I wished to find a boy to fall in love with and to be safe. And here I was, my heart thudding into Velvet's back each morning as we awoke together, safe and snarled in our little bed. Magic is real.

You might wonder how, if all this is real, it was okay that Velvet stole my deck from an actual voodoo store. I figure it's really Velvet's karma, technically speaking, since he stole it and then *gifted* it to me. That's actually the way you are supposed to acquire a deck of tarot cards; they're meant to be given to you. So it's Velvet's karma, and since he doesn't believe in karma, then the whole thing is moot, right? Anyway, I always tell my clients to go to that particular voodoo store and buy their own tarot cards, so I'm really doing them a service, a service I never would be doing were I not plagued by guilt and a nagging fear that my understanding of karma might be perilously off.

THIS ONE AFTERNOON I had had many customers, perhaps because it was overcast—bulbous, iron clouds darkening the sky!—and then, right in time for the sun to set, the clouds began to float away, revealing electric pink and orange above the church's three steeples, turning the drifting rain clouds indigo. My last customer had laid her money on my scarf and was digging an extra five-dollar tip from her bag because my reading had encouraged her to be hopeful about love, and that is why most everyone seeks a tarot reading, at least in my short experience: They want to be encouraged to be hopeful about love.

"You can't get hung up on this person," I'd counseled, jabbing my finger at the gloomy cluster of swords on the card that represented her crush. "The point of this person was just to show you how powerfully you can feel and experience love. There is so much love inside you. You'll find different vessels to pour it into, people who want it and love it." I flicked my fingers around the other cards—a person staring hopefully into a globe, a whole world of love! Two people shyly exchanging great golden cups—a little on the nose, but people like that. *The Magician* with his red cape, casting love spells at his garden altar. After I was finished, the woman grabbed my hand with a thankful squeeze, and then the sunset caught both our eyes, and we stayed mesmerized by it for a moment, the glow and the colors imprinting themselves on our brains, and we emerged from it together, a bit dazzled and laughing at how we were holding hands. In that friendly feeling, she leaned in close.

"Can I ask something?" she began, and then she simply asked: "Are you a runaway?"

My body seized up a little bit, like I forgot to breathe. My eyes darted over to where Velvet leaned against a wrought iron fence that surrounded the statue of Andrew Jackson that sat in the middle of the park like a dining-table centerpiece.

How was I supposed to answer this woman? Like, was she going to get me in trouble? It was against the law to run away. I imagined getting hauled to the police station, spending an uncomfortable night in jail, shivering on a cot while my parents flew on a plane to bail me out. My eyes skidded over to Velvet, and he could see in them that something wasn't right, because we are connected. My thoughts found his thoughts, and as he moved away from the fence, the woman gave my hand a squeeze before letting go. "I don't care if you are, and I don't care if you're gay," she said. "But if you are *either*, there is this organization, Patsy's Place, and they can help you out."

"Help how?" I asked.

Velvet was at my side now, eyes alarmed. "What's up?"

"Housing, food, maybe jobs or money—I'm not sure," the woman said. "They're in the Marigny. Just so you know it's there. In case you need it."

"We're good," Velvet said, his voice disparaging. "Thanks for your concern, though."

The woman looked at us and gave a tight smile. She didn't seem so terrible. Her hair was a fake blond that gave it a touch of frizz, and she dressed like she didn't give a crap, her brightly colored clothes sporting rips here and there, tattooed skin poking through.

"Enjoy the sunset," she said, and she hauled herself off the ground, brushing dirt off her butt as she strolled away.

"What was that about?" Velvet asked.

"I don't know," I said. "She was nice, actually. Maybe we should check out the place she was talking about."

"*Patsy's Place?*" Velvet said it in this *way*, like it was the stupidest thing in all the world.

"Do you know it?" I took a hunk of fringe from the edge of the scarf and twirled it in my fingers.

"There are places like that everywhere. Like, homeless shelters for gay kids."

"There *are?*" This was the first I'd heard of such a thing. First I'd ever heard of anyone, anywhere, giving a crap about a gay kid who maybe needed something. "This is a normal thing? A normal government service?"

I could tell I must have looked like a real dope, a rube, by the way Velvet stared at me, head cocked, a laugh poking out from behind his smile.

"No, it's like, you know, some cities have them. Places like New Orleans, places that have a lot of gay runaways, I guess. It's not the government. It's, like, *do-gooders*." Again with that tone, spitting the words onto the sidewalk.

"Are they, uh, Jesus people?" I asked. Jesus People were always trying to help everyone, but obviously they had a terrible agenda, and all their help came with a price. Jesus People couldn't give a homeless person a sandwich without warning them that their soul was in peril. As if homeless people don't have enough to concern themselves with!

"No," Velvet scoffed. "Jesus People don't help queers. These do-gooders are, I don't know. Just, like, college graduates who made it their jobs to try to take care of runaway queers, like we can't take care of ourselves."

Velvet crouched down and put his arm around my neck in a tough little hug. I shivered with the feeling of his skin against my skin, my destiny against his destiny. The feeling of being in cahoots with him was delicious. And at the same time, we were on the verge of being kicked out of his sister's home. You could feel it: There was something about the way the air felt in the humid little rooms when both Velvet and Manny were at home; it felt charged with a malevolent electricity, like a storm was brewing. The air smelled metallic, and I could see something in their eyes growing closer, like a monsoon you watch coming over the mountains and straight for you, pulling its gray slab of rain through the sky. I don't know if working with the tarot cards was turning me into a psychic witch like Joy, but it gave me feelings that agitated my whole body, and as far as I was concerned, Stacia couldn't boot us out soon enough. This urgent feeling did of course collide with the reality that we had nowhere to go, and Velvet's insistence otherwise—the way he had started talking about my dream of a gay uncle, ever since that first night—well, this added a whole other emotion to the mix. Maybe a gang of college-educated do-gooders with a soft spot for gay runaways was just what we needed. Maybe Patsy's Place was our place, too.

"I want to check it out," I declared. I'd been rolling along with Velvet's plans this whole time with nary a complaint. No matter what new type of peril he landed us in, I stuck with it; it seemed rude to complain when I couldn't provide a reasonable alternative. But maybe our era of stealing from perverts and cab drivers and drag queens was over, and we could get back on the proper side of the law. We could find some type of stability, a legal way to get money. Velvet had a niece or nephew forthcoming; we could focus on becoming upstanding gay uncles ourselves.

"Those spots are so dumb." Velvet shook his head. "They have curfews. You have to be in by like five o'clock, before it's even dark out. And then they kick you out in the morning. You can't have drugs—"

"But we don't do drugs," I interrupted.

"Yeah, well, I don't think someone should be denied shelter just because they have a drug problem."

"But if you don't even like these places, why do you care so much that they won't let druggies stay there?"

"Don't call people druggies, it's fucking rude," Velvet said rudely.

"Well, okay, sorry, people who are high on drugs or whatever—"

"People who use drugs aren't *defined* by the fact that they use drugs. It's not their *identity*."

"Well, it makes sense that they don't want people doing illegal things at a shelter."

"Being a runaway is illegal." Velvet said, then nodded at me with his chin: "*You're* illegal. They just want to control people."

"They probably want to make sure people aren't stealing—"

"That is a myth, that people who use drugs steal." Velvet shook his head, like he could barely stand me.

"Yeah, right, true," I said, fuming. "I mean, look at you, drug free and the biggest thief in the world."

I had wanted to make Velvet stop, but then once I did, it all felt terrible.

"Yeah, look at me," he said. "Just getting your ass around the United States, making sure you don't starve to death or get murdered by some pervo creep. Sorry, I should have figured out some type of socially acceptable manner to get us here. Yeah, right."

Velvet turned his back on me, started punching the wrought iron gate that ringed the Andrew Jackson statue. Little punches that made a faint, pinging sound.

Velvet had plans to deface the statue. He talked about it a lot, how he wanted to paint the words SCUMBAG KILLER across it. As president, Andrew Jackson had signed the Indian Removal Act, which allowed white people to shove Native Americans all over the country, marching them away from their homes, and of course thousands of people died. I learned this from Velvet, who learned it from his mother. She was Native American, and she told Velvet and Stacia about their history in this country. I wondered what it must be like to grow up knowing all along that this country is a terrible country, rather than being blindsided by it later, as I had. I guess it makes you a bit hard, but isn't that a better way to be? Here I was, pampered and deluded, working double time to play catch-up, to harden myself to this country that Velvet always knew was trash.

"I'm sorry, Velvet," I stammered. "I—"

He spun around. "Why don't you call your fucking gay uncle and have him come get us, huh? Maybe I'm actually sick of having to take care of the both of us. I thought when I dropped Harlon I was finally free, you know? But you're even worse than him. You've got zero sense at all. You're like some sort of inbred cat that got tossed into the woods. You're gonna get eaten."

This felt like the worst thing anyone had ever said to me. "I am *not* an inbred cat," I said, in shock.

"Look right there." Velvet pointed to an honest-to-God pay phone nestled into the corner of a building over yonder. "I want you to call your uncle. Right now."

"No, Velvet," I stammered, clattering around in my mind for a good reason. "He's so busy, he never picks up. I just go to voicemail. I don't want to waste my money."

"That's *our* money," Velvet corrected me. "Everything I have, I share with you. I got you those tarot cards. We're a team. You have to go call your uncle, right now. Tell him to get us. Tell him we're in trouble."

"We're not in trouble," I said uneasily.

"You are. You're in a lot of trouble. Aren't you?" Velvet looked at me hard, like there was newsprint all over my face and he was trying to get a sense of the story. Whatever he found there sure made him chuckle.

"You know, I have always been so honest with you," Velvet said. "I'm honest with you, I tell you everything about my family, about Manny, I share whatever I have with you, I fucking save your *life*, and you just sit there, all wrapped up in your privilege, all quiet, like you don't have to tell me nothing. You just take and take and take like you're entitled to it. I want you to call your uncle. I want him to help us."

"My *privilege?*" I repeated. This was more outrageous than the inbred-cat insult. "I got gaybashed so bad I landed in the hospital! And then my own closet-case father lied and told my mother that *his* gay porn was *my* gay porn!" I looked at Velvet, my eyes buggy like they were going to burst from my head, and waited for some softness, some humility or tenderness to leach into his handsome face. Tick. Tock.

"Are you done?" Velvet finally asked, which caused my mouth to unhinge with a tiny gasp. "Is that all? Someone at school was mean to you? And you got in a fight with your mommy and daddy?"

"Yes!" I was shrieking now, and all the psychics in the square were swiveled around and gaping at the two little faggots screaming at each other. "Someone was *horribly* mean to me! And my parents are *monsters!* Sorry if it's not extreme enough to get your sympathy!"

"You want my sympathy?" Velvet laughed. "You are so stupid! Why didn't you beat that kid up, back? Why didn't you light his fucking house on fire! Why didn't you tell your mom your dad is a fucking fag? Why don't you fucking take care of your own shit?"

"I fucking take care of my own shit," I said in a low voice. "Look at me! Here I am! I said fuck it all! I ran away! And that—" I pointed my finger at Velvet righteously. "That is harder than just living on the streets with your dad, okay? You never had anything, Velvet. I did! And I stood up for myself! I ran away from it!"

"Spencer," Velvet said. "You're just going to go home. You're slumming."

"No I'm not," I said. "But, just to be clear, what does that mean?"

"It's like you're having a little bad-kid vacation," Velvet said, the lightness in his voice not matching up with how heavy his words were. "None of this is real for you. If you got arrested, or if you really ran out of money, you'd give up and go home. But if I ran out of money, if something went wrong, and you ditched me—"

"Velvet," I said, "I wouldn't—"

"Sure you would," Velvet nodded. "You will. You'll ditch me. You'll wind up back home. This will be some wacky story you tell your husband someday."

"You think I'll have a husband someday?" I gasped. It wasn't the point, but Velvet was such an authority, him just saying the impossible could make it so. He stared at me then, a liquid hurt slowly pooling in his eyes.

"Fuck you, Spencer," he said, and turned away, walking. I leapt after him.

"Velvet, I'm sorry."

I reached out for his arm, but he pulled it away with a glare, like touching him was the worst, creepiest thing I could do, even though I had just woken up *this very morning* with my arms wrapped all the way around him, my nose full of the smell of him, his hair tangled with my own. "Velvet, I want *you* to be my husband," I said, embarrassed at how whiny it sounded, how desperate. But it was true, wasn't it? I think it was true.

Velvet spun and took my eyes by his own.

"Someday," I said. "I want you to be my someday husband."

He didn't shake me off now when I grabbed his arm. He didn't take his eyes off mine, even as mine suddenly erupted with tears that shot down my cheeks. The stupid shaking, heaving tears that babies get when they have a tantrum. I felt tired, suddenly aware that I'd barely slept last night on the tiny bed, and hungry for a leftover hunk of muffuletta, and embarrassed, because probably everything Velvet had said to me and about me was true. I probably *would* be dead on a set of Texas train tracks if not for him, I *was* an inbred cat, privileged and dumb, and I didn't deserve him any more than he deserved to be living in an abandoned train car with his dad, or cast out from Stacia's just because her boyfriend kissed him, and I didn't deserve Velvet and he didn't deserve any of it, and I wished with my whole heart that this whole life was a dream, and I would wake up bandaged and bruised at the hospital in Phoenix. I could give it all another try.

"Your uncle," Velvet said.

"He's not real," I said. "I made him up. He doesn't exist."

Velvet chewed on this for a moment. The wind picked up and rustled the scarf and cards behind me, picked one up on its breeze and blew it flat against my leg. *Ten of Swords*. A person dead in the street, ten blades in his murdered back.

"You should get your cards, Spencer," Velvet said as the wind continued to shuffle them. "You should go home."

28

ON THE WIDE stone steps that led down to the Mississippi River I sat and cried. Of course I was crying for and about Velvet and the fight that we'd had. Arguments make me nervous, generally, and when I'm nervous, tears spring to my eyes; I can't help it. Also when I'm angry. Basically, all emotions trigger tears—lucky me. The aftereffects of the conflict were inside my body, and I felt turned around, as if I'd just exited an amusement park ride, one which had gone horribly awry, an evil, cackling carny allowing the ride to continue even though my door had flipped open and I was dangling by half a frayed seat belt. Not to be dramatic. This is how I felt in my body, okay?

I put my head between my knees and tried to steady my breathing. I didn't want any beignet-scarfing tourists to see me and begin to worry that someone as young looking as me was alone and in distress by a body of water. I did not want the authorities alerted. The thought of jumping into the waterway did occur to me, letting its thick, gray muscle push me to my saddest destiny. But it was just imagination, more drama. I did not and never have wanted to die, not really. I just wanted to be in a different place, a tremendously different place. And now I was there, looking out on ships moving and lingering, picking up specks of conversation from the tourists popping over for a glance at the famous river, the air sweet and oily and carrying brassy sounds of music from buskers scattered around the neighborhood. It could not be more different than Phoenix, a place starved for water. New Orleans, where the air itself is wet, molecules of the river suspended in the air. I guess I'd proved my point and could go home, like Velvet had said.

There was the issue of my uncle, however. There was the issue of his Provincetown house and its paint, crackling away, worn off by the salt in the air; the issue of his garden that bloomed in the spring, the yellowy honeysuckle flowers that tumbled over his fence. There was the issue of his front porch and the little swing that swung there, the pillows nestled upon it, the tiny table to place your cup of lemonade. There were the hydrangea bushes and the rose bushes and the one lilac tree in the corner; there was the issue of the anchor decor and the glass ball in its frayed netting. There was the street he lived on, the village's one main street, which curved slowly through the town and managed to hug everything to it, the lapping ocean on the one side and the flowery cottages on the other, giving way to outdoor restaurants where tourists—visitors, really, pilgrims—slurp oysters and other creatures of the sea, and little shops selling T-shirts and housewares, designer clothes and pizza, tarot cards and cupcakes; anything anyone could ever want was for sale in Provincetown in the summer, lobster at the lobster restaurant and a length of chain or wood paneling at the hardware store, old coffee cups from retired airlines at the army-supply store and the latest literature at the bookstore. I had become an expert on Provincetown, and between my internet knowledge and my advanced vocabulary, I could write a convincing travel essay for a magazine about all the things a person could do there. Especially a gay person, a gay person older than myself, could go and meet other gay people at a certain beach, or poolside at a certain hotel, or at a tea dance, which I surmised was like a disco but during the day. On the curving street that held all of this, people moved in slow, sun-stunted shuffles right down the middle of the street, clutching their shopping bags or slurping their milkshakes, occasionally making way for the cars that crawled behind them. It seemed like a parade, always, a parade made of normal people, a parade you joined just by being there, your whole being proclaiming that you were gay, and no one would beat you up for it, no one would even hiss passive-aggressively in your direction. Indeed you would only receive praise from strangers, approving winks, maybe a *You go, girl!* as you marched down the street.

    In my imagination, I could see my uncle's crisp and natty fashion, the neat and glossy swoop of his hair. I could sense the rhythm of his walk, a light bounce beside me. I could feel his hand in my own, protective and proud. But I did not know what my uncle's face looked like. And as I sat by the river, I felt it fade away, replaced by my own snotty, wet face, which I held in my hands as I tried to get it together. I didn't realize what saying the truth to Velvet would do, how the moisture in the New Orleans air would take my words and hold them, hang them in the air like art on a wall; how they'd vibrate, absorbing the humidity like a sponge, growing fatter, floating upward until they were the gray clouds that hovered over the river. It was like my sweet gay uncle had died. I didn't have an uncle, I never did, there was no one in Provincetown to receive me, which didn't matter, because Provincetown may as well have been France or Thailand or Atlantis or the moon. I was never going to be able to get myself there, and the crash of disappointment in my body made me understand how real I'd let the whole fantasy become, and it scared me. And I wanted Velvet, who was never scared, until I scared him away.

    After my face had calmed down and those terrible, infantile hiccups had ceased, I pulled myself up and away from the river. At the bottom of the stairs, back on the street, I asked a man on a stool in what direction the Marigny stood. The man was selling tickets to see wild alligators in a swamp outside town, and he himself looked a bit like an alligator, with cracked skin and a bit of a snout. He regarded me with cool alligator's eyes and pointed a finger, and I began my walk.

In my pocket I still had the earnings of the day's earlier tarot readings, and I felt a pang of worry for Velvet, who I had not given any bills to. I had the cards, too, wrapped in Stacia's scarf. All I needed was a hobo stick to tie it onto and I was practically the character on the first card of the deck, zero, *The Fool*, a card without a number, a card that means nothing, and that was how I felt as I drifted down the bumpy, busted sidewalk from the French Quarter to the Marigny. A band played in the street, and a crowd gathered around them with hot dogs and cups of beer; I peered among the people, looking for Velvet, his okapi arm stretching out to pluck a wallet from the unsuspecting derriere of some *tourist*. But there was no Velvet there, no one with his gleam and elegance and saunter, only regular people swaying to the music or to their own drunken equilibrium.

I made it through the crowds, and the street became calmer, tree roots cracking up the pavement alongside houses so squat and colorful they seemed fake, like toy houses, though every so often there was a person sitting on their stairs talking on a phone in the sun. As if the paint jobs weren't enough—lavender and pink! Teal and mango!—some houses had sun-dulled Mardi Gras beads twined around their railings or woven through the bars on the windows. Beads also dangled from the trees, shining in a faded way like they'd been out there in the wind and the rain, in the sunshine and the hurricanes, like they'd seen it all but still caught the light, and the gusts only served to knot them more securely in the branches so they'd live there forever now; even the ones whose strings had snapped hung like tinsel from a holiday tree. And so many of the houses, already rainbows, had rainbow flags stuck in their windows or hanging from their awnings, fluttering in the damp breeze; the houses, so very gay, each and every one of them, not wanting to trust the communication of their colors but wanting, really, to shove it down your throat—the worst thing a gay can do, shove their gayness down the tender throats of the nongay!—*I'm gay we're gay this is a gay house a*

LITTLE F—

gay home a piece of gay architecture a gay space a gay structure a gay street a gay city gay gay gay—the houses singsonged their colors down the street until I came to one with a wooden board swinging from a pole above the door, a chunk of splintered rainbow, *PATSY'S PLACE* swishing across it in swirling pink letters.

29

THE FRONT ROOM of Patsy's Place looked like a regular office got ran over by a Pride parade. From it, a long hallway grew little rooms that people lived in, like leaves from a flower stem. Gay people lived in them, young gay people, more or less like me. There was a room with a television and a kitchen with snacks, and down the street and around the corner was another house just like this one—two, actually—side-by-side, pink and blue, and the front rooms in those houses held Ping-Pong tables and trunks of flashy costumes. I didn't really relate to the intense dyed-chicken-feathers aesthetic, but I was drawn to the feeling that perhaps every day was a holiday if you're gay—that normal holidays, like Christmas and Halloween, are for straight people who meter out their exuberance, whose lives are so sad that they can only muster up the joy and generosity a holiday requires a few times a year. But despite our myriad hardships, gay people are simply *bursting* with joy and generosity and exuberance, and so any and every day is a potential holiday, even if you are the only one celebrating, sashaying around in a feather boa and a pair of rhinestone sunglasses. So though I did not personally find myself drawn to the style, I appreciated the occasion.

The day I checked into the Hotel Patsy, as some of the residents call it, Kimberly was working the office. She looked like an older, more polished version of Joy—a woman that Joy would maybe someday grow into. Her hair was sleek and shiny black, and her eyeliner darted out from the corners of her eyes. But the thing that really got me was the pentacle necklace dangling around her neck.

"You're a witch!" I gasped, and burst into tears.

"Oh!" Kimberly—though I didn't yet know that was her name—gasped in turn. And then another "Oh," this one more thoughtful, and finally, a sympathetic, cooing "Oh."

"Honey, I'm not a bad witch," she said in an accent that was part New York via Hollywood, part Betty Boop. Was that her real voice, I wondered? I stared at her through my latest batch of tears and waited for her to speak again. "You know, most witches are not bad witches. Most witches are good witches." Yes, that was definitely her voice, and I guess it didn't matter whether it just came fluted from her throat like that or she'd willed it into existence. At the end of the day, it was her voice.

"Oh, I know," I hiccupped into the wad of tissues she'd plucked from a cardboard box on her desk, kept around, no doubt, for weeping homeless people like myself who, meeting a kindly face, fall apart. "I know—my best friend back home, Joy, she's a witch, and she has that same necklace, and that's how I knew. And then it made me really miss her."

Kimberly smiled and nodded, fingering the encircled star charm. "When was the last time you saw her?" she asked in her gentle, squeaky doll voice. "Where were you, then?"

And so I told Kimberly all about it: all about Phoenix with its Martian canyons and lack of moisture, so different from where we sat, here below sea level. I told her about Douglas Prine, and I swear her own eyes got runny as she listened, but it might have been the veil of drying tears I was still looking through. I told her about my father and she looked properly horrified; I told her about all my stupid, imaginary plans, and then the one I hadn't planned for at all, Velvet and how not imaginary he was, how real real real were his warm skin and floppy bangs and everything he knew, what the world had shown him, and what he'd made of it.

And Kimberly chewed on her lip and listened; she nodded and scrunched her face in sympathy, like Peyton had but different. Like an anti-Peyton.

"I used to go to therapy," I told her. "Before all of this happened."

"That's good," she nodded, encouraging. "Therapy's good."

"You're like my therapist, but better," I said, and she burst out laughing.

"But I haven't said a thing," she said, smiling.

"Neither did my therapist," I told her. "But I could feel your silence better."

Kimberly smiled and plucked herself a tissue from the box, dabbing beneath the arc of her eyeliner. "This job." She shook her head and then blew her nose with a terrific *honk*. "This job."

I HAD TO fill out some paperwork, yes, and I had to promise to not do certain things I wasn't planning on doing anyway, and maybe Velvet would have found that it impinged upon his freedoms too greatly to agree to such things. But Kimberly never locked me in my little room come any certain hour, and she never kicked me out when the sun came rumbling up the sky each morning. Neither did Benny, another staff member who had a big hoop earring that went right through her nose and a pile of dreadlocks bunched on top of her head; and neither did Wolf, who always wore overalls and a sun hat so big and shadowy that I don't think I ever really knew what they looked like. Kimberly and Benny and Wolf were only ever nice.

For over a week, I'd wake up in my assigned room and for that first moment have no idea where I was. My assigned dresser, old but not antique, possibly having belonged to a child in a past life, given the gummy rings of old stickers patterning the painted wood. The wardrobe, aluminum, with a mirror embedded on one wonky door. The little nightstand that teetered on its one short leg when I knocked into it. My room in New Orleans.

I stayed locked in these four walls, emerging only when the

halls were silent of joyful gab and the tinny music leaking from bedrooms, the blast of the shower, the mechanical pop of the toaster. I listened to the life outside my door with my ear pressed up against the wood, and I thought, sometimes, about my mother, and I realized that in my mind she was still there, through all I had been through, the terrain I'd covered and experiences I'd experienced. I imagined her with that same cigarette, exhaling smokily into a forever dim living room. Hiding out in her own sad way. And the tears would come again, and then would go, and I knew they would be back.

I did wonder about my roommates, of course; I'm a curious person and not unfriendly. It had just taken so much out of me to explain my situation to Kimberly that the thought of going through it again, and perhaps again, made me want to take to my bed. I knew there was a girl with a shaved head who wore a dog collar like a necklace. A tall, lanky boy with long braids who seemed to always have a pair of oversize woman's sunglasses on his face. A super chubby girl with long purple hair who accessorized with items from the trunk in the front room. She reminded me of Joy, which gave me a pang that ricocheted through my body, sad feelings of love that shot from my heart and bounced off my lungs and landed in my kidneys.

In the mornings, I would listen to them and sometimes peek through my own keyhole to watch them dash around like characters on a sitcom, stealing bites of each other's Pop-Tarts, trading lipsticks, cracking in-jokes that made no sense to me. Occasionally, they would pause at my door, and I would freeze, a wild animal spotted by something higher up on the food chain.

"Is missy ever coming out of there?" asked Sunglasses.

"Hope they're checking to make sure he's not dead," grumbled Dog Collar.

"Don't be so macabre, Belle," said Purple Locks. "Remember when *you* first got here? And I said hello to you? And you *hissed* at me?"

"Whatever. I wasn't used to people being nice to me. I thought you were up to something."

"I *was* up to something!" Purple Locks waggled her eyebrows, and everybody laughed. I used the noisy moment to shift my weight on the creaky floor, but I lost my balance and thudded against my door, cringing. The trio froze, all of them facing me, or my door.

"Hi, scaredy-cat," Purple Locks waved at me through my little keyhole. Her fingernails were razor-tipped claws stuck with something that caught the light. "Come on out, we won't bite."

Sunglasses slid his sunglasses down his long nose. It seemed like his wide, almond eyes were looking right at me. "We're here when you're ready, sugarplum." He poked the others in the shoulder. "Come on."

They shuffled down the hall and out into the sunny day. I took a deep breath and leaned my full weight against the door. The wood of the old house around me creaked and groaned. *Missy. Scaredy-cat. Sugarplum.* These were all my names.

WHEN KIMBERLY, Benny, and Wolf finally sat me down and urged me to take some shifts at My-O-My, the nonprofit coffee shop that helped fund Patsy's, it wasn't like they were kicking me out or making me work. Even though it must have driven them mad to watch me slump around the house that first week and a half—weeping or not weeping, missing various people, real or imaginary, who were now gone forever—they never grabbed me like a woman in an old-fashioned film and slapped my cheeks and demanded I *snap out of it!* Nope. They were almost timid in their approach and gave me lots of room to refuse. Their mention that the other residents did shifts at My-O-My wasn't a peer pressure move; it was more like they were offering me a route to actually meet my roommates.

And in the end, I decided they were right: I should get the hell out of my room and join the world again. I was sick of myself and the unchanging walls. Had I run away from home, tumbled through all the intensity of the past days, only to become a boring, bored recluse?

So I followed Benny over to My-O-My, hustling to keep up with her long strides. Outside the house, it was a perfect day. Not too hot, the sky clear blue, a little breeze like the air was welcoming me, holding my hand as I stepped out into a New Orleans that felt oddly new. A New Orleans without Velvet by my side.

"We named My-O-My after this old, old drag bar that used to be here in New Orleans," Benny told me, sunlight bouncing off the silver bouncing in her nose. "Old like in the 1930s. Probably some of the performers were trans women, some were queens. They were all beautiful. And talented! They'd sing and dance, no lip-synching back then." Benny laughed like she'd been to one of the shows. She was old—like in her late twenties—but not *that* old.

"How do you think they would know whether they were drag queens or trans women?" I asked. I'd read about trans people on the internet and basically was asking the question to let Benny know that though I was a young gay from godforsaken Phoenix, Arizona, I was also worldly. But Benny didn't seem impressed. She shrugged.

"I suppose just knowing yourself from the inside," she said.

You could smell My-O-My as you approached it, that almost sweet, somewhat scorched smell of coffee. People left the café clutching white cups, the name stamped onto the paper in an old-fashioned style. A rickety screen door slammed behind us as we entered, and Kimberly looked up from her task of rearranging the morning's pastries inside a glass case.

"Well, look who's here!" she chirped brightly.

"Don't make a big deal about it," Benny warned in a low voice. I touched her arm.

"It's okay. I'm really happy to be here. I'm really glad you guys got me out of my room. Thank you." I felt suddenly and unexpectedly shy at my own expression of gratitude and turned my burning cheeks down toward the wooden floor.

"It's a fine line between taking some 'me time' and self-isolating," Kimberly nodded knowingly. And it was true. While at first it was a relief to close the door on my sparse but cozy little room, at some point it just seemed impossible to open it back up. I really was glad for the intervention.

"Let me introduce you to everyone!" Kimberly clapped her hands together. "Belle!" she shouted, and the girl with the shaved head and the dog collar slipped out from a back room.

"Hey," she said, popping her hand in the air but not waving it. "I'm Belle. You're Spencer, right?"

"Yes," I nodded. "I love your choker." I didn't actually know that I loved Belle's choker, or if a dog collar could even be called such a thing, but I presumed that a person wearing such an extreme accessory must want some acknowledgment for their daring, and I was happy to do that for her. However, she just nodded and slipped back into the room behind the counter.

Sunglasses came up behind me with a tiny stack of crumby dishes and sticky mugs. He placed them on the counter with a clatter and made a big show of wiping his hands on his jeans. He pushed his sunnies up so they sat on his braids and looked me in the eye. "Hello Spencer, I'm Johnny. I'm *so glad* you've come to Patsy's Place and that you're here today at My-O-My. Are you going to be joining us?"

"Um, yeah," I said, suddenly unsure of what that even meant. I jumped as the screen door slammed and Purple Locks came shrieking into the café.

"*Eew-eew-eew-eew*, raccoons or something in the garbage. I cleaned it up; you're all welcome, but now I'm disgusting. *Eew-eew-eeew—*"

She stopped in front of me, hands held out to her side.

"Oh for heaven's sake, of all the days. I've just been waiting to squish you in a big hug but I don't want to contaminate you.

Don't move!" She ran behind the counter and through the door Belle had slunk to.

"That's Fiona," Johnny laughed. "And she's *always* like that, even when she doesn't have raccoon cooties."

I laughed and nodded. "I know," I said. "I hear you in the halls a lot."

Johnny squinted his eyes at me and dropped his sunglasses back on his nose. "I knew you were spying on us, you little sneak." He said it in a nice way, though, and I had a feeling that, even though I hadn't been with them these past days, maybe I sort of had been.

Fiona came clattering out of the back, the heels of her sandals hitting the floor like tap shoes. Her hug smelled like pastries and coffee and flowers and dish soap. "Yay, we're so glad you're here!" She slid her hand into mine possessively and turned to Kimberly. "Kimmy, can I train him? Puhleeze?"

"Ask Johnny," Kimberly said, putting her hands up like she had nothing to do with it. "He's the manager. This is y'all's business, you sort it out."

"Can I?" Fiona turned to Johnny, who hugged his hands to his chest and did a little twirl.

"'Mommy, can I keep him, can I?'" Johnny teased. "Yeah, sure. Get him on the espresso machine, show him some drinks. Belle can show him how to use the register, and I'll go over everything else. I *am* the manager," Johnny spoke to me conspiratorially. "Meaning I've been here the longest and know the most. So if these nancies get on your nerves, come talk to me about it."

SOON IT WAS just me and Fiona behind the counter, packing dusty espresso into tight little pucks and clicking them into the machine by their handles, watching as the brown liquid dribbled out into the tiny cups. There were Americanos and cappuccinos and lattes and cortados, and I couldn't keep them at all straight, but I did like the sturdy way the handle attached to the machine and the reliable trickle of espresso. When Fiona peeled a thin slice of yellow from the ball of a lemon and singed the edge with a lit match, I was most impressed. Was I in Europe? I was stepping into an ancient tradition, the preparer of an elixir that had gathered humans together for millennia, inspiring their thought, certainly prompting the eureka moments of countless inventions. The brewing of espresso was noble work indeed, and I felt proud, and grateful, to be suddenly privy to its secrets.

My excitement about my new—my first!—job grew over the week, certainly enhanced by the coffee elixirs I myself sampled and the way they made my thoughts slide faster and smoother through my mind, and the way they made my chest light up and hum like a hive of bees suspended in globs of honey. I felt excited and sort of wonderful. By my fifth shift, I felt like I'd been working at My-O-My as long as Johnny. I recognized customers by their daily order, and *they* recognized me, too, greeting me like an actual friend. *Heeeeeey*, some would singsong, like they were happy to see me, like we were *friends*. *Hey, Gay*, said Petey, a baseball-hatted regular who had a crush on Fiona and who would give me a high five as they approached the counter. I was shocked, frankly, to be called *Gay* so openly, in such a casual tone, and even as some part inside me flinched, I smiled, too, because I *am* gay, just like Petey and practically everyone at My-O-My. And we played with this word, *gay*, and others—*queer, girl, queen, mary, daddy*—like feathered birdies, batting them back and forth at each other, laughing because they were so silly, such fun words, really, and how had I—how had anyone?—thought they could hurt us? We all went from being *drink daddy* pulling espresso to *cash queen* ringing up pastries to *garbage butch* hauling bulging bags of trash out back throughout the day. I felt like I was suddenly part of the best club, both incredibly elite yet also open to every single person who walked through the door. I felt suddenly, extravagantly happy.

And then I felt sad. Because I had nobody to tell about it.

LITTLE F—

I COULD TELL Fiona, of course. It was immediately clear that anybody could tell Fiona anything, and she would listen with her arm wrapped around your waist, nodding in time to your words. I could tell Johnny, and he'd probably be happy to hear it, and I could even tell Belle, who would probably take it in with a nod and say, "Cool," before disappearing into the back where I guess she did important things like manage the books and order sacks of coffee. But what I wanted to do was tell Velvet. Velvet who knew so much, and now I had something to offer, too, something I could maybe tell *him* about, instead of him always showing the world to me.

I wanted to tell Velvet, and I wanted to tell Joy. The thought of Joy, every creeping reminder of her, threatened the cascade of tears that had erupted when I first met Kimberly, and so I kept thoughts of Joy at bay, because really, life was hard enough, I didn't have to torture myself with longing for my long-lost best friend who I might never see again. That thought, the *might never see again* part, brought about a hollow feeling in my chest, like the inside of those hollow chocolate Easter Bunnies, where you take one bite and it all caves in. That's how I felt inside, like the thought of Joy could take one chomp from my sweet-seeming exterior and I'd fold all into myself, crumbled and crumpled. I'd be back in bed, locked in my little room, where I was the last time I let myself really indulge in how badly I missed her.

"Honey boo, what's the matter with you?" Fiona, who'd been polishing the big machine that churned out the espresso, was suddenly back by my side, her colorfully lidded eyes huge, her hand upon me, gentle so those witchy, bedazzled claws didn't sink into my skin. "Are you okay?"

I was too startled to answer. Startled that my insides were showing on my outside without my knowing, and startled that anyone around me would care to point it out. In my family, we made a point of ignoring each other's interior experience, and if anyone was sloppy enough to let a feeling leak out from a crack, the rest of us gave them the dignity of pretending we hadn't noticed. But *was* it dignity? Or was it something else, something scared and ashamed? Velvet has seen inside me in all sorts of ways, and Joy, too. And it always felt a little weird but never bad. Fiona's careful touch made me want to tell her everything. Pretending everything was okay all the time was sort of exhausting.

I started to speak, but my eyes suddenly spilled over with tears, and I busied myself trying to restore my dignity, flicking them away.

"Oh gosh, I'm sorry, I'm so sorry," Fiona said, pulling away from me and shaking her head. "This is my fault; I always do this. I'm psychic, you know, sort of anyway, like I can pick up on energy real strong. But that doesn't mean it's any of my business, or that it's *consensual*."

"You reading people's minds without their permission again?" Johnny clucked at her, pulling his glasses down his nose so she could register the disapproval in his eyes.

"I know, I know. I'm working with a psychic in the quarter who's helping me learn to control my *gift*," Fiona said, still cringing at my tears. "It's not much of a gift if it makes people cry now, is it?"

"I really miss my friend," I hiccupped. "Her name is Joy and she's a witch. I can't believe how long it's been since I spoke to her—I can't use my cell phone. She doesn't even know I'm in New Orleans or anything."

"Well, honey, you've got to call her!" Fiona exclaimed. "Doesn't he, Johnny?"

Johnny nodded. "Yeah, call her on the landline. Just don't stay on too long, okay? Just let her know you're all right."

"Really?" I asked. Telephones everywhere, in the office at Patsy's and right here behind the counter, and I didn't even think I could use them. Why didn't I think that? I was filled with a rush of urgency now, to talk to Joy, like yesterday.

LITTLE F—

"I won't be long, I promise," I said, and grabbed the phone from the receiver.

I knew Joy's phone number by heart; I almost danced to the specific little melody her particular arrangement of beeps created when I punched in the digits. As it rang, I wondered about the time. As in, what time was it, even? I didn't know the time right there in New Orleans, let alone Phoenix. Would she be at school with horrible new friends, the popular kids she once found so pathetic? Was she at home casting spells for my safety? Perhaps she'd forgotten all about me. That thought brought back the hollow-chocolate-Easter-Bunny feeling again. But then the phone stopped ringing. Somebody had answered.

"Joy!" I gasped into the phone.

"Spencer!" the phone gasped back.

"Oh my God, oh my God, oh my Godddddd!" I squealed. "Girl, I have so much to tell you!" Maybe I had never called Joy "girl" before, but now that I was gay and free, it seemed like the thing to do.

But the voice on the other end of the phone snapped: "This is *not* Joy." And *girl*, my blood ran cold.

"Mrs. Jenkins?" I ventured, all my exuberance shrunk into a tiny croak.

"Spencer, where *are* you?" asked Joy's mother. "Where have you been? Do you even know what is happening?"

"No, I-I—" I was at a loss. So *much* was happening. Had happened. Mrs. Jenkins, like everyone in Phoenix, thought Phoenix was the center of the universe. How could they know that New Orleans, actually, and My-O-My specifically, was the center of everything? Phoenix was a snow globe whose plastic flakes would slowly drift down after the little upset my disappearance had caused.

"Spencer, Joy is *gone*," Joy's mother spat into the phone. Her voice held a tremble that was all too familiar. I imagined she was either crying or furiously trying not to.

"What do you mean, gone?" I asked.

"She's gone, Spencer!" the woman hollered, and it was clear from the lash of her anger whose fault she thought it all was. "She went off looking for you! Off with some *man!*"

"What? But I don't know any men," I said dumbly. "Joy didn't, either."

Joy's mother didn't seem to hear. "She wrote me a whole letter about it, as if she's twenty-five years old and can do as she pleases. Well, I have the cops looking for both of them. I am not"—Joy's mother took a breath—"fucking around."

I'd never heard Joy's mother use a swear word, let alone the f-bomb. I felt a new, wormy anxiousness.

"Does she have her cell phone?" I asked, confused.

"Spencer, this is her cell phone, you dummy. You just called it. She left it behind on purpose so I couldn't track her. Like I'm a goddamn forensic scientist." Joy's mom gave a bitter laugh.

"She thinks I went to Provincetown," I said. "But I didn't. I'm not there."

"So she's not even going to find you. Great. Just great. Well, where are you, then? We can get the word out. Maybe it will reach her, and she'll come after you."

The phone line crackled gently between us. The bluesy music the café piped out through speakers lodged high in the corners wrangled around in the air. People chatted quietly. Silverware clinked.

"Spencer," said Joy's mother, "If you don't tell me, I swear to God. I swear to *God—*"

"I'm in New Orleans," I said before I could stop myself. Before I could hang up the phone and pretend I'd never dialed that number. Before I could turn my back on the whole drama I had caused, and just sink all my Joy-love feelings into Fiona, just as I'd planned to put all my sad Velvet-love feelings into Joy. Couldn't one person cancel out another? What good was loving or people

LITTLE F—

when life or fate or your own stupid self could tear them away from you, so that they were gone but all the feelings were left in your body, slowly turning rotten?

"I'm in New Orleans," I said again in a whisper, and then I gently hung up the phone.

30

"WELL?! HOW DID it go?" Fiona's bright face was brighter with anticipation of my good news and lifted mood. But her psychic antennae must have picked up on a problem, because I watched the cheer go right out of her face. Or maybe she wasn't really psychic at all. Maybe I was just an open book, with every passing problem plastered across my face.

"You don't need to tell me," she said, squeezing her eyes and shaking her head so that her purple hair fluttered and shook. "It's up to you."

"I think—" I began, and then halted. "That is, I know. I know I'm in a lot of trouble. I don't know if I can keep running from it."

"Girl!" She gripped my wrist, this time not even bothering to keep her magnificent claws from jabbing me. "Did you kill someone?"

"No!" I exclaimed.

"If you killed your abuser," Fiona continued as if I hadn't spoken, "we will all help you, okay? You don't have to worry. We got you."

"Oh my God," I said, processing the overwhelm. "Well. That is *nice*. To know. But I haven't killed anyone, Fiona! God!"

"Well, I wouldn't blame you if you did," she said ominously.

I detailed the terrible problems of my life to her, and she laughed.

LITTLE F—

"Girl!" She shook her head with a chuckle. "Girl. This is no big deal. We *all* ran away. Why you think we're at Patsy's? Running away is messy. You're running away from a mess, you're making a mess. It's all okay, boo. So long as you didn't kill anybody, it's no big deal."

"I didn't kill anybody," I said.

"But if you did—"

"You got me," I nodded. "Thanks."

I almost didn't tell Fiona about Velvet. Even though I liked her—liked her a lot—and the bigness of her, the extra-loud and effusiveness of her was part of why I liked her, I also was afraid of the big deal she'd make of it. Fiona, I now understood, made a big deal about everything. If I couldn't handle something emblazoned across the sky as if written there by an airplane, I probably shouldn't share it. But my floodgates were open. Had they ever been closed?

"Wait." Fiona stopped me with the universal signal for *stop*, an elegantly clawed hand in my face. "Is he, like *hot*? Like, super-hot?"

I thought about Velvet. Was Velvet hot? Super-hot, even? I sure thought so.

"Sometimes I couldn't even look at him," I confessed. "Because once you start, you notice more and more beautiful things, and you can't stop looking, you can't tear away, and then you're staring."

"Nobody likes that," Fiona agreed.

"And he's beautiful *inside*," I said, and then felt incredibly stupid. But Fiona was nodding her head, quite seriously.

"You can tell," she said. "That's the kind of outside beautiful he is. You know there's so much more beauty than you can even see."

"Wait," I said, slow as always. "You know him? You know Velvet?"

"A little tattoo under his eye?" she asked, nodding. "Like a delicate little etching? And his arms?" She made slicing motions with her hands, not in a rude way, almost like speaking it out loud would have been the rude thing. The silence was respect.

I nodded.

"I have some of that, too," Fiona shared, lifting the hem of her minidress. There on her thigh was a ladder of shiny welts, just like Velvet. "Were you a cutter, too?" she asked. "Are you?"

A cutter. Somehow, I knew that that was what Velvet's shiny stripes were, even though he'd never told me. Somehow, I'd known not to ask, had intuited they were attached to something puzzling and sad, and if he wanted to tell me about it he would, and he might not ever. I shook my head at Fiona. "Good," she said, and flung her arm around me. "It's a bad habit. You never really break it. It's always there in your head, like, *hey, feeling stressed, want to hang out?*"

I didn't share how I envied her and Velvet, just a little, for having someplace so clear to put their pain, a purposeful action, a ritual almost. And how it made something so invisible visible. But I could tell these were the immature thoughts of a privileged, suburban, middle-class gay boy, and everything else that Velvet was right to call me. I guess it was something to know it, at least. To know to keep your mouth shut. That's a thing.

"He was coming in here a bunch," Fiona said. "Sometimes he sat outside and didn't buy anything, which is fine. We don't bother people. Sometimes he got, like, a coffee. He wouldn't talk to anyone. We're all friendly. Well—Belle's not, but me and Johnny are, and this kid was not friendly back. I was like, okay, whatever, you do you. But now I know. He was looking for you."

Like an eclipse inside my chest, something huge passed over my heart's sun, a shadow of confusion that only made the light burn brighter when it passed. I gripped Fiona like my legs were about to give out. "Do you think so?" I asked. "Do you really think so?"

"I do," said Fiona. "But that doesn't mean you should go off with him. Y'all sound like twin flames. You know what that is?"

"Uh-uh," I said, shaking my head.

"It's like soul mates," she said. "But evil. Like you're the perfect, miserable match for each other. Like, really passionate, like you can't let each other go, but you're the worst thing for one another."

I thought about it. "I don't know that it was like that," I said. "I think Velvet is good for me. He sort of saved my life maybe."

"Yeah," Fiona said. "Classic twin flames."

"We were sweet, I think," I said, not quite confident.

Fiona closed her eyes. "Something is coming, that's for sure."

I wondered what *something* felt like to her, if it was a vibration or a sound or a feeling. But I didn't need to have Fiona's psychic powers to know that something was coming. I imagined Velvet sauntering up to the counter in that easy way he moved inside his body. I imagined myself staying professional, staying calm: *Can I help you?* I'd take his order *and* fill it, clicking the handle into the machine with a bored flick of my wrist, dispensing a cup of brewed coffee with a yawn. Languidly I would interact with Johnny or Belle, chuckling at an inside joke, addressing them with an intimate *girl*. I'd avoid making eye contact with Velvet's dazzling, curious eyes. I'd avoid the tattoo beneath his lashes, I'd avoid his mouth I'd filled with kisses, his arms that radioed survival, I'd turn my nose away, toward the espresso machine, huffing the bitter stink of steaming grounds just to make sure none of his own smell, grubby and sweet, reached me. Because if any of that stuff happened—if I smelled him, or saw him, or saw him seeing me—I know I would hop over the counter and tackle him with kisses and promises and apologies and tears. Which sounded uncomfortably like a real twin-flame thing to do.

I sighed, and I leaned my head on Fiona's shoulder. I did hope, before it all came crashing down, that Joy and Fiona would get to meet one another. I knew that they'd really, really love each other.

31

ON THAT LAST day, I woke up in my bed at Patsy's Place, and I knew where I was. Knowing this was a new feeling. In all the mornings leading up to that day, I would awaken in my twin bed, the blankets kicked to the floor, sun or haze coming in the window, and without opening my eyes I would sense around the space for that familiar feeling that reassures you of your place, your time. It wouldn't come. At first I'd imagine myself at home in Phoenix, but that wasn't right; maybe I was with Velvet, in a train car or stranger's bed, but my nose was empty of his soft smell, and my arms even emptier. On that last day, though, I could feel my surroundings before opening my eyes, recognized the patter in the hallway as Johnny and Fiona and Belle's morning preparations. What I'd forgotten was that I was among them, now.

Fiona reminded me by swinging my door open. With her purple hair piled on her head and accented by some fuchsia chicken feathers harvested from the feather boa in the costume trunk, she looked like a bird or maybe a parade float. Her dress was probably originally intended to be a nightgown when it was manufactured a few decades ago, but it didn't look wrong on her. Everything about Fiona looked exactly correct.

"Get up, Spencey, no more hiding out in your bedroom, remember?"

"Oh my God!" Johnny gasped in a scornful tone, pulling my

door shut and vanishing Fiona. "Girl, you cannot do that! Privacy is important! You knock and get permission to enter, okay?"

Fiona's nails drummed across my bedroom door, like a sudden pelt of rain. "Spencey, can I come in?"

"Sure," I assented from beneath the blankets I'd rescued from the floor. I felt a breeze as the door pushed open and the sag of my mattress as Fiona made herself comfortable. A hand clutched the blanket above my head.

"Girl!" Johnny yelled. "What is wrong with you?"

The hand retracted. "Spencer, come out," Fiona said. "I had a dream about you."

I peeked my head above the covers.

"More," she commanded. "Sit up."

I did as instructed. Fiona looked me over, my mussed hair and the garish T-shirt I slept in, some sort of swag from a corporate-sponsored gay marathon, it seemed. It was in the pile of free clothing Kimberly gave me when I first got to Patsy's. I hadn't wanted to insult her, but none of it was anything I'd ever wear, though the T-shirts made for good enough pajamas.

"Oh, Spencer," Fiona said, dramatically averting her eyes. "You *are* a real boy! Look at you! Your hair is a mess! You have, like, lines on your face from your pillow! And that shirt! That tacky shirt! Oh!"

She pulled me to her polyester bosom in a big hug.

"I was afraid you were a perfect, preppy android. But now I see you are actually a human being, like the rest of us."

"Fiona!" I said, blushing and swatting her away. "Of course I'm not perfect."

"Well, you look like you are. You look like a little richie-rich Ivy League New Englander who never had a struggle in his *life!* It's good drag," she nodded emphatically, "just odd for a runaway shelter, you know?"

"Spencer, are you coming in to the café today?" Johnny asked.

"Yes," I said, still knocked off-kilter by Fiona's observations. I was sort of proud of myself for having such a strong look—*drag*, she'd called it—and while I never would have thought of it that way, she wasn't wrong. It was nice, dignified to have kept it so together at my biggest crumble. But it also made me think of my mother and father, their appearance impeccable while their insides came apart at the seams. Is that how I wanted to be?

I thought of Velvet again, and the stripes of everything he'd survived, a tattoo on his *face*, for goodness sake. What more could one do to say plainly to the world, I am not of you, and do not wish to be among you?

LATER THAT MORNING, when they'd left for work and I was getting ready in the bathroom, I thought about my hair. It's true that I had trained it into obedience so that even without the various creams and pomades I abandoned in Phoenix, it mostly did as it was told. But it had been a while since my last haircut. It was harder and harder to keep it brushed back and tamed.

When I dipped my head, my bangs swung into my face and made me think of Velvet. How once, as he was falling asleep at Stacia's, I'd taken a chunk of that hair that fell over his eyes and twisted it into a little braid. He'd kept his eyes closed until I was done, and then he opened them and went slightly cross-eyed peeking at it.

"Very cool," he'd said, and kissed me, and went to sleep.

In the morning, the braid was miraculously still there, even with the slippery texture of his hair and his nightly tossing and turning. He would wake me up throughout the night, his knee or his butt banging into me, but I never cared, because every time I opened my eyes I'd see *him*. My boyfriend, or whatever he was. My Velvet. And I would be all filled up with something that was definitely happiness, it had to be, and I would snuggle into Velvet's new position and doze there until he bumped me off him again.

But the braid. He'd run into the bathroom with the end of

it pinched between his finger and returned with a tiny elastic band pilfered from Stacia's jar of hair things. He kept the braid for days, even though it looked a little funny. Awkward. Velvet was cool, he was so cool, but things kept turning up in the braid, like a sprig of jasmine tucked into the weave or a piece of yarn tied in a bow. I felt like he was wearing my love for him and ornamenting it, feeding it, dressing it up. Then one day the elastic fell out, probably while we were sleeping, and the braid unraveled, and that was that.

Thinking of the braid, I looked at myself in the mirror. My cutoffs were raggedy enough from the last few weeks that if I did not take the time to pare down the fringe with scissors and carefully fold them into neat little cuffs, they looked like haggard jellyfish tentacles waving on my legs. Thinking about Velvet, thinking about what Fiona had said about my preppy drag, I took one of the stupid logo shirts I'd been sleeping in, chopped the sleeves off, and turned it inside out. My hair I allowed to flop where it may. Then, coming upon a dull nub of Fiona's eyeliner on the bathroom sink, I attempted to outline my eyes in it. I thought, doing it, about the last time I had my face painted, by Velvet. We hadn't attempted anything so precise as eyeliner. I do think that if given the proper tools—a pencil sharpener, for instance—and if I'd permitted myself to go slowly and carefully, I could have sketched out a marvelous, dramatic eye for myself, something an Egyptian queen—or a Hollywood starlet portraying an Egyptian queen—would be proud of. But because what I was doing felt rash and ridiculous, the only way through was to scribble swiftly upon my lids before some other, more sensible part of my brain—the part inhabited by my mother, perhaps—perked up and realized the terrible mistake I was making. So it was a rush job with an inferior tool and none of my inherent artistry. The fat line of kohl went wavy round my eyelid and buckled at my lash line on my lower lids, and all I could do was take my knuckles and smear it all around my eyes. But still. That in itself was something, was *a look*. And when I'd brought my hands away, the smudged affect was, frankly, quite awesome. I imagined myself lounging behind the counter, pulling shots and looking pouty and mysterious and very New Orleans.

FIONA AND JOHNNY appeared to be in the midst of a faint argument outside My-O-My's as I approached.

"It's like we're leaving little engraved invitations in the dumpster: *Come raccoons. Come one, come all!*"

"Just show me what you're talking about." Johnny was laughing and shaking his head.

I caught all their eyes as they were starting to make their way behind the building.

"Oh hey, *you* look amazing," Fiona said in her normal way, which always sounded like she was flirting with or teasing the world.

"Oh, ah, thanks," I said, looking down, suddenly shy about it. I made myself look up, tried to access the confident pout I'd spied back in the mirror. Hand on hip. Eyes rolling, then squinting.

"Yes, this is *so* good," Fiona said, nodding. "You've *got* to reinvent every now and then. I mean, we think the self is this stable, rooted thing, but it's not. We're deeply influenced by what we experience, and that should show, no?"

"Okay, Dr. Fiona." Johnny put his hand on her shoulder and aimed her toward the raccoon-infested dumpster. "Let's see if you can apply some of that analysis to, like, pest control."

"They're not pests!" Fiona protested. "We do have to figure something out, but we need to start from a place of honoring these intelligent and resilient creatures!"

"Fine," Johnny nodded. He took a last look at me. "That *is* a surprisingly good look on you."

"Thank you," I said. Everyone around here was so nice all the time that it was hard to trust them. Would they even tell me if I looked stupid? But, then, maybe they had truly elevated their way of thought to a place where there *were* no stupid looks, only expressions of art and personality. The vibe of acceptance was that powerful. I didn't know that it was a state of mind I would ever be able to reach, unfortunately. Maybe for other people I could, but for myself, personally, I knew in my heart there were really stupid ways to look, and I never wanted to look like any of them.

Inside the café, Kimberly was leisurely chatting with the gray beard who owned the cat-infested used bookstore on the edge of the quarter. Though there were plenty of coffee spots closer to his job, he made a point of hiking out to My-O-My's to support our business, often with a stack of secondhand gay books for the library Kimberly wanted to install in one of the rec rooms.

"Spencer, you've met Willie before, right?"

"I do not think so," the man said, though I'd in fact met him numerous times at Patsy's. He offered his hand for a shake.

"We've met," I said shyly. "I just look a little different today."

"You do," Kimberly nodded. "You look great." That was it. I appreciated her not making such a big deal about it. We traded places behind the counter.

"Willie has some local writers who are going to offer writing workshops for the kids at Patsy's," she said. "Is that something you'd be interested in?"

"Maybe," I shrugged.

"So teenaged." Willie chuckled. "Classic."

"Why don't you grab a pastry or two, cut them up, and put them out as samples, okay? Belle is in the back researching women-owned coffee roasters, and I don't know what happened to Fiona and Johnny."

"Raccoons," I said.

"Ah. Right. Well, good." She stuck her arm through the crook of Willie's, as if they were both about to skip down the yellow brick road. "See you tonight!"

I sliced into a puffy chocolate croissant, wondering about

the writing workshop. I didn't find the bookshop owner terribly inspiring, but the idea of writing a story, maybe even *my* story, that was something. And thinking about everything, everything with my family, with Velvet, thinking about Joy and Douglas Prine and even the hippies who'd kicked me out of their car as characters in a story—*my* story—that was something, too. Something that made my body buzz like I'd just gulped down a cortado.

I was arranging the flaky, buttery chunks of pastry onto a plate when, I swear, I felt the air shift around me. Molecules receded to allow for the introduction of new molecules, molecules that felt familiar on my skin, that brought a warm smell into my nose, into my nose and down, swiftly, to my heart.

My head shot up. Velvet, there before me, in my place of employment. My mouth opened and shut, opened and shut, as if I were doing those face-toning exercises my mother once did. Maybe still did. Maybe was doing right now, from her forever perch on the dimly lit couch, her cigarette like an eternal flame, perpetually burning.

32

IT TOOK A MOMENT for Velvet to recognize me. I liked that, I'm not going to lie; it harkened to my fantasy of pretending not to recognize *him*. While part of me felt a little pang at the obvious imbalance of, fine, call it obsession between us, with me being able to sense and smell his presence as if psychically attuned to his energy field, he was capable of standing right in front of me, looking me dead in the eye, and with a bit of cosmetic camouflage and a different hairdo, I didn't exist. Insulting, sure. But in that feeling of not being known was some power. Yes, I was everything that Velvet knew me to be, all the embarrassing things, protected and moneyed and white and housed, naïve, slumming; everything he'd ever said was true. But there was also more, like I possessed secret drawers that not even I had known about until I tripped them. It didn't make all the embarrassing things go away—nothing could—but it shifted them around some, made me less afraid of them, less afraid of myself. Whatever I was, I could work with it. Even if it was bad, I could know about it and maybe lessen its power somehow. A knuckle full of smudged eyeliner wasn't going to do that work, but it was something. A symbol, a start.

Velvet spoke before I'd even fully looked at him but while some internal alarm system had been tripped by his unmistakable presence.

"Empty the register," he said in an exaggerated crook voice, like a cartoon stickup. He held his bag, the same one that dangled on this shoulder or crisscrossed his torso, the one he'd used as a pillow, the one that smelled like his head (yes, I'd smelled it.) He held it open like a mouth and tossed it across the counter at me. Was he serious? Was this happening? How could he not recognize me? Wasn't he in here to find me? Or had he just been working up the nerve to rob the place?

I put down the plate of croissants. I shook the crumbs from my fingers. I approached the register, my eyes wide. Maybe it was then, the gleaming of my widened eyeballs bulging out from the mess of makeup.

"Spencer!" Velvet gasped.

"Velvet," I said, and then I hit the X button that barfed open the register. There were the neat stacks of bills, all the presidents facing the same neat directions, neatly tamped down by the metal bits. There were the tiny dishes of loose coins sparkling like sequins, and the heavy tubes of rolled coins, some in paper, some in shrink-wrapped plastic. I went for those first—they felt so real in my hands—I plopped them into the bag. Then I grabbed the bills. There weren't so many of these, but I took all there was, the metal tongs slamming down on the plastic with a cracking sound. I scooped palmfuls of change, even the pennies, and I dumped it all into Velvet's bag like a big money stew, and I pushed it back over the counter to him.

"Go," I said.

I didn't have a plan. I didn't know what I was going to say to Johnny, to Kimberly, about where the money went; I didn't know how I was going to make change for the next café au lait a customer ordered. I looked to the back door. No one used the back door because the frame around the pane of glass was rotting and the glass shook frighteningly as it moved. In fact, the whole door appeared to be melting away in the wet Louisiana heat, with splintery cracks spidering out around the dead bolt and the doorknob. It was the closest exit, but it only led to the dumpster—would he be able to get out? Both my hand and Velvet's hand lay upon the loot-filled bag, and I could feel our energy running through it, his essence of something tickling the tops of my fingers.

"Come with me," he said.

"What are you doing!" snapped Belle from behind me. I didn't know how much she'd seen, but it was enough to lunge for Velvet's bag, which I deftly yanked away so that her hands landed with a smack upon the counter.

"Spencer, *what the fuck*?" Belle looked at me with outraged betrayal all over her face, and I wanted to stop and soothe and explain. But obviously something else had taken over my instincts and reactions, something that allowed me to *spring over the counter like a spider monkey*, in a parkour-like move I had never, ever attempted. I landed in my loafers beside Velvet, knocking into him upon my landing—oh, how nice he felt, the brush of his worn T-shirt upon my arm!—and I registered the customers frozen at their tables, all eyes on us as they realized that something was *going down*. It would only take a moment for one of them to turn vigilante and attempt to tackle one of us—I pegged the white guy in the Gulf Shores baseball hat as the hero to do it—and so, grabbing Velvet by the hand that was not holding the loot, I pulled him toward the rotting back door, and like the Kool-Aid Man, I smashed right through it. With a shove of my shoulder, it all caved like a slab of wet cardboard, the pane of glass finally dislodging and shattering on the patch of cement and glass outside.

At the dumpster, as I yanked Velvet through the portal, Fiona and Johnny stood, their hands wrapped around what appeared to be *baby raccoons*. Is there anything more adorable in this world than a litter of baby raccoons? I cannot say; I was not able to pause and consider. I only felt a fleeting surge of gratitude for their precious fragility, as Fiona and Johnny, registering immediately that something catastrophic had happened, looked frantically back and forth and up and down, from me and Velvet and the shattered door to the mewing raccoons fuzzy in their hands to one another's faces, hoping to read an obvious next move in one another's eyes, but before they could metabolize all this information, we were *gone*, Velvet and I, dashing down the alley and out of sight while the raccoon babies still kicked their dumb little legs, while Fiona and Johnny still felt the animals' beating hearts against their fingers. Belle was after us as well, but like a girl in a horror movie, *Belle fell*, and I wasn't exactly happy about this, because I am not a monster, I do not want anyone to fall upon a death trap of shattered eighteenth-century glass, especially Belle, who I must admit, I liked very much.

"I'm so sorry, Belle!" I screamed over my shoulder as I dashed, hearing the glass tinkle like a wind chime as it rearranged itself over the skid of her certainly bleeding body.

"Come on." Velvet was pulling me now, and I followed him, although soon we were running side by side, and I was responding to his tugs on my wrist to go right or left as we booked it, our feet slamming down on the cracked, gray street. Above and all around were jelly bean houses with lacey black balconies, and there was the smell of garbage as we brought the breeze of our motion past dumpsters and fat buckets of trash. We were heading back into the French Quarter with its warren-like mazes of streets and throngs of tourists; it seemed like the perfect place to hide from my friends at Patsy's. My friends. What the hell had I done?

It wasn't even noon, so we must have spun onto Bourbon Street, where every other human held a tall, plastic drinking contraption glowing with alien colors, burping daiquiris in the humid air. Velvet had a plan, as Velvet always did; I could see it in the set and the focus of his brown eyes. He took quick, jab-y glances back at me, and I turned away and shook hair into my face.

We came to a stop outside Big Daddy's. The swing pushed

the shiny, plastic mannequin legs through the window again and again. Above us, the new sign gleamed dull beneath the sun. Velvet stuck his head inside and hollered. A woman with big hair and tall shoes clunked out, squinting against the brightness and wrapping a flowered robe around her body.

"You boys are *too young*," she snapped, shaking her head. "I can't barely see a thing out here, but I can see *that*."

"I'm Stacia's brother," Velvet reminded her. "Velvet?"

She squinted harder. "Oh, sure, sure. But, Stacia's not here, honey."

"I know. She told me to meet her here, though. To wait for her."

"Oh, no, baby," she said. "Management is here, I can't let you in. Plus Stacia isn't working anymore. She's showing too much. It disturbs the customers."

"Can we just wait for her backstage?" he begged.

"Sorry, kid, I smell a rat." She stepped backward back into the bar. "I love Stacia to death, and any brother of hers is a brother of mine, but I wouldn't let my little brother in this place, either." She turned on her massive heels and vanished.

Velvet bit his lip. A perfect, pearly little tooth, gnawing on that sweet, red pillow. I sighed. He looked at me and leaned against the building, nearly getting kicked in the head by the mechanical feet.

"We have to hide somewhere," I said, my voice spiky with panic. Velvet shrugged, gestured briefly at the hordes of passersby stumbling down Bourbon Street, drinks aloft, radiating, every one of them, a type of up-to-no-good-ness that spanned from cheerfully mischievous to lecherously sinister.

"We're fine," he said, then looked deeply at me. "Spencer. Why'd you do it?"

"What do you mean?" I asked dumbly. "What else could I have done?"

"Said no," Velvet laughed. "Said, 'Are you nuts, you little rat, get out of here!'"

"Is that what you wanted me to say?" I asked.

"Maybe. I don't know. I didn't even know it was you. I was just sort of... flirting, maybe, just being a goon—"

"You were flirting but you didn't know it was me?" I asked, stung. "So, you weren't actually robbing me?"

"No!" Velvet yelled. "I wouldn't rob, like, a gay coffee shop in the Marigny! Where I hang out sometimes, and people sort of know me? If I wanted to hold someplace up, I'd go out on the 10 and hit a gas station or something, oh my God!"

I stared at Velvet. "Are you *mad* at me?" I couldn't comprehend this. I'd just robbed my work for him, more than my work, my home, the most stable place I'd been since Dougie Prine kicked me in the face what seemed like years ago. He hadn't even asked me to. And now he was upset.

"No." Velvet turned and gripped my arm, and I got goose bumps. "I'm not mad at you, Spencer. I'm confused. Everything happened so fast. It's like—*was* I robbing the café? I swear, I was just joking, and then, it was you—it was like I was brought there to you. Like it was all meant to happen."

I nodded. "Yeah," I said. "That's what it felt like to me, too."

"I knew I would see you there," Velvet admitted. "Not today. I really didn't know it was you. But I figured you went to Patsy's Place, after we fought about it. And I know those kids work there. I knew I'd find you there eventually."

"But not like this," I said, still not quite able to believe it all.

"No. Not at all like this."

"I guess it's our energy," I said, sounding like Joy, or maybe Kimberly or Fiona. Were all girls witches, or just the ones who wanted to be my friend? "I guess it's just what happens when we come together. Chaos."

"Mayhem." Velvet nodded. "Crime."

With that, he reached out and pulled me into him in a long, tight hug. Through my tears I watched the blurred, black pumps of the swing stripper fly by. My tears rolled down my face, cutting tracks in my makeup and sploshing wetly on Velvet's arm.

"What's the matter?" he asked.

"I missed you."

"I missed you, too." He paused, breathed. "I made out with Manny again."

My tears came harder, and I tried to squirm away from his grip on me.

"No, listen, it didn't mean anything. It was like, like making out with the past. With another version of myself, to see if it still fit. And it doesn't fit. I didn't like it. I just felt sort of confused and mad at you, and I went back to Stacia's and she was out and—"

"And it was the first time the both of you were alone and you couldn't resist each other," I spat. Tears were leaping from my eyeballs as if on powerful little frog legs. Just hurling themselves off my face, splattering Velvet's T-shirt.

"It wasn't like a soap opera," Velvet said. "And, like, I didn't even need to tell you. I just—"

"Oh, right, really great of you, Velvet. You're like, so upstanding."

Velvet sighed. "I hate fighting with you. It's so stupid. Look what happened last time we had a fight. You wind up in some gay-ass shelter, and now we're on the run *again* for a whole new crime."

I laughed through my snotty tears. "You don't want to be boyfriends with Manny?" I asked.

"No way," he said. "I just want you to know everything. I feel like, ever since I met you, I have told you everything. I told you about my dad, right? I never told anyone that Harlon was my dad. I always made up some story. I told you about Manny, which nobody knows but Stacia, and I know she didn't tell anyone cause she doesn't want anyone thinking her boyfriend is a fag." Velvet's bangs had gotten so long that he could slide them behind his ear, and he did. His beautiful face shone out at me, like a poem. I don't know if a face can be a poem—that seems like a poem in itself, really, not that I've ever read a poem outside school. But looking at Velvet sort of made me want to read a poem, or even write some.

"When I first met you, I felt like I could tell you anything, because you didn't matter." I blanched, but he shook me in his hands, "Wait, listen to me. I pegged you, right, and I was sort of correct. You're a white kid from the suburbs, and you've never really seen the world, and I figured you were going to get scared pretty quick and be gone, so it didn't fucking matter what I said to you cause soon enough I'd never see you again. It was like an experiment, being that honest." Velvet's eyes dug into mine, like they were begging me to understand. His face shot out toward my face and he kissed me, quickly, on the cheek, and I gasped, and his hands held me tighter.

"But then every day you stuck around, even when things were crazy, and then when things were chill—"

"Things weren't ever chill," I interjected. "Things aren't ever chill."

"Spencer, you're *here*. And it's like all the secrets I told you piled up and turned into something. I didn't know it would happen. I feel like—you're the person that knows me best in the whole world."

"Velvet," I started, overwhelmed with the possibility, the responsibility of being that person, the person who knew Velvet the most. "Velvet, *whoa*."

"Am I that for you?" he asked. "Do I know you best of anyone?"

I thought of Joy. Probably it was Joy who knew me best. But when I tried to remember her, I recalled incense and lighting, but not her face. I guess Joy used to know me best, before Velvet happened. But I was a different person now, and not only did Velvet know *this* me the best, he had helped me become this me. He was all over me, like smudgy eyeliner or a lattice of scars.

"It's hard to say, because I'm not sure I even know myself anymore," I said. "But I think so. But—I love you." I could see relief in his eyes, and that made me cry some more. "I'm sorry I'm such a crybaby."

"I love you, too, Spencer," Velvet said, and even though I must have looked the worst I'd maybe ever looked in the history of me having a look, he kissed me. It tasted like sweat and coffee, wet and salty and bitter and sweet.

"Get a room!" slurred a passerby as we came up for air.

"We are *trying* to get a room!" I shouted, a little embarrassed at how high-pitched my voice is when I'm loud.

"I know that voice!" came a shout from somewhere beyond the kicking mannequin.

I craned my head, prepared to run, and there was Joy.

33

I DON'T KNOW that I'd even stopped the crying inspired by Velvet-provoked emotions, but there I was crying all over again, or continuously, now soaking the spaghetti strap of Joy's brightly tie-dyed tank top and getting the skin of her shoulder all gooey. Of course she did not care; I seemed to be very good at selecting friends who will not judge me for being a crybaby or get repulsed by the way my feelings get all over them.

Joy and I hugged and hugged, leaping up and down while hugging, and then we pulled away to look at one another and express some deep fact, such as "I was afraid you were dead!" (Joy) or "I forgot what you looked like!" (me), to which Joy made a face and socked me squarely in the arm, demanding, "How could you forget *this?*" and shoving her face—familiar! So familiar! Etched on my heart; how could I not have recalled it!—into mine. What was *not* familiar was the pinky-blue eyeshadow, the glossy lips. Most of the purple had washed out of her hair, leaving it simply blond with a bit of lavender highlight.

"You look..." I reached for the right word.

"Basic?" she teased. "It's okay. I'm into it! I avoided looking like this for so long that it actually seems kind of taboo and transgressive."

"It's not," I laughed. "You just look regular."

"Well, you look very *irregular*," she stated. "What, is it Freaky Friday?"

LITTLE F—

"Maybe," I said, squinting at her. "Maybe *I* have all the witchy powers now."

"You look like you do." She nodded. "But fashion does not equal witchcraft. *Color* is magic, too, you know. Every shade I'm wearing is a deliberate spell to bring you to me and into my protective bubble!"

"Am I in your protective bubble?!" I gushed.

"You never left it," she said, and then she started to cry, too.

Velvet was behind me—I could feel him with my new, Velvet-related psychic powers; I would have to tell Joy *all* about this so she could stop pooh-poohing my witchery—and I grabbed him and pulled him by my side.

"This is Velvet," I introduced. "He has to be in the bubble, too."

Velvet gave a little wave, and Joy waved away his wave and brought him in for a big hug. "Are you guys... friends?" she asked with uncharacteristic nervousness, like a weird mom.

I looked at Velvet, who *seemed* to be blushing, though it was hard to tell, especially since he'd freed that lock of hair and it was swinging over his face once more. "We love each other," I told her, and she leapt into the air and did a fist pump. Velvet's smile cracked across his face as he looked back and forth between Joy and me.

"I'm sorry," Joy said, wiping her tears with one and patting Velvet with the other. "But this one—" She thumbed toward me. "He's needed some love in his life—for reals—for a long time."

"God, Joy, can you not make me sound pathetic?"

"Pathetic! Oh, no, Spencer, you are a *hero!* You are *legendary!* You don't even know what happened! Like three other kids came out and accused Douglas Prine of, like, *abusing* them. He was fucking with other people—not just you. He's in a *lot* of trouble. But he confessed to everything. So everyone knows you didn't do anything wrong, at all. But that you ran away? It's so fucking cool! Kids are like, 'My uncle in Minnesota saw him at a truck stop!' 'Uh-huh, I have a cousin who had coffee with him at a coffeehouse in New York City!' 'Yeah, well, my grandmother said there was a kid buying cigarettes in front of her at the drugstore in Texas!'" Joy shifted her body and tone to mimic each voice. I missed her so much.

"I was in Texas," I confessed, "but I don't smoke! So that Nana is a liar!"

We were cracking up when I heard a noise like a throat being cleared, but one of those throat clearings that go on for so long you know the person's throat is actually fine but they want some attention. We all looked up to see a tall person, a guy, standing just behind Joy. Her face lit up at the sight of him.

"Oh my gosh! You guys! This is Travis!"

"Hey, little brothers."

That voice. That face. But where were the dreadlocks? It was the good hippie from the terrible hitchhiking fiasco but with a choppy, short haircut. One side of his head was actually buzzed close while the other side was longer and floppy, like he'd been shaving his head and got bored.

"Travis," I said slowly, trying to remember if there was any reason I should hate him forever. That terrible day when I almost drowned in a river felt lifetimes ago. But as I was wracking my brain, he got down on one knee, the bare skin of his kneecap landing just south of a little pile of classic Bourbon Street vomit.

"Little brother," he began, with such sincerity in his voice and earnest sadness in his face that I couldn't help but burst into laughter.

"Is he going to propose to me?" I asked Joy. "What is this?"

"This is serious," she nodded, and looked at Travis, nodded her head at him.

"Little brother, I gave my word—my *word*—to this powerful woman. Joy." He looked at her, and it was clear in an instant that if he was going to be offering marriage to anyone that day, it was Joy.

"I promised her that I'd keep you safe," Travis said. "And when

LITTLE F—

I said it, I meant it. But I didn't keep you safe. Did I." Travis looked forlornly at the ground. It wasn't a question, except maybe one he was asking of his own conscience. When he looked back up, he too was crying. That was the fourth face full of tears I'd experienced in the past five minutes. Good thing New Orleans is so weird that everyone passing us by just assumed we were a pack of friends having some drunk drama and walked in huge arcs around us.

"When I made that promise to you, I meant it," Travis said, punching himself in the heart. "What I didn't know was the hold Jackson had over me. I'm not blaming him. I have a lot of unrecovered childhood trauma that I'm only just beginning to understand, bro. Just, like, a bad dad situation, right? And it makes me vulnerable to dudes like Jackson. I, like, give them all my power. And that's what I did that night, little brother. I did the wrong thing. I should have punched Jackson in the face, not that I believe in violence. I mean, I believe in it sometimes—"

"Even Buddhists believe in violence sometimes," Joy interjected.

"Exactly," Travis nodded. "The Buddhist thing would have been to sock Jackson in the jaw or do whatever I had to protect you."

"You could have at least helped me out of the river," I said.

"It's true." Travis nodded somberly. "I could have *at least* helped you out of the river. I didn't care that you ate the hummus, bro!"

"Uh-huh," I nodded.

"Anyway, it's not about Jackson. Jackson has his own path, right? But this is my path. I bailed from that trip with Jackson the next day, somewhere in Texas. I made it back to Arizona, to my parents' place in Phoenix, and I just couldn't stop thinking about you"—he looked at Joy—"and about you. But you know that. I had nightmares every night. All kinds of things were going wrong. My mom gave me her car, and the battery died."

Velvet scoffed and rolled his eyes: These were exactly the kind of "problems" that fired him up. I smiled tightly, containing my glee. I *knew* Velvet! I knew him! I squeezed his hand and rolled my eyes, too.

"Seriously, though, it was uncanny. Computers getting viruses. My cell phone screen shattered, and I hadn't even dropped it, bro! I got food poisoning from fresh, vegan food! And I knew what it was. It was Joy's curse. And I knew I had to make it better, for you and for me. And for her. Because I knew she really loves you, bro. And if you weren't good—and I was afraid you weren't—then she wasn't gonna be good either. So I went to the next full moon gathering, and I saw her there. She was making manifestation offerings, right?"

"They were all wishes for you," Joy said.

"I knew they were. And I went up to her, and I said, 'Excuse me'—"

"And I said, 'You scumbag motherfucker!'" Joy took over. "I said, 'You think I was fucking playing when I said I'd curse you?'"

"And I was like, 'No, no!'" Travis picked back up. This was obviously going to be their *meet cute* story. I sighed. But it was interesting. Maybe because it was about *me*.

"I told her, 'Your curse worked! My life is falling apart! I dream of that little brother every night. I feel awful, I didn't protect him, I didn't do right by either of you!'"

"He was crying," Joy said.

"That tracks," I said.

"I didn't care, though. I pushed him into the fucking bonfire. I was going to kill him. I thought you were *dead*. I thought he was *dead!*" She said this to Velvet, who slipped his hand into mine and squeezed.

"We both got asked to leave," Travis said.

"Which is *so* fucked up, right? Like, thankfully, Travis is a good guy—"

"You think so?" he asked, in a begging sort of voice. "I still don't know."

"Obviously," Joy snapped. "But don't take up so much space with it."

"Right," Travis nodded.

"This is taking too long," Joy said impatiently. "We both got kicked out—which, it's a public canyon so I don't know how they can even do that, and I am definitely going to complain to the Facebook page for that event when this is all over. But anyway, we left together, and Travis was so upset, he was sort of desperate. I had him meet me at the twenty-four-hour Waffle House, and he told me everything. He told me how he was determined to find you and help you and make sure you were okay, and—get this—he said I did not even have to lift the curse on him, because he really deserved it."

"Dra-ma," Velvet mumbled.

"But I believed him," Joy said. "I could tell he was sweet. He just fucked up. Like a lot of people do."

"That's true," I nodded. Travis flashed me a tiny, grateful smile. "You can get up," I told him, waving my hands like instructing a dog. "This is too much. Plus, that vomit is migrating."

"Ooh," Joy wrinkled her nose and took a few steps sideways. We all followed.

"I told him what I knew about your plan, about how you were going to go to Provincetown, Massachusetts, and convince some gay man to be your uncle. And Travis said he would drive there right then, and I said I would come with him. But only if he got rid of his dreadlocks, because they were *so* culturally appropriative, I couldn't be seen in the world with him."

"Bro, I didn't even know what that *meant*," Travis said, shaking his head.

"Anyway," Joy continued, "I called my mom from Virginia just to let her know I wasn't dead. I mean, here *I* was feeling so bad and worried about you, and I was doing the same thing to my mom!"

"That's what I love." Travis gazed at Joy. "Just, like, the self-reflection, and the accountability."

"And when I called, you know, she'd just spoken to you. She couldn't believe you told her where you were. *I* couldn't believe it."

I thought about that moment at the café, how trapped and confused I'd felt. Maybe I'd wanted it all to end.

"I didn't want *you* to be in trouble," I said. "Your mom was so worried."

Joy made a dismissive face. "She always worries."

"Yeah, but things can happen, Joy!" I said. "You're not, like, invincible."

"All's well that ends well," Joy said dismissively.

I laughed. "I'm glad you think this ended well," I said. "Maybe it did for you. But me and Velvet just accidentally robbed a café I was sort of working at."

"How do you sort of work someplace?" Joy asked.

"It's like a nonprofit that helps homeless queer kids—"

"And you *robbed* them?" Joy said *very* judgmentally.

"It's complicated," I defended myself. "I was confused. I still am confused!"

"A place that helps homeless gays, though!" Joy responded.

"I am a homeless gay!" I screamed in the middle of Bourbon Street.

Joy sighed and put her arm around me. She looked at Travis.

"The Spencer I know would *not* have done something like that," she told him. "I hold you responsible."

"I'm sorry, little brother," Travis said sadly.

"It's really not your fault," I assured him.

"It's probably more my fault," Velvet offered.

"More than Travis, yes," I agreed. "But it's not even your fault, Velvet. I'm my own person. I do things. Sometimes they make sense, sometimes they don't." I looked at Joy. "I'm not the same person I was when I left home," I told her.

She made a face and rubbed her hands up and down her arms.

"That legit gave me chills," she said. "But for reals, nobody is. I'm not. Travis isn't. Your parents aren't."

LITTLE F—

"What do you mean?" I asked. "How are my parents different?" I can't explain how being there with Joy—someone who actually knew my parents—made them suddenly real to me in a way they mostly hadn't been. My mother had been frozen in her dramatic smoking vignette in the living room; my father, he was forever throwing me under the bus in the fluorescent glare of the laundry room. But they were both more than that. "Are my parents okay?" I asked.

Joy and Travis looked at each other like they were speaking telepathically.

"Joy!" I grabbed her arm. "Tell me! Are my parents okay?"

"Yeah," Joy nodded. "They're fine. They're here. They're at a hotel down the street."

34

THE HOTEL MY parents were staying in was on a corner, brick, with one of those New Orleans balconies wrapped around it, lacy looking and decorated with fluffy plants and stray strands of Mardi Gras beads. Looking up at the porches, I could imagine partiers shrieking at a passing parade below or mellow travelers kicking back on the furniture, observing the city's constant flow of dense life. But I could not imagine my mother or my father.

Ahead of me, Joy walked with quick purpose, Travis by her side. She'd told me that if I didn't want to talk to them, she'd let them know. She'd be my messenger, the go-between. But, she continued, maybe I wanted to think about what my plan was. Did I have a plan?

I looked at Velvet, still carrying his bag of stolen money. Money stolen by me. Velvet was my plan. Could a person be a plan?

The hotel's doorway was set into the old bricks. Joy paused at the entrance. "I'm in room 101," she told me. "I'll be out on the veranda if you need me. Travis is in 104." She rolled her eyes and shook her head. "Such a waste of money. For what? Some show of propriety. Your parents are in 108."

She blew me a kiss and went inside. Travis followed, also blowing a kiss. Awkward.

"Okay," Velvet said. "So—goodbye. Do you want any of this money?"

"What?" I asked. "No, Velvet, no goodbye. No goodbye. Will you come with me?" I paused. "You have to."

"You're going home," he said, more a statement than a question. "We both knew you would."

I nodded. "I might be. I probably am. But not without you."

Velvet laughed. "Okay," he said, shaking his head like I'd said something *soooo* funny. "Yeah, sure. Totally."

"I mean it," I said, and I did have a plan. And it *was* Velvet. "You're my person. I won't go anywhere without you. I really won't. I'll stay here in New Orleans. We can keep robbing cute gay coffee shops." Velvet laughed again, but a real laugh, not one that sounded like a scoff. "I'll sleep on the side of the river with you, I'll sleep in an alley, we can break into Big Daddy's and sleep on the stage."

"Big Daddy's doesn't close," Velvet informed me. "Not even on Christmas."

"Velvet, I'll go anywhere with you. We'll probably wind up in jail—"

Another scoff-laugh from Velvet, but I grabbed him and shook his shoulders. "We *will*," I insisted. "But I don't even care. I'll run around with you until we just can't anymore. We can do that." I stared hard into Velvet's eyes, like I was beaming my sincerity, my *love*, into his brain. He nodded, slowly. Maybe getting it.

"Okay," he said.

"But I think it might be hard," I kept going, my hands on his shoulders, our faces close. "And—I think it would end." I took a breath. "Can't you see that? We'll end up not being able to be together. Eventually."

"Everything ends eventually," Velvet shrugged, bouncing my hands from his shoulders.

"Stop being so cool," I demanded, my voice going up. "Stop

acting like you're so over everything, like you don't care. I know you care, Velvet. I know you care about me."

"I wish I didn't," Velvet said, and there were tears in his eyes. "This whole thing is so stupid."

"It's not. It's not stupid. Maybe it's time for *my* plan now, okay? Please? Will you trust me?"

"What, you want me to move to the suburbs and live with you and your parents?" Velvet asked incredulously. He held his arms out like, *Look at me.* His striped arms and long hair and tattooed face. His bag of stolen cash hanging off his body. I started laughing. Velvet of the train-station bathroom, knife-wielding Velvet, train-car Velvet, my Velvet. Yes, the thought of him in my suburban high school life back in Arizona was absurd, as if I'd caught a mythical creature. Velvet, the unicorn by the swimming pool. But there was no other way. And maybe it was so absurd it was genius. I laughed out loud, and Velvet began to smile, like he could see through my eyes into my brain. He started to nod.

"Okay, he said. "Okay. Fine. The suburbs. This is for sure the craziest thing I have ever done."

MOTHER OPENED THE door when we knocked. She looked like hell. She must not have been keeping up with her Botox, or even with her hair—the roots were a dark gray. Her clothes were sort of amazing because all she owned, really, were fancy-ish clothes, so it had the odd effect of a pauper playing dress-up in the queen's wardrobe. She opened the door and blinked at me. *Blink, blink.*

"Spencer?" she asked, though she knew it was me. She had to say it out loud, my name. She had to claim me. "Spencer," she repeated, this time no question, and she grabbed me and clutched me in a tight hug. I smelled all of her smells, her hair spray and her perfume, the scent of the makeup she spread across her face, all these remnants of smell that were hanging around her, plus a new smell: cigarettes. I guess she's been keeping up with her new bad habit.

"Ma, you've got to stop smoking," I said into her neck, and she squished me tighter. "It's so bad for your skin." She laughed onto the top of my head.

"I will," she said. "I will. I promise. Oh, Spencer. I'm so sorry."

"Don't," I said, suddenly, swiftly, deeply uncomfortable. "Just forget about it."

"Spencer, no," she said sternly, in mother mode. "We *all* have some apologies to make to you. I'm sorry if it makes you uncomfortable, but we are going to make them. It's up to you if you accept them or not." I just lived in a world of crying people now, I guess. I hadn't encountered a person and *not* seen them cry in, oh, about twenty-five minutes.

"Mama, this is Velvet," I said, grabbing Velvet's hand and pulling him close.

My mother looked at Velvet, and not in the tight way she'd gazed at Joy when they'd met, like an electronic scanner shooting an imperfection-seeking laser up and down her body. She looked at Velvet and seemed to see him. Mother had been tenderized, like a hunk of meat whacked with a mallet.

"Hello, Velvet," she said, offering her hand. Velvet held my mother's hand in the air as if he didn't quite know what to do with it. He gave it a quick shake and dropped it.

"I won't go anywhere or do anything without him," I said. "Anywhere I go, he goes."

"Oh," my mother said. She squinted at me, then at Velvet, chewing her lip the whole time. "Oh. Hmmm. Well. We certainly have the space. I guess we can speak with Velvet's parents, and—"

"Not necessary," I told her.

"I'm emancipated," Velvet explained. Which was sort of a lie but also not.

"How old are you, dear?" my mother asked.

"Seventeen," he replied.

"Okay. Well. You'll have to be in school. Like Spencer."

"I'll get my GED," Velvet countered. Were they negotiating? My mother gazed at Velvet and cocked her head, like she was taking in a new species of boy. Finally she nodded.

"Okay," she said. "That will be fine. A GED, and we'll take it from there."

"Maybe," I suggested, "I could also—"

"No." Mother cut me off. "*You* will be attending high school. But I don't want you to worry. Nothing will happen to you there." Mother looked at me intensely, shook her head like a regret-filled woman from a soap opera, and wiped a plump tear from her eye. "Nothing bad will ever happen to you again at that place, Spencer. We settled out of court."

"What?"

Mother brushed me off. "All in due time," she said. "Now. Are you willing to see your father?" I nodded. "You do know I know everything, yes?" she asked.

"I think so?"

Mother sighed. "You're a homosexual. Your father is a homosexual." She looked at Velvet. "I suppose you're a homosexual, too?" Velvet nodded. "Well. Everyone is a homosexual, except me."

"It's not too late," Velvet quipped.

The air was still, and then my mother laughed, reached out and ruffled his hair. Her fingernail polish was chipped. This had clearly been very hard on her. "Nothing would surprise me, at this point."

MOTHER FINALLY OPENED the door and we shuffled in, like meeting a dignitary. A very undignified dignitary. The room was classy, with brick walls and gold-framed painting, and the bed had a polished, antique-looking headboard with a quilted, crimson comforter. My father sat upon it in a pair of khakis, his head bowed. He looked up as we entered, and in a flash, we made eye contact. He dipped his head again. A neat ring of baldness sat on the top of his head. His shoulders slumped. I'd never seen him look so defeated. He had probably propped himself up with his closeted persona for all of his life, and now that it was gone, he maybe didn't even know who he was. I felt a surge of feeling for him, and for the first time ever felt grateful that I *couldn't* hide my gayness. I'd rather end up in the hospital for a beating than wind up my dad's age with a broken spirit.

"Spencer," he said, still looking at the floor. He started to speak a few times, and stopped.

"Dad," I said, "this is Velvet. My boyfriend. He's going to live with us."

Father raised his head. He looked from me to Velvet to me to Mother. Mother rolled her eyes and shrugged.

"Well—it seems your mother is okay with this. So, okay." He sighed, and offered a little smile. "Hello, Velvet." Poor, sunken Father. Each time he lifted his head it seemed his skull was made from marble.

"Spencer," he started again. "That was the lowest moment of my life. Not your mother finding me out. But what I did to you."

The utter coldness of that moment, the frenzied face of disgust he showed me, it all came back, and I felt dizzy.

"You looked like you hated me," I said, with force, trying to push the sick-sad feelings from my body. "Like you thought I was disgusting."

"I was disgusting," Father said. "I hated myself. I hated myself so much, Spencer, that it was easy to just do one more hateful, horrible thing. Why not? Why not just become a monster?" He laughed a shaky, nervous laugh. "It's not funny, of course."

"It's not," Velvet said.

"I knew I was gay, Spencer, from the time I was your age. Younger than you. I've always known."

I imagined a small father, a stiff, somber child, tense and protective with his terrible knowing. I wondered how much, or how little, I'd resembled him.

"There was just nothing to do with it," he went on. "Nothing I could see. I wanted to live, to have a life, to have children, be happy. That didn't seem possible. Do you know, people were given electric shock treatment? If they found out you were..."

"Homosexual," Mother supplied.

"Ma, that's not a word anyone actually uses," I said. "You can say *gay*."

"Fine," she said, rolling her eyes and crossing her arms tightly across her body, a big X, warding off the family gays.

"You seem—resentful," I said, carefully. It was one thing for Velvet to talk to my parents like they weren't his parents. They weren't. But me? I realized that just as I'd become new and somewhat mysterious to myself, Mother and Father surely had as well. And we were all going to have to get to know each other all over again, while we got to know ourselves.

"This isn't all going to magically resolve itself overnight, Spencer," Mother said. "I've accepted that everyone is homo—*gay*. I'm letting your boyfriend move into our house, which will now be like a gay compound, really. I'm not resentful, exactly, I'm just..."

"Flustered?" Velvet offered.

"It's not what I expected," she said. "It's taking me a moment to adjust."

"And you can have all the time you need," Father said to her. "You have been wonderful. Truly, Spencer. Your mother is wonderful."

"So, are you guys getting a divorce?" I asked. "So you can be gay now?"

My parents looked at each other.

"I'm very old-fashioned," my mother said. "As you know, Spencer. I don't believe in divorce."

"Not even in the case of a gay husband?" I asked.

Father cringed. "I'm still getting used to this, too," he said.

"Maybe you should be in therapy," I suggested. It was rich—so rich! After what he put me through with Peyton—but I meant no snark. I truly wanted my new gay dad to get help.

"I'll be going to therapy," Father said. "Your Peyton is putting a list of possible therapists together for me."

"I asked her to do that," Mother butted in.

"And your mother is going as well. We probably all should. Family therapy."

"Yeah, sure." I nodded. "Therapy's great."

"Your father and I will remain married," Mother pronounced. "Though marital relations will be . . . discontinued."

"Well," Father said, "it's not like they'd been that—"

"Ew, stop," I gasped, letting go of Velvet's hand to slap my own hands over my ears. "I don't need any of the grisly details, okay? Just be parents. Ugh."

"I think what your mother is trying to explain is, we'll be friends. Close friends."

"Best friends." My mother nodded, and for a moment, there was such sweetness in her face she looked like a girl. Hopeful.

"Separate rooms, all that, but we'll support one another. In life. And with you, raising you, Spencer."

I shrugged. "Okay," I said. "But don't you want a boyfriend?" It occurred to me then that we were alike, my father and me. Stuck with the terrible consequences of being gay before ever getting to experience the joy. It was so worth it, though. I wanted to tell him it was worth it. I scooped Velvet's hand back into my own.

"I don't think I'm ready for that yet," he said. "Therapy, you know. I have to learn to love this gay man." He pointed at himself. "Then we'll see about loving another."

"Well, you already do love one gay man," my mother pointed out.

Father looked alarmed. "No, I promised you, I never acted on—"

"Your *son*," Mother said.

"Oh," Father said, and he looked at me in a new way. He cocked his head. "Yes. Indeed, I do already love one wonderful, gay, young man."

The look he had on his face—it was the look of my dream uncle, the pink-shirted one by the sea in Provincetown, Massachusetts.

"You're about to love another gay man, too," I said, bumping my body shyly into Velvet. Velvet bumped me back.

"Indeed." Father nodded, smiling. "Indeed."

POSTSCRIPT

JUST SO YOU KNOW, we returned all the money to My-O-My. Father wrote a check for the door I'd smashed, and on top of that made a donation to Patsy's Place. Mother acted very suspect toward Kimberly, Belle, and Wolf for harboring runaways, but Father expressed much gratitude toward them for keeping me safe. Incredibly, no one was mad at me for having robbed the café. Well, Belle was mad. I think. She always seems sort of mad, so it was hard to tell. I felt so sad saying goodbye to them all, especially Fiona, but I felt ashamed, too, of the robbery, and it was sort of too much to have so many worlds colliding, all of Phoenix there with all of New Orleans. I was happy when we left, though very glad that Joy and Fiona got to meet because of course they loved each other, and now they're going to be pen pals, and Fiona inspired Joy to go back to having purple hair because she always looks so good. I get to hear about what's happening at Patsy's and My-O-My through Joy, which I love, because it is proof that life is entirely weird and you never know what is going to happen.

STACIA HAD A baby, a girl, though Velvet pointed out that we really don't know what gender the baby will wind up being, or even what genders will exist by the time she's old enough to start caring about it. Stacia said fine, but until then she's a girl and her name is Ruby Lara Anastacia Frias-Clancy Deon. Stacia sends us pictures of her all the time, and someday they're all going to come and visit us, that's what they say even though Velvet insists they never will, and that's okay, too, I guess, because it means we'll have to go visit them, eventually, in New Orleans, and maybe by then I won't be quite so ashamed and can visit everyone there, because I miss them all so much sometimes. I miss that strange place, so unlike anywhere else it feels like I dreamed it, like I brought Velvet back from a dream.

VELVET AND ME live in my bedroom, in my parents' old double bed, which is maybe weird, but the whole thing is honestly sort of weird, and we're all just going with it. Mother forbade us from dumpster diving our interior design after we dragged home a lavender end table that swiftly revealed itself to be infested with termites. But she's okayed us bringing home things from the secondhand shop after getting the lady at the counter to *promise* that everything there is vetted, inspected, cleaned, and sanitized. The lady shrugged and made a face at me and Velvet after Mother walked out, which could have been a face of sympathy that we live with such a demanding germaphobe, or it could have signaled that she had been totally lying about their vetting process. We shrugged back at her, and we went on to fill a cart with wreaths of plastic flowers, this silky orange fabric with pink swirls and dots all over it, beads that reminded us both of New Orleans, and a big, purple glass ball that reminded Velvet of a crystal and reminded me of my fantasy uncle in Provincetown. For a minute I felt ashamed all over again that I had let such a fiction take root in my brain; it seemed like the mechanism of a crazy person. But, the more I thought of it, the more philosophical I became. Like, if I *wasn't* so delusional, I might have never left Phoenix, never met Velvet. Not only would I have stayed so sad and lost but my parents would have, too.

Maybe there was something special about my brain and its wild imaginings. Maybe I will write a story about it all someday—maybe the true story of Velvet and my love, or maybe a

LITTLE F—

made-up story about a despondent gay teen and his super cool, nautical gay uncle.

WE'RE ALL GOING TO therapy. Even Velvet comes with us because it's family therapy, and Velvet is now family. And I get to see Peyton, and Father sees his therapist, and Mother really could use one, if you ask me, but she insists that three therapists is enough for one family. She is pretty busy with P-FLAG meetings, the group for parents of gay kids, and she loves to tell me how much more horrible other parents have been to their gay kids and how we, Velvet and me, should be super grateful. Father talks about joining a support group for gay men who came out later in life—I guess it's a real thing—and his therapist really wants him to join, but Father is quite a slowpoke. You'd think that after waiting so long, he'd just want to get *out there*, but that's not his personality. And that's fine. I try not to look like I'm having too much gay fun in front of him, but it's really hard, because I am honestly having so much gay fun.

AFTER EVERYTHING THAT happened, my school was pretty embarrassed and on the news and whatnot. Some of the less miserable teachers created a Gay Student Alliance, and there isn't a president of it or anything, but if there was it would probably be me, not to brag. I have a lot of good ideas for events, and even all the straight kids want to be allies now, so the GSA is basically the funnest, coolest thing about school, and everyone knows it. Even Velvet gets sort of jealous sometimes and wonders if he should go back to regular high school. But then he actually sees all the kids, like at an event, and they drive him a little crazy.

Velvet is like from another planet. He's seen and done so much that he's just not a normal teenager, and so he can't be expected to live like one. Mother is helping him look into college courses, which he'll be able to enroll in once he aces his GED test, which he will because he's brilliant. My favorite part of the day is after dinner when we are both at the dining room table studying, and I can just look at him with his head in a book, chewing on his pencil or silently mouthing words to a tricky problem. Velvet is a math/science person—who knew?

Sometimes he gets restless, and the rules he has to abide by to live with me here rankle him enough to rant.

"It's just, like, not *real*," he spit out one night, his tossing and turning keeping us both awake. "It's like I'm *pretending* that I can't just leave. Like, 'Oh, right, yes, a curfew, of course. I'm just a child, I have no business roaming the streets in the middle of the night.'"

"So go roam the streets," I groaned. I pulled myself out of bed and went to the window, unlatched it, and heaved it open. The hot, dry air hung there right outside our comfortable room, like I'd opened a portal to a whole other atmosphere.

Velvet froze, sitting up in bed. He looked caught somehow. Like he'd wanted something and got it, and now maybe he felt weird about wanting it. I slapped my hand lightly on the windowsill. "Go for it," I urged him. "Just please don't get arrested."

He paused to kiss me before ducking beneath the glass.

"And please come back," I said.

He did, of course. With some flowering succulent he'd dug up somewhere, leaves like plump gummies shooting up a stalk of dangling lavender blossoms. He'd replanted it in one of Mother's cereal bowls.

I KNOW IT'S ridiculous to think we're going to live happily ever after forever and ever—I mean, who does that? Nobody does that anymore. And the ones who go live happily ever after forever, they seem pretty miserable about it ultimately. Maybe we'll get older and get really sick of each other, or maybe we'll get bored or be like, *I need to be out on my own* or something. Because yeah, we are really young, I know that the odds are that we'll grow apart or one of us will do something terrible to the other,

LITTLE F—

even though we can't imagine that right now. But it seems pretty common in the world of adult relationships, and soon enough we'll be adults for real.

But I can't help thinking, or rather feeling, deep in my heart, that Velvet and I have something special, something so very special that even if the wicked world tries to tear us apart it will only bring us closer together, make our magical love flare up and grow stronger. Joy gave me a tarot reading about it, and it basically said that Velvet and I are going to get married and be together till the tragic day one of us dies a million years from now. And I believe Joy. She is, in fact, a very good witch. So even though there is no way to say this with 100 percent accuracy, I am going to go out on a limb here and say that Spencer and Velvet did in fact live happily ever after.

ACKNOWLEDGMENTS

Thanks to the folks at Loghaven, who gave me a spot to finish this work. It remains one of my favorite experiences! Thanks also to the Tin House Summer Workshop, which very much revitalized it. Thanks to Jeanne Thornton for really astute and sharp-eyed edits, and Rachel Page's close and helpful edit. And thanks to everyone at Feminist Press—I feel so lucky to have this long relationship with such an outstanding and important publisher! And thanks to Alison Lewis, for being the very best all the time.

MICHELLE TEA is the author of over twenty books of fiction, memoir, poetry, and children's literature. Her autofiction *Valencia*, a cult classic, won the Lambda Literary Award for Best Fiction. Her essay collection *Against Memoir* was awarded the PEN/Diamonstein-Spielvogel Award for the Art of the Essay. Tea is also the recipient of awards from the Rona Jaffe Foundation and the Guggenheim Foundation. The founder of Drag Queen Story Hour, she has received honors from the American Library Association and Logo Television. Tea curated the Sister Spit Books series at City Lights Publishers and founded the ongoing imprint Amethyst Editions at the Feminist Press.

The Feminist Press publishes books that ignite movements and social transformation. Celebrating our legacy, we lift up insurgent and marginalized voices from around the world to build a more just future.

See our complete list of books at
feministpress.org